'The doctor in... nurse for a few... I can think... Ravensworth said, and his voice became like heavy silk sliding over her skin.

'You know of my faults, and your conversation is more amusing than most. Should you wish the position, it is yours. I will pay half as much again as your present employer.'

'Lord Ravensworth!' Daisy stared at him in astonishment. If she went to work for him, she might as well forget about ever being a governess in England again. She could well imagine how the interviews would go if he gave her a reference. The slight tutting, and then the news that the post had been filled. 'You are unmarried!'

'Double what Mrs Blandish is paying you. You drive a hard bargain.'

His eyes were molten gold with flecks of amber— eyes that Daisy knew she'd dream about for months to come—eyes which silently urged her to say yes.

'It should be more than sufficient to make you swallow your principles about being employed by an unmarried man.'

'Without my principles I am nothing. I am a governess, not a nurse. Therefore I must refuse, Lord Ravensworth, and urge you to seek a suitable person for your needs.'

Author Note

This book came about because of the gleam in my senior editor's eye when I mentioned governesses, and the image of a half-naked man lying in Irthing River which haunted my brain for several nights running. And, as I had recently finished reading Alex Von Tunzelmann's *Indian Summer*, as well as *Kipling Sahib* by Charles Allen, I knew the story had to have an Indian connection. India remains high on places I want to visit. And some day I will.

I found *The Victorian Governess* by Kathryn Hughes and *Other People's Daughters—The Lives and Times of the Governess* by Ruth Brandon really useful for background information about governesses—plus their front covers are endlessly inspiring.

Because Daisy's friend Louisa Sibson came up and tapped on my shoulder, demanding her story be told, and thankfully my editor agreed, her story will be appearing soon.

As ever, I love getting reader feedback—either via post to Mills & Boon, on my website, www.michellestyles.co.uk, or my blog, http://www.michellestyles.blogspot.com

All the best.

COMPROMISING MISS MILTON

Michelle Styles

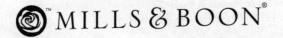

All the characters in this book have no existence outside the imagination of the author, and have no relation whatsoever to anyone bearing the same name or names. They are not even distantly inspired by any individual known or unknown to the author, and all the incidents are pure invention.

First published in Great Britain 2010
Harlequin Mills & Boon Limited,
Eton House, 18-24 Paradise Road, Richmond, Surrey TW9 1SR

© Michelle Styles 2010

ISBN: 978 0 263 87584 3

Harlequin Mills & Boon policy is to use papers that are natural, renewable and recyclable products and made from wood grown in sustainable forests. The logging and manufacturing process conform to the legal environmental regulations of the country of origin.

Printed and bound in Spain
by Litografia Rosés, S.A., Barcelona

Born and raised near San Francisco, California, **Michelle Styles** currently lives a few miles south of Hadrian's Wall, with her husband, three children, two dogs, cats, assorted ducks, hens and beehives. An avid reader, she became hooked on historical romance when she discovered Georgette Heyer, Anya Seton and Victoria Holt one rainy lunchtime at school. And, for her, a historical romance still represents the perfect way to escape. Although Michelle loves reading about history, she also enjoys a more hands-on approach to her research. She has experimented with a variety of old recipes and cookery methods (some more successfully than others), climbed down Roman sewers, and fallen off horses in Iceland all in the name of discovering more about how people went about their daily lives. When she is not writing, reading or doing research, Michelle tends her rather overgrown garden or does needlework, in particular counted cross-stitch.

Michelle maintains a website (www.michellestyles.co.uk) and a blog, (www.michellestyles.blogspot.com) and would be delighted to hear from you.

Recent novels by the same author:

THE GLADIATOR'S HONOUR
A NOBLE CAPTIVE
SOLD AND SEDUCED
THE ROMAN'S VIRGIN MISTRESS
TAKEN BY THE VIKING
A CHRISTMAS WEDDING WAGER
  (part of *Christmas By Candlelight*)
VIKING WARRIOR, UNWILLING WIFE
AN IMPULSIVE DEBUTANTE
A QUESTION OF IMPROPRIETY
IMPOVERISHED MISS, CONVENIENT WIFE

To Pauline Tomlinson;
because everyone needs a Pauline in their life!

Chapter One

July 1837—Gilsland, Cumberland

The carriage's abrupt stop jolted Adam Ravensworth, the third Viscount Ravensworth, from a fitful sleep, and sent his cane clattering to the floor of the carriage. Adam gripped the horsehair seat with his long fingers, narrowly preventing his body from tumbling after it.

'In the name of all that is holy, what sort of driving is that? You are paid to avoid potholes, not drive through them!' Adam banged on the roof.

Silence filled the unmoving carriage, only to be broken by the tramp of heavy feet and muffled voices. Adam froze, listening. Not poor driving but something far more sinister.

With a practised hand, he reached towards where his pistol was stored and encountered—air. A loud oath dropped from his lips.

Adam forced the remains of sleep from his mind. The pistol was there. It had to be. He had carefully placed it alongside the necklace before they had left the coaching inn this morning, an integral part of his ritual. His hand groped for the ruby necklace. His shoulders relaxed slightly. That at least was there.

Adam reached out again, fumbling in the dark with the latch of a hidden compartment, but despite his frantic groping the space and indeed the carriage remained empty of all weapons. Gone. Vanished.

What else had they done? And when? The fog of sleep clawed at his mind, making it difficult to think. Adam shook his head, noting the vile taste in his mouth. Drugged. He swore at his own stupidity. Meticulous planning had gone into this unscheduled stop, but this was where it would end. It would not reach the desired conclusion. He would see to it. Personally.

'Down from the carriage!'

'Here, what is this all about?' His new driver Hawkins's protest was a heartbeat too slow, too certain.

'We mean business. Stand aside.'

A single shot rang out.

Adam grabbed the ruby necklace and slipped it into the waistband of his trousers. Everything else was replaceable, but not the necklace—his talisman, a reminder of who he was and what he had done. If he lost the necklace, he might as well be dead.

'Step out, my lord,' Hawkins said.

Adam's neck muscles relaxed slightly. Hawkins lived. But how loyal was he? His words held the barest veneer of civility.

Rapidly Adam searched on the floor for the pistol, hoping that in some mad moment of sleep, he had dislodged the weapon. Nothing. His hand closed about his cane, a weapon of sorts, something to even the odds.

'Get out, I say!' The door rattled again and Hawkins's voice became harsher. 'Get out or I will drag your lordship's carcass from the coach.'

'When I am ready.'

Adam tugged at the sleeves of his frock coat and straightened his stock. He tucked his cane under his arm and knew he looked the perfect gentleman, perhaps a bit foppish and overly concerned with clothes, but not someone who waited for an opportunity to strike.

Taking a deep breath, he stepped out into the night and surveyed the scene, weighing his options. Seven men, far too many to fight and have a hope of success. Whoever had planned this had left nothing to chance, but someone always made a mistake.

The leader snapped his fingers and Hawkins plucked the cane from Adam's hand. 'Sorry, my lord. The cane is required. We wouldn't want anyone to get hurt.'

'Is there some problem, Hawkins?' Adam kept his voice calm and unhurried, the epitome of an aristocrat who frequented the environs of St James's. 'Why have you stopped the coach? I need to get to Newcastle to catch the packet to London. The Atheneaum's annual election waits for no man.'

'Outlaws. Road was blocked ahead and I slowed. These men grabbed the horses' heads.' Hawkins shifted from foot to foot as the lantern cast strange elongated shadows. The cane with its hidden sword was now clasped lightly in Hawkins's unsuspecting hand. 'It weren't my fault. Not expecting it, like. There was nothing I could do. Honest my lord.'

'Join me, Hawkins.' Adam held out his hand, and willed the driver to place the cane into his palm. 'It is not too late. I will save you, Hawkins.'

Hawkins took a step backwards, shaking his head. 'I'm sorry my lord. They…they threatened…my wife and child.'

'Indeed? And here I thought you a single man without a relation in the world.' Adam lowered his voice. 'How much did they pay you, Hawkins? How did they get you—drink, gaming or was it opium? Did you think about your wife or child, then?'

Hawkins raised the cane, but Adam caught it before the first blow fell and pulled Hawkins towards him.

'Whatever it was, it couldn't have been enough.' Adam saw the man's face contort with uncertainty and fear.

'Leave Lord Ravensworth to me. I have waited a lifetime for this moment.' The leader's muffled voice rang out again. 'Back to your place. And this time take his cane out of his reach.'

The driver yanked the cane away and turned on his heel.

Another wave of drug-induced tiredness attacked Adam. He fought against it, struggling to stay upright. Survival first. Retribution later.

'You have something we want. Something you stole.' The leader's voice was rough, but held a tone that Adam's brain faintly recognised. 'A treasure beyond reckoning. Give it here.'

He lifted his hand and Adam saw the tattoo of a blackbird between the man's thumb and forefinger. The ground shifted beneath Adam's feet. He knew the tattoo. Once it had had a meaning, but that was more than a continent and half-a-dozen years away. The gang of particularly murderous thieves who sported the tattoo and who preyed on innocent travellers were dead. The last ones had danced from the end of a noose after he had testified in Bombay.

'You are making a serious error,' Adam said. 'I have no idea what you mean.'

'Wrong answer.' A blow struck the side of his head, sending him staggering towards the dark edges of his mind. 'A rich nabob like you. You brought the treasure from India. You thought yourself beyond the curse. It has taken us a long time, but the goddess will be satisfied once we have tasted your blood.'

Adam put his hands on his knees and attempted to breathe. Ghosts did not possess cudgels and curses were for the weak-minded. These men were flesh and blood, but who? And why now? When had the tattoo been revived?

Another blow rained down on his back and shoulders—heavier, harder. He stumbled and fell, lay still, then waited. A tiny portion of his mind told him to offer up a prayer for help, but any higher being that existed had forsaken him after India. He knew that.

'Here, you'll kill him. They never said nothing about killing. That's murder, like!' Hawkins squawked.

'It's a dirty business. You knew that.'

'It is not here,' a voice called out

'Search the carriage again!'

'What about him?'

'Him?' A contemptuous kick landed on Adam's back. 'He will be dead before sunlight. Did you see him stagger as he came out? They did their work at the inn.'

'You will get what you deserve,' Adam muttered under his breath, but he kept his body still and his face in the mud, waiting.

'I'll check his person.'

'It won't be there. It will be in the coach. He didn't have time, like,' Hawkins protested. 'He always takes the necklace when he travels. He has a special compartment for it, see. He didn't have the time or the wit to get it.'

'Just the same.' Hands tore at his coat, ripping it from his back.

'That was a mistake. My tailor hasn't even sent the bill yet,' Adam said as he flipped over and brought his boots up into his attacker's chest and kicked hard.

The man flew backwards, colliding with another.

Adam crouched for a heartbeat and then began to run. Behind him, he heard the screech of the men calling their dogs. But Adam did not stop until he reached a small cliff, lit silver in the moonlight. He checked his step as a stone bounced down and hit the river.

The dogs howled again, closer. Two shots rang out.

Adam kicked off his boots, grabbed them with one hand and jumped, allowing the current to take him.

'Miss Milton! Miss Milton. You must come. A man is lying by the river. Without any clothes on! Undressed—that is to say, naked!'

Daisy Milton glanced up from her sister Felicity's latest letter about their niece and the unwelcome return

of her illness. She was alarmed at her young charge's
words. A naked man? Here in this peaceful spot? Nella
Blandish was supposed to be gathering flowers for a
botany project, not spying. She had been given the
strictest orders. But Nella had returned with her hat
ribbon askew, pinafore stained, no flowers and another
outlandish tale.

There were times when a governess was forced to
make a judgement. Her sister's problems would have to
wait.

'Truly, Miss Milton, there is a naked man! I saw him
with my very own eyes.'

Daisy folded the letter and placed it in the wicker
basket, each movement precise and unhurried. 'Is this
another of your fables, Prunella Blandish? This one
does bear some semblance to last week's tale about the
lion eating buttercups.'

'It is the truth…this time, Miss Milton. Honest,
there is a naked man. You could see everything—all the
way to kingdom come.' Nella's bottom lip stuck out
and she shook her golden curls. 'I watched him and
watched him and he has not moved. He lies there, feet
dangling in the water, head resting on a log.'

'And what was this naked man of yours doing
before he started lying there? Swimming?' Daisy
strove to keep her voice calm. She refused to enquire
about what this everything-to-kingdom-come that
Nella had seen was. If Nella's tale was true, and if they
did encounter this man on the way back to the house,
she would explain in a quiet but firm voice about
common decency and the necessity of wearing something when bathing.

Nella's reactions were only natural, the result of being a lively twelve year old. But what would Mrs Blandish say once Nella related the tale? And Nella's sister? A tiny pain appeared behind Daisy's eyes. She needed this position and its wage.

No one ever set out to be a governess, least of all her. But Felicity had to look after their niece, and the annuity from her father was barely enough for one to manage on, let alone three. There was little to be done about falling sickness, but she completely agreed with Felicity that Kammie must be kept at home. It was Felicity, not she, who bore the hardest burden. Daisy's sole contribution was to provide what funds she could.

'How should I know, Miss Milton, what the man was doing before I saw him?' Nella adopted her butter-wouldn't-melt face. 'You always tell me to refrain from speculating.'

'It is a lovely afternoon in July.' Daisy kept her voice light and tried to regain some of her authority. 'I do hope you came away without saying anything. It would have been the height of bad manners, Prunella, to interrupt a man's bathing.'

'He wasn't bathing. He was lying there in his altogether...' Nella's brow wrinkled and she clasped her hands under her chin, the very picture of injured innocence. 'That is the very honest truth, Miss Milton.'

Daisy frowned, tapping her fingers against the basket.

How many times had she heard those words—'the very honest truth'—over the past few months, only to discover that Nella had managed to exaggerate or somehow twist the story until it bore little resemblance to the actual sequence of events? This tale would stop here.

'You solemnly promised your dearest mama no more tales or untruths.'

'I know what I saw, Miss Milton…' Nella pushed her bonnet more firmly on to her head. 'I'll prove it. Don't you want to see the man? Judge for yourself?'

To see the man? Daisy set her bonnet more firmly on her head and smoothed the pleats of her black stuff gown. Nella made it seem as if she was some sort of sex-starved spinster who had nothing better to do than spy on men bathing. She had a healthy appreciation of the masculine form, but the consequences had to be considered. Someone had to contain Nella's enthusiasm.

'It is not a question of want, Prunella, but of decorum.'

'It would be the Christian thing to do.' Nella's being positively glowed as the idea took hold in her brain. 'To see if he was in trouble and needed our aid. He could have gone over the waterfall, or have been attacked by brigands…or…'

'I do know my Christian duty, thank you, Prunella. And I endeavour to do it. Always. As you should.'

Daisy checked the little watch pinned to her gown. Nearly half past three. Did they have time to investigate? She could then deliver the 'Importance of Always Telling the Truth' lecture for the seventh time in as many days when Nella's falsehood was revealed.

'It is time we returned to the house. Your dear mama and sister will wish to know where you are. There may be arrivals to greet. Gilsland Spa is quite the rage this year as London remains in solemn mourning for our late lamented king.'

'Susan isn't interested in new arrivals. Susan's sights are fixed on Lord Edward because he is the younger grandson of an earl and she wants a title.' Nella paused and wrinkled her nose. 'But Mama says that if anyone more eligible comes along, Susan had best be prepared to change her mind. Papa is worried about Lord Edward being to let in the pocket. Susan agreed eventually. A carriage is worth more than a handsome face.'

'Nella!' Daisy stared hard at her charge. 'Your sister cannot be that mercenary.'

'Susan told Mama the very same thing this morning.' Nella swayed on her toes. A broad smile crossed her face as she lowered her voice. 'I listen at doors.'

'Then your sister is to get her London Season after all.'

'Susan is quite convinced, though, that Lord Edward can be brought up to snuff and has begged Mama to keep the house for another month. It will save the expense of a London Season next year and the water will soothe dearest Mama's nerves.'

Nella's voice replicated the exact intonation of Miss Blandish's overly refined tone. With difficulty Daisy forced the laugh back down her throat.

'You should not listen in on private conversations. It is neither clever nor useful.' Daisy practised her best governess stare. 'And you should certainly never repeat them to anyone.'

'How can I learn anything interesting otherwise? Nobody tells me *anything*.'

'It is far from ladylike. Your mama wants you to become a lady. You will want to make a good match, just as your sister does.'

'Who wants to get married? Marriage is all practicality and good breeding. I want to be a lady explorer.' Nella waved her hand with airy disdain. 'I am going to discover lost continents and find buried treasure. And I have not been anywhere yet—even Susan has been to France.'

'Even lady explorers are ladies first. And explorers pay attention to their geography lessons.' Daisy winced slightly at her prim words, so reminiscent of her own governess's—glittering dreams were well and good, but they often vanished in the cold light of reality. Once she had dreamed of exploring the world. Now she settled for independence.

Nella tilted her head to one side as her eyes shone with mischief. 'Do you think Susan would be interested in seeing my naked gentleman?'

'Prunella! Control your mouth and your thoughts! A lady acts with propriety and honesty at all times. The man in question does not belong to you. And you have no idea of his antecedents and so cannot make a judgement about his status.'

Nella screwed up her nose. 'But do you think Susan would be interested in my discovery?'

'I doubt it.' Daisy struggled to keep her voice withering. She could well imagine Susan Blandish's face squeezed up as though she had tasted a particularly sour plum if Nella mentioned the word naked. 'Knowing things and informing other people of them are two different things. Discretion and tact should be your bywords, even when you are a lady explorer.'

'I am glad I have you, Miss Milton.' Nella reached out a grubby hand and squeezed Daisy's pristine glove. 'You never worry about such things as fashion and how to catch a viscount. You understand about exploring and never wanting to get married.' Nella batted her lashes. 'I wouldn't have interrupted you for any other reason. I know how much you enjoy your letters from your sister. It is just that I feel one must try to help and do one's Christian duty. Mama gave me a lecture on the very subject yesterday after I objected to meeting Mrs Gough, the vicar's wife, who smells distinctly of lemon barley water.'

Daisy permitted a tiny smile to cross her face as she recognised Nella's tone. Perhaps after all she would reach some sort of *rapprochement* with her pupil. The whole episode would provide fodder for several letters to her friend Louisa Sibson. 'Where is this sight that you wish me to see?'

Daisy climbed the short ridge and looked down on the winding river. The sound of Crammel Linn waterfall crashed in her ears. In the sky a hawk circled. All was at peace. Nothing could possibly be wrong here.

She shaded her eyes and then she saw him, the body, lying in a pool of water just before the waterfall. His body was half in and half out of the water, caught on a log.

Once when she had been about ten, she had travelled to Italy with her mother and sister to improve her Italian. In Sorrento, she had spied a statue like this man. Not young or a hardened warrior, but an athlete, poised to throw a javelin. The perfection of masculinity personified, her governess had declared, with a clasp of her gloved hands before sweeping Daisy onwards towards more suitable views. She had not quite understood the meaning of the remark until now.

'You see. I spoke the very honest truth,' Nella called out in a sing-song voice. 'A naked man by the river.'

'Except he is far from naked. He wears a shirt and trousers.'

Nella put her hands on her hips. 'Mama always says that a man might as well be naked if he is not wearing a stock or a coat, and this one isn't. He does not have boots either. Or a waistcoat.'

'He is still wearing clothing, Prunella.' Daisy rolled her eyes heavenwards and struggled to keep her face stern.

'I preferred it when he was naked.' Nella rocked back on her heels. 'It made it seem all the more exciting. It is very easy to imagine that he had no clothes on and I could see everything. See how his shirt moulds to his back. He has a very pleasant back.'

Daisy swallowed hard, remembering the statues in Italy with their unclad shoulders and tapering waists.

'The man is clearly in need of assistance. Excitement does not come into it,' Daisy said firmly. A governess was never ruffled. Or surprised even when confronted with such a sight. A governess was prepared for everything.

She put her hand to the side of her face and tried to think straight.

Help—she needed help and fast. Strong backs and arms to carry the man from the river.

She picked up her skirts and prepared to run, but

halted before she had gone two steps. Was it her imagination or was the log rocking against the stones, preparing to carry its cargo down the waterfall?

Her mouth went dry. By the time she returned with help, the man would have been washed downstream, and any hope of survival gone. He needed to be lifted clear of the river immediately.

'Do you think he is dead? He has not moved.' A thoughtful expression came into Nella's eyes. 'I have never seen a dead person before, not even when Grandpapa died and they laid him out in the best parlour. I was considered too young.'

'I have no idea.' Daisy watched the man for another breath. The faint breeze ruffled his hair, but she could not discern the rhythmic lifting of his chest. On one of his hands the dull gleam of metal showed. What had happened to him? A swimming accident? Had he misjudged the swift current? Surely no robber or thief would have left a ring. 'It is impossible to say from here. But there does not appear to be any blood. A closer look is needed. Remember, Nella, hard facts and not guesswork. Ladies do not make assumptions.'

Daisy shifted the basket so it was tighter against her hip and the blanket secure. A narrow bramble-strewn path wound its way down to the river and if she was careful she would be able to reach the man…the corpse without too much difficulty.

'Shall I come with you? Or am I needed elsewhere?' Nella asked, pulling her bonnet towards her nose. 'I mean, I think I would rather go back to the house. Mama may have need of me.'

'What a clever idea, Nella.' Daisy forced her voice

to be brisk. Propriety demanded that Nella be kept
away. 'It would be best if you stopped at Shaw's Hotel.
Tell the innkeeper about the man and ask him to send
some assistance. You can do that, can't you, Nella? You
can find your way?'

Nella stood straighter and positively glowed. 'I know
the way. I am twelve and not a baby of ten, after all. We
came here last year for Mama's nerves. Mademoiselle
Le Claire often had a poorly head and so I wandered
about on my own. The innkeeper and I became great
friends.'

Daisy clamped her lips shut. She knew all about
Mademoiselle Le Claire and her habits. The woman
had returned to France and Nella had been through
three other governesses since, each with their own
particular quirk. 'Nella, you should walk quickly and
not run. A lady always proceeds at a dignified pace—
even lady explorers.'

A mutinous expression passed over Nella's face, but
she obviously thought better of it. 'Of course, Miss
Milton.'

'That's a good girl. Remember to tell the innkeeper
without delay or *embellishment*.'

'I will, Miss Milton,' Nella sang out, lifting her hand
in farewell.

Daisy pushed the slight sense of trepidation from her
mind. Nella would enjoy the attention of being the
heroine of the hour. Nella set off walking at a quick
pace, but before she had gone thirty paces, the girl began
to run. Daisy shook her head and turned her attention
to the injured man. It was definitely not her imagination.
The log had started to move towards the waterfall.

Daisy put her boot down on a loose rock, half-slid and half-ran two more feet. A distinct ripping sound resounded as the black stuff fabric in her skirt gave way. Daisy winced. Another bit of mending to do. And she hated to think about the state of her gloves. Felicity and Kammie had given them to her for her last birthday. Kammie had carefully stitched the daisies about the cuff. She wouldn't have worn them, but, after last week's thorn-bush incident, the pairs of serviceable gloves she owned were distinctly limited.

As she reached the riverbank, there was a huge creak and the log pulled free of the anchoring rock. With hesitating, Daisy plunged in, grabbed the man's arm and tugged. His body refused to move as the current began to pull the log ever closer to the waterfall. Daisy watched as two black objects broke free, swirled once and then went over the waterfall to their doom.

Daisy closed her eyes, readjusted her hold on him and pulled with all her strength. At first the log seemed to be trying to carry her with it as well. She went further into the river, and planted her feet more firmly. Suddenly his body moved with her, coming up against her. Immediately Daisy redoubled her efforts and forced her mind not to think about the impropriety of having his chest so close to hers. She stumbled backwards, and his heavy body landed on top of her. Her hands pushed him, rolling him off her. He gave a faint groan.

She turned her head in time to see the log crash over the waterfall, splintering as it hit the rocks. A violent shiver racked her as she thought how narrowly he had escaped.

He gave a violent cough, bringing up water. Daisy rapped him sharply on the back until his breath appeared to come easier.

His linen shirt was translucent and moulded to his back. He wore a pair of fawn-coloured trousers and so gave the illusion of being naked. He lay on his stomach, head turned away from her. His black hair curled slightly at his neck. His chest rose and fell slightly. Alive. A soft noise arose, a cross between a snore and a snort, and he mumbled something incoherent about clubs and railways—the same sort of noise that her father had made in his wingback armchair after several glasses of port.

A deep rage filled her. She had risked life, limb and reputation to save this man and he was drunk. More than likely uninjured. She should have let him drown.

She coughed softly, but when he did not move, she tried again, reaching forwards to prod him with her basket as water dripped from her gown.

At the sound of her squelching boots, his lashes fluttered and his amber gaze pierced her. His eyes were a myriad of shifting browns and golds and his lashes provided the perfect frame.

The sound of laughter filled the air—his laughter, low and husky as if they were sharing some private joke.

'Are you hurt? Or merely drunk?' she asked through gritted teeth. 'I have spoilt my best gloves and soaked my gown in the rescue attempt. The least you can do is answer civilly instead of laughing at the spectacle.'

The man groaned and buried his face in his arms. 'Do you have to speak so loudly? You would wake the dead, ma'am, with your tones.'

'Not the dead, just you.' Daisy raised her eyes heavenwards. English, and with the arrogant tones of someone well bred. That was all she needed—a rake who had made a drunken wager to swim the Irthing. All she asked for was a bit of common decency, but when had a rake ever possessed such a thing? 'Do you know how you came to be here?'

'Not by choice. Wrong sort of clothes to swim in for a start. Always swim in my birthday suit.' A great cough racked his body. 'Swallowed most of the river as well. Definitely not my preferred tipple. It lacks a certain something, don't you agree?'

Daisy wrung out the hem of her skirt. Definitely a rake and one of the worst sort. Her only hope was that he would begin to make a certain amount of sense and she could leave him. 'Have you any idea why you are here?'

'Carriage halted. I escaped and the dogs followed. So I went into the river.' His frown increased and his hand fumbled about the rocks as if he were searching for something. 'My boots! What have you done with my boots?'

'I have not touched your boots. A pair may have gone over the falls, but forgive me as I was otherwise occupied with saving you.'

The man swore, loud and long. Daisy made a tutting noise at the back of her throat, so that he would understand that curses were always unnecessary in the hearing of a lady. She then made a great show of picking up her basket.

'Someone stole those boots.'

'You still have your signet ring.' Daisy pointed at the

dull gold band he wore on his little finger. Did he take her for some green girl? Easily conned by a smile and a pair of fine eyes? As if she would take a pair of boots. He was probably the sort that could not take his boots off without a valet. More than likely the boots were with his friends.

A frown appeared between his two dark eyebrows. His fingers curled about his ring. 'Not that. Curious.'

'Why did they do that? Why not take it if they were thieves?' Daisy shifted the basket to her other hip and watched him through narrow slits.

'You would have to ask my attackers. I was too busy trying to stay alive.' The man's sardonic voice echoed in her ears. His long fingers explored the back of his head. 'And while you are at it, you can ask them why they left me with a lump the size of a goose egg on the side of my head. The violence was unnecessary.'

'If that is the case, then perhaps I had best go and find them immediately. You are obviously in no need of assistance from me.' Daisy opted for her most withering tone.

'Why did this attack happen?' His hand shot out and encircled her wrist. 'The truth this time, phantom of my mind, or I shall be forced to destroy you.'

Chapter Two

Adam fastened his gaze on the slender wrist and the embroidered glove of the woman. Until his fingers closed around her, he had been nearly convinced she was another apparition, part of the never-ending parade of ghosts and phantoms that had plagued him ever since he had found a log to cling to, to keep his head above water. Always mocking him and then vanishing, always keeping that elusive answer of why the attack had happened beyond his reach.

He glanced upwards, following the line of the shiny black sleeve to the white collar fastened at her neck with a blue cameo and finally coming to rest on her glorious eyes. For a brief heartbeat, her features blurred and merged with the shadows, becoming the countenance of one of the dead. He blinked and the image vanished.

He swallowed, tasting once again the foul residue in his mouth. It had been at the last inn where his driver had insisted they change horses. Newcastle by mid-morning, Hawkins had said with a laugh, pressing a pint of foul ale on him. Had Hawkins survived? Or had the thieves saved Adam a job and slit his throat?

He pushed the thought from his mind. Later there would be the time for vengeance and retribution. Now, he had to survive. To get away from here. Alive.

His captive moved her hand upwards and silently tried to break free.

Adam regarded her with a jaundiced eye. The fates were definitely laughing at him. He had asked for help as he had struggled against the current, and this is what had appeared—a governess, someone who was more concerned about propriety and giving lip service than actually aiding anyone. Or, worse yet, a parody of a governess intent on harm. She had been about to search him for valuables. He was certain of it. The woman was no angel of mercy, but a black-hearted harpy.

'Who sent you here?' he asked, grinding out the words. 'You might as well confess. I will find out in the end.'

'Let go of my wrist,' the woman said, her hideous straw bonnet slipping to one side and her golden-brown hair tumbling free.

Her tones were clear and precise like a bell, echoing in his mind, reminding him of someone, someone he should know. Adam willed his mind to clear. He had never seen this woman before. Ever. He would have remembered the eyes and the heart-shaped face.

'Let. Me. Go. Now. Before I scream very loudly indeed.'

Adam concentrated on tightening his grip. It would come to him in a moment, the connection. He drew in a breath and his body protested once again at the pain of moving. He had thought lying in the river that he might have been in India again, lying in a pool of blood, waiting for the final blow, when he had been unable to get to Kamala, but had desperately wanted to. When he still thought Kamala might have feelings for him and he could redeem his earlier failure.

He was supposed to die then but didn't. If he could cheat death once, he could do it again. But he had to know if this woman was friend or foe.

'I am warning you.' The woman tapped her foot and her eyes shot sparks. 'Cease this nonsense immediately.'

'I doubt anyone will hear you, save the odd sheep. Possibly a hawk.' He permitted a smile to cross his lips and promptly regretted the pain. 'Unless you have friends nearby.'

'Friends?' Her voice went up an octave and her being quivered. 'Do you think I would have dragged you from the river if I could have sent a man? I saved your life—an act of mercy and one I will regret to my dying day.'

Adam levered his body to a sitting position and concentrated on the frivolous daisies embroidered on his captive's gloves. Would a governess really wear such gloves in contrast to her severe costume? Not any that he encountered. But then the ones he remembered had too-big teeth or casts in their eyes. And their figures were not like this woman's.

Suddenly he wanted done with it, to face his enemy instead of having him lurk in the shadows. He nodded towards the river and empty riverbank on the other side.

'Go head, scream. Or else keep silent.' Adam glared at her. 'My head aches enough as is. I have no desire to hurt you. I only require a few answers— Answers you will give me sooner or later.'

She caught her bottom lip with neat white teeth, worrying it, but no sound emerged from her throat.

'Thank you for confirming my view that you have no intention of screaming,' Adam continued. 'It always pleases me when I read women correctly.'

Her lips curved upwards, transforming her face, making it seem far too lively. 'You harbour odd beliefs.'

'It is never good to make threats that you do not intend to follow through. If you were going to scream, you would have screamed immediately and without warning. Perhaps you are hoping for a kiss.'

'Do you always follow through on your threats?' Her voice held the faintest tremor.

'On my threats and my promises.' Adam dropped his voice to seductive purr. There was more than one way to get an answer from a woman. 'The kiss is a promise.'

Her cheeks flushed. 'I have no desire…'

'Ah, you wish to test my theory.' Adam smiled. This supposed governess was behaving exactly like other women. It was disappointing in a way. He had hoped for more.

'Please,' she whispered.

Adam touched her shoulder and felt the black stuff give way under his touch and the warmth rise up from her. Her large grey-green eyes met his. A sense of satisfaction went through him.

Her next move would be a few false pleas combined

with batted lashes and a single tear down her face to elicit pity and to appeal to his better nature. But that nature had vanished seven years ago in India. He would discover which of his enemies had sent her. And then they would pay. Slowly.

'Shall we begin?' he asked. 'And I want the truth.'

She leant forwards, so that her mouth was inches from his. Her eyes danced with a sudden light. 'Yes, let's.'

Her piercing shriek rose and echoed back from the rocks above the waterfall, paining his ears.

He raised an eyebrow and glared up at her, concentrating on the few escaping tendrils of dark brown hair rather than the superior expression. 'Did the scream make you feel better?'

'Only if it hurt your ears. Like you, I keep my promises. I have been a governess for long enough to know how to handle awkward children.'

'I am not a child. I am a grown man.' The instant the words were out of his mouth, he regretted them. He sounded like he was not yet in long trousers. He concentrated on keeping hold of her wrist.

'Behave like one and let me go.' Her eyes flashed, transforming her face and making him want to stare. There was something so alive about the woman. 'Shall we repeat the exercise or do you release me?'

Most women of his acquaintance would have fainted by now, or at the very least declared their intent to faint, but not this woman. She appeared positively triumphant in her scream.

He cocked his head slightly, his body stilling. Adam's fingers itched to shake her shoulders until she revealed everything, but he remained in control of his emotions and waited for her next move and to see what aid came to her rescue.

The woods were silent. No one was coming. Was she innocent? Could he take the chance?

'Are you always this stubborn? Who knows who you could have alerted?'

Her chin tilted upwards. 'It is my intention to alert someone. There are laws against this sort of behaviour. Molesting women.'

'Someone? Someone in particular? Who?'

'Does it matter?' Her bonnet ribbons trembled slightly.

'You can tell me. Who sent you? What secrets am I supposed to tell?' He pulled her close, so that each one of her eyelashes was highlighted against her pale skin. Up close and unencumbered by the shadow of the bonnet, her face was striking—thin curved eyebrows, a straight nose and full lips that did more than hint at passion. 'Give me his name. Who is your lover? Where does he hide? What does he want from me? What does he seek?'

'I am unmarried, sir!'

'Marriage has never been a requirement for taking a lover.'

'It is with me.' Her nostrils quivered with indignation and her cheeks flamed pink. 'That is to say, I wish for no other lover than my eventual husband.'

'And does he have a name? This fiancé of yours?'

'I have no fiancé.'

'No lover, no fiancé and no prospects. Is it any wonder you are a governess?'

'I am a virtuous woman, whereas you are naught but a scoundrel and a rake.'

'A woman of virtue! Truly a rare prize!'

'My elbows are quite sharp.' Her voice became shrill. 'And I will not hesitate to use any means at my disposal to fight you. To the death if necessary. What is a woman when she has lost her virtue?'

'What is she, indeed?' Adam lifted his other hand and traced a finger down the rim of her bonnet. An errant curl brushed against it, surprising him with its softness. 'More interesting? Yes, a woman who has lost her virtue is infinitely more intriguing.'

'Let me go. I am…am not that sort of woman. Nor will I be—ever.'

'Rest assured, ma'am, I have no designs on your virtue.' He allowed his hand to drop. 'But I will keep the suggestion under advisement.'

The woman's mouth opened and closed several times. 'You are impossible.'

'My nurse proclaimed me a devil at the tender age of two.' Adam permitted a smile to cross his face. He leant forwards so his head touched the brim. 'I have made no attempt to improve.'

'I saved your life, sir! Do not ruin mine! Let me go and I will answer your questions.'

The governess gave one last frantic tug and he let her go. She tumbled backwards and gave him a view of a neatly turned ankle, far neater than the dress suggested. The woman had something to hide. He could feel it in his bones. He would discover her secrets and destroy her if needs be.

'Are you satisfied? You are free.' He gathered his

legs under him and wondered if they would have any power.

She gave a loud disapproving sniff and scuttled backwards. 'You did not have to let me go that quickly.'

'A proper gentleman never refuses a lady's reasonable request. My dear mama taught me that.'

'Are you a gentleman?' She tilted her head and then shook her head in wonderment.

'I was born one.'

'Then behave like one.' Her eyes slid away from his. Almost imperceptibly she began to inch towards her basket, shuffling backwards on her hands. Her fingers reached out towards it and then hesitated as she saw his face. Her white teeth worried her bottom lip and her eyes slid between his face and the basket. Then she gave a small sigh. He realised with a start of surprise that she intended on keeping her promise. A woman of integrity. Most unexpected.

'I will answer all your questions, but I can shed no light on why you are here,' she said with quiet firmness.

Adam frowned. He prided himself on being immune to feminine wiles. How many times had he seen the false pleas, the crocodile tears for yet another bauble? But this woman was sincere and willing to keep her promises. 'You have no idea why I might have been attacked?'

She nodded vigorously, sending her bonnet sliding to one side of her face. 'I give you my word as a governess and a lady brought low by family circumstance.'

The last words—family circumstance—hung in the air. Adam immediately recalled India. Then, too, Kamala had claimed to be a lady, brought low by family circumstance. She, too, had begged and pleaded with him to save her, but he had refused to act. Then he had taken her proof to his commander and had lost her for ever. Even now he heard Kamala's voice whispering, begging him to forgive her. He refused to have another death on his conscience. The parade of ghosts was long enough already. He shook his head and willed those particular shades to go.

Adam looked up at the sky. He attempted to regain his balance, his famous cool demeanour. The events seven years ago had nothing to do with today.

What was it that was said about him in the clubs in London? Adam Ravensworth never loses his temper and always maintains control. Hah! Here he was attacking governesses, or whatever she was pretending to be. Had he fallen that far?

'Why do you feel compelled to wear such ugly clothes? What are you attempting to conceal? Your magnificent figure?'

Two bright spots appeared on her cheeks and her hands went to automatically smooth her skirts and straighten her bonnet, hiding the glorious gold-brown hair that had spilled free. 'Are you always this rude?'

'I ask the questions. You answer them. It was our bargain.'

'Your question is…personal.' Her hand plucked at her skirts. 'I *am* a governess. I wear what I wear because…it is appropriate. Your time is up.'

'My questions are not finished.'

'But I am.' In one swift movement, she picked up her basket and started to stalk off. 'I have no doubt that you will find your own way back to whatever hole you crawled from.'

His head pained him as he attempted to rise and sank back down again. Adam loudly cursed his weakness. The woman merely lifted an eyebrow and continued walking.

Adam winced. With her went his best hope of getting out of this hellish nightmare alive.

'Thank you for saving my miserable life,' he called out. 'Allow me to show you my gratitude.'

Daisy hesitated. She had planned on running, but the wet black-stuff material made moving swiftly next to impossible.

'Change, become a pleasant person now that you have been given a second chance,' Daisy retorted and knew the instant the words left her mouth they were mistaken. She should have ignored his plea.

'I did not ask for the carriage to be set upon.' His soft words sent a warm pulse down her spine, holding her there. 'Nor the beating. I am an innocent man. On my honour as a gentleman, I need your help desperately. Must I be reduced to begging? Forgive my sins and trespasses. At first I was convinced you were an apparition sent to plague me. Then I was certain you belonged to the gang. I suffered from malaria when I was in India.'

An apparition. Tears pricked Daisy's eyelids. She remembered her brother Tom using the same sort of words when he was home on leave from the East India Company and suffering from a recurrence of the ague. She looked back over her shoulder and saw the man sitting there, bruising beginning to show on his face.

She glanced upwards and saw the hawk was now but a speck in the sky. Had all this happened so quickly?

Could she blame him if he had thought her somehow

involved? How would she have behaved if she had been thrown into a river and left for dead? If she had not been sure a person was truly there, or their intent was peaceful?

You are too quick to judge, Daisy my girl. Give people a chance to prove their worth before leaping to conclusions. You might be pleasantly surprised. Her brother's voice reprimanding her for some long-forgotten misdemeanour echoed in her brain. Her brother would never have left anyone in this condition, and neither could she.

Daisy retied the strings of her bonnet, making sure it was firmly on her head, reminding her of her position in the world. 'You have not improved with age. You have ended up like your nurse predicted. The very devil.'

'Hoisted by my own words.' He shivered as he shook his head in mock despair. 'There are devils and then there are demons.'

Daisy resisted the impulse to smile. His hair had flopped forwards, making him seem like a little boy. But there was nothing boyish about his mouth or his hooded glance. Here was a man who was aware of the seductive power he could wield over a woman. Daisy forced her shoulders to relax. He would be surprised when she proved immune.

'I will listen to your story and then decide if you are deserving of my help. But I want facts and not embellishments. When did this start?'

'There are simply not enough hours in the day to begin to explain, even if I knew where to begin.' Adam ran a hand through his hair. A vast tiredness swept over

him. Where should he begin? In India with Kamala, the
necklace and its aftermath? But everyone save him was
dead now. There could not be a connection. If he knew
the why behind the attack, then he could give the
woman some reason. No, it was best to keep things
simple. 'But like any law-abiding person I object to
being beaten and robbed.'

Her full lips became a disapproving line. 'Are you
always this irritable? Or did drink contribute to this
situation?'

Adam regarded the waterfall with its treacherous
rocks. He should have died last night. He could see that
now. A few inches to the right or left and the log he had
clung to would have gone over. His head would have
been dashed opened on the rocks. He closed his eyes,
unable to bear the glare of the water any more. Arguing
with this woman was the only thing that was keeping
him from collapsing in a heap.

'I don't generally make a habit of jumping into fast-
flowing rivers at night—drunk or sober.'

'It is good to hear that you can be sensible.' The
woman's voice dripped with sarcasm. 'Are you from
around here? How far do we have to go before I can
bid you adieu?'

'Where is here?' Adam gazed at the crashing waterfall and the broad-leaf wood. How far had the coach
had travelled and in what direction before they had
stopped? He wanted to think the time had been short,
but all his brain could summon was confused images.
The carriage stopping, the shouts, the rude awaken-
ing from confused dreams.

'You are near Gilsland in Cumberland.' She put her

basket down and shielded her eyes. 'Shaw's Hotel is no more than two miles from here.'

Gilsland! Adam raised his eyes heavenwards. The tension in his shoulders eased slightly. His attackers had made an error. In Gilsland he was known and could procure the means to go after the gang with relative ease, provided he could discover their lair.

'The area is not noted for its thieves,' he said slowly. 'The border raids stopped over a century ago.'

'Then you must have enemies.'

Adam considered the question. Who hated him enough to want him dead? He had broken with his mistress before he had left for Scotland, but she had received a good pay off and had gone into the arms of a baronet. The poor fool was welcome to her. His business associates would not dare. There was no one. No reason he could think of. His imaginings about the Indian thuggee—those long-dead murderers who attacked innocent travellers—were hallucinations brought on by the drugged beer. Had to be. But who wanted the necklace enough to bribe his driver? Who would take that sort of risk?

'None that I felt would take such drastic measures.' Adam pinched the bridge of his nose and bade the pains in his head to go. 'It must be this area.'

'Impossible, despite Sir Walter Scott's tales to the contrary.' The governess began to straighten her hideous bonnet as she expounded on her theme of the area being safe and very refined. Adam inched his way over to the basket. He touched the handle and secreted the necklace in between the lining and the wicker basket. Later when they had reached safety, he would retrieve it, but for now, it was best that it resided there, hidden. If she had no connection to the gang, then she would not be in danger. If she did, the thieves would deal with her.

'A very pretty speech, but I was attacked here and, therefore, discount your theory,' he said, bringing the recital of Gilsland's virtue to a close.

The governess gave a loud sniff and straightened her mud-splattered gloves. The ring finger split open. She wrinkled her nose. 'Bother!'

Adam lowered his voice to a seductive purr. 'Allow me to get you another pair.'

Her cheeks flamed. 'I could not possibly accept. It is not done. Ever.'

'You have decided that I am a ruffian.' Adam put a hand to his head and winced at the lump. Each breath he took pained his ribs. But he would procure another pair of gloves for the lady and she would accept them. It was the least he could do.

'I am being practical.' The governess picked up the basket and primly held it in front of her. 'Without a formal introduction, I have no knowledge of your antecedents.'

'It is my fault your gloves have become spoilt; even you will have trouble denying that.' Adam regarded her with a practised eye. His manoeuvre had been a success. She suspected nothing. 'Miss…'

'Milton. Miss Daisy Milton…governess to Miss Prunella Blandish.' She ignored his outstretched hand.

'Adam Ravensworth, the third Viscount Ravensworth.' He inclined his head. Lord knew, right now he needed an ally. He might be near Gilsland, but

he was not in the hotel. He could remember the walk
to the waterfall from the hotel took nearly the entire
morning, not a prospect to be undertaken lightly, even
in the best of health.

'I had not realised that the second viscount—Lord
Charles Ravensworth—had died.'

'My grandfather died two years ago.'

'Ah, that explains it. I recollect his despairing of his
grandsons. Which one are you? The elder one who
would not settle or the younger one who went to India?'

Adam started. Of all the responses, he had not
expected that one. His grandfather had been well
known once, but his gout had made it difficult for him
to go out in the final years. Sometimes, he had spoken
querulously about everyone but his immediate family
considering him long gone from this world. Had he
once long ago met this woman? It would explain the
strange air of familiarity. He half-smiled—nothing to
do with India and everything to do with Warwickshire
and home. 'How did you know my grandfather?'

'He was a client of my first employer. Years ago. He
came to dinner once.' Miss Milton gave a distinct nod.
'You have a certain look about your nose and eyes that
recalls his features. He, however, was a perfect gentleman.'

'Why did you sit next to my grandfather?' Adam
ignored the gentleman remark. He never thought he'd
have occasion to bless the old man, but right now, he
blessed his grandfather's foresight in attending that
dinner party.

'They needed a spare woman to make up the dinner
party and felt I had the necessary qualifications.'

'Your employer was…'

'His solicitor.'

'Which one of Marsden, Flyte and Wainwright?' Adam held up his hand, stopping her words. 'Allow me to guess—Flyte has two little girls. He recently remarried after being widowed, but is reckoned to have an eye for the ladies.'

Miss Milton drew in her breath sharply and her cheeks flamed. Adam made a mental note to send Mr Flyte's wandering eye a case of the best port once he reached civilisation.

'The late Mrs Flyte gave me a good reference when I felt it necessary to depart, as well as invaluable advice on the proper attire and conduct for a governess.'

'I take it you did not plan to become a governess.'

She picked at the edge of her glove. 'My father was a solicitor. After his death, quickly followed by my brother's, it was apparent that my annuity would not cover everything.'

Adam did not need to see the slight nod. Her story was probably a familiar one. Dead father with little or no family. Forced to become dependent on the good will of others and her spirit crushed. Not completely, he corrected his thoughts, but only allowed in small flashes. How could anyone enjoy such an existence? But it would take a more determined man than he to free her from the shackles of governess servitude.

'You may consider me safe. I was the one who went to India and returned with a fortune.' He gave a wry smile. 'My brother died in a boating accident. The gloves are a promise, Miss Milton, as you spoilt them to save my life. You will admit that we have a connection.'

'But our slight connection does not permit you to replace my gloves.' Miss Milton drew back.

'A pity.' Adam ignored the pulling on his shoulder. 'You will have them and you may then throw them in to the fire. But never let it be said that I did not honour a debt.'

'Indeed.' Her lips became a thin white line. Adam wondered why he kept glancing at them, and at the outline of her figure. Despite the hideousness of the gown, she could not quite conceal her curves. 'And what else do you want for these *gloves*?'

'I need your help, Miss Milton. I ask for it based on your past friendship with my grandfather.'

'What sort of help?' Miss Milton put her hands behind her back and took a step backwards, stumbling over her basket. She picked it up and held it out in front of her like a shield.

'I want to get away from here, from this river.'

'You want me to hide you.' A frown appeared between her eyebrows. 'You want me to protect you from the law.'

'No, I want you take me to Shaw's Hotel in Gilsland.' Adam bit out the words. Slowly. 'Your involvement will end there. I will endeavour to see your reputation does not suffer from being alone with me.'

'You want nothing more from me?' She tilted her head to one side.

'Nothing at all.' Adam ignored the vague pricking of his conscience about the necklace. What she didn't know could not hurt her. 'Do we have an agreement, Miss Milton?'

Chapter Three

Daisy trudged along the faint path a few steps in front of the infuriating Lord Ravensworth, silently cursing the fact that her conscience had been pricked. As a young girl she had rescued stray cats, dogs and even on one memorable occasion a ferret. She had thought that she had outgrown the habit, but now she was rescuing this man.

He seemed content to follow behind her, making caustic observations about the amount of brambles and rocks. Impossible man. She had thought he would be grateful. She was taking him the easier way. But having decided to depart, he first had had to stop and wash his mouth out, to get rid of the taste. Then they had had to try the other way before he believed her assessment.

Daisy concentrated on keeping to the faint path and ignored the way her black stuff gown clung to her back. Ladies never sweated or perspired. Heat never bothered them. She would look on this as a test of her fortitude and would endure without a murmur.

Lord Ravensworth's curse echoed off the rocks and trees.

Daisy stopped, and crossed her arms. And she wished she could say something equally as strong. 'Losing your boots was not my fault.'

'Lost boots are the least of my worries.' He stepped and cursed again, this time louder and stronger and far more forthright. He then executed a perfect bow as his eyes danced with amusement.

Daisy gritted her teeth, lifted her chin and adopted her most governesslike voice, the one she reserved for situations of dire emergency. 'Pray keep a civil tongue in your mouth when ladies are present.'

'I can see you have taken the late Mrs Flyte's words to heart. Governessing is a calling you are eminently suited for, Miss Prim and Proper.'

'Keeping the niceties of civilisation takes only a modicum of thought and courtesy, something which your character sadly lacks, my lord.'

Lord Ravensworth's eyes glared at her as he rubbed the bottom of his foot. 'And, what pray tell, is the correct word for when one steps on a thorn in bare feet?'

'Stoic forbearance.'

Daisy lifted her chin a notch higher and promptly stumbled over a rock. The hem of her gown tore a bit more and her boot became entangled with a bramble. She pulled slightly, but her foot remained caught. A small oath escaped her lips.

'Stoic forbearance?' Lord Ravensworth's barking laugh rang out.

Daisy glared at him with her best governess expression. He immediately sobered, but his eyes danced. Daisy tried to keep a straight face, but she struggled against a smile. Finally she gave in and laughed.

'Sometimes, stronger measures are necessary,' she admitted.

'Precisely, one does not have to be a governess all the time.' He bent down and his long fingers closed around her boot, releasing it from the bramble. 'With a cool head, things become simple.'

Daisy pressed her hand to her eyes, and attempted to ignore the pulse of warmth that had invaded her insides. This man was everything she should despise about aristocrats, but one touch turned her insides to mush. 'We should be through this bit soon and then there is grass, which will be easier for your feet.'

'I hope you are right.'

His hand reached out, forming a barrier across her path, preventing her from moving forwards.

'Is there something wrong? Have you stepped on another rock? Are you going to faint? I can't carry you, Lord Ravensworth.' Daisy attempted to keep her voice calm. 'You will have to walk.'

'No, I hear voices.' His tone was the sort that she used with Nella when Nella had failed to do something for the third time—patient and exaggeratedly slow.

'Voices? What sort of voices?' Daisy stared at Lord Ravensworth. She had heard nothing, despite her entire being listening. Was he suffering from another delusion? She had heard nothing. No shouting, no calling of her name and promises of help, nothing. She listened again.

Silence except for the faint yap of a dog.

'Do you often suffer from hallucinations, Lord Ravensworth?'

His tawny eyes glowered at her. 'All my senses are working, Miss Milton. Listen, instead of filling the air with noise.'

Then, from far away, she heard the shouts. Louder, and not childlike at all and becoming more distinct by the breath. She put her hand to her throat and moved closer to his solidity. 'Perhaps I was mistaken. Someone is out there. And they are definitely searching for something. They...they are not coming from Gilsland. They are coming from the opposite direction, from above the waterfall.'

His warm hand landed heavily on her shoulder and she gave a small squeak.

'We must be cautious. They could be the aid you sent for, but there again, they could be my attackers. If we keep moving, we might make it to Shaw's before we encounter them.'

Daisy swallowed hard and tried to concentrate on everything but the way his shirt gaped open, revealing a shadowy place at the base of his throat. 'It is the most sensible suggestion I have heard.'

'I will protect you to the best of my ability, Miss Milton.'

'I was not worried about that. I have always been able to look after myself.'

'Nevertheless.'

Daisy glanced over her shoulder to where the trees loomed large and shadowy. The woods had seemed so peaceful, but did they hide anything? She should have insisted on staying closer to the hotel. She had, of course, read Sir Walter Scott's books about the area, but had dismissed his tales of robbers and such as pure fantasy. But now… A shiver went through her as she remembered how blithely she had sent Nella to get help. What if…? The world seemed to spin. 'Who are they? Thieves? Murderers? I should never… Poor Nella!'

'Miss Milton, giving way to panic never solves anything. Remember to breathe.' His hands forced her to turn. She put out a hand and encountered his damp shirt front. Clung to it. 'Deep breaths now. If you faint, we will be lost. How tightly have you done up your corset?'

'I never faint.' Daisy forced the air back into her lungs and ignored the image of his long fingers unlacing her corset. 'Ever. There is little point in it for governesses. Nobody is ever there to catch you when you fall.'

'Poor Miss Milton, not having any support,' he murmured in her ear.

'And corsets are not something one discusses with gentleman. They are unmentionable. But rest assured, breathing is required in my profession.'

'Then you might be able to run or at least walk at a brisk pace.'

'I attempt to be sensible in all things, but it is not my movement that is the problem. You are the one who nearly drowned. Can you run?' Daisy lowered her lashes and stepped back from Lord Ravensworth. 'What do we do next? Hide? Turn back?'

'I want to re-acquaint myself with civilisation as quickly as possible unless you can think of a reason why I should not.' His voice slid over her like silken velvet, but she could also hear the underlying steel. 'You are speechless, Miss Milton. Is there hope for me yet?'

'Do not seek to twist my words.' Two bright spots began to burn on her cheeks. She twisted the handle of the basket. 'I did not ask for this alliance.'

'The state of your arm is the only thing I am concerned about.' He raised an ironic eyebrow. 'Are you offering something else?'

'You are impossible.'

'Silence!'

'I…' A hand over her mouth prevented her from saying more as her body was hauled back the hard planes of his. Her hand went slack, sending the basket tumbling to the ground.

Moving more rapidly than she considered possible, he pulled her into a hollow beside an oak tree. He pressed her into the tree, so they were shielded. His scent enveloped her. She could see the markings of the beating clearly, and the smooth column of his throat. Stubble caressed his chin, giving him the appearance of a highway man, much like a hero from one of the Minerva Press novels that her sister Felicity loved. Her mouth went dry as her world seemed to be swallowed up in his eyes.

What would it be like to be kissed by him? To have his arms hold her close? And for her body to mould against the hard planes of his chest?

Daisy screwed up her eyes, blotting out the sight and regaining control of her thoughts. She pushed against his immovable shoulders, indicating that he should remove himself and find another place to hide.

He shook his head and pointed. Shapes moved around on the other side of the river. But then she saw it; her basket had come to rest in full view with the book of poetry half in and half out of the top, getting ruined in a mud puddle. She had purchased the book just before they had left for Gilsland, an extravagant purchase, but she had also sent little presents to Felicity and Kammie. And it was going to be ruined all because of this man's infuriating caution.

Daisy summoned all her energy and forced him off her. He raised an eyebrow as a dimple played in the corner of his mouth. 'You did not like the position. You prefer to remain in control.'

'I have to get my basket and my volume of poetry. It's Shelley. I happen to like the Romantic poets.'

'Where is your blasted basket?'

Daisy pointed and her ears rang with his furious oath. 'Those men are not searching for me, and my sister gave me the basket. If they see that basket, they will search the area for its owner. Do think ahead, Lord Ravensworth.'

Without waiting for an answer, Daisy marched over to the basket. Her hand curled around its familiar handle as three flat-capped men crashed through the undergrowth on the opposite of the river. An overly thin dog ran alongside, sniffing, and occasionally barking. One of the men lifted his cudgel, swore at the dog and then hit it.

Daisy swallowed hard and kept her head up, fighting the temptation to sink low. She gazed up at the branches and not back at where Adam crouched.

'Hello, over there,' the thickset one called and signalled to her.

Daisy inclined her head. She forced her movements to be unconcerned. She put her hand to her head and discovered her bonnet had come off and her hair tumbled about her shoulders. Bits of oak leaves stuck to it. She must look like a wild thing. Or worse. Desperately her hands searched for a pin.

A soft crunch behind her caused her to turn.

A thin man with deep-set eyes dressed all in funereal black stalked into the glade. His bony fingers were clasped around a large stick. Every few steps he hit the bushes with it, poking them. Each time he lifted the stick, a tattoo of a blackbird on his hand moved. He paused, several bushes from Lord Ravensworth, and regarded her up and down. 'And you are here, why?'

'Is there some problem?' Daisy kept the basket in front of her like a shield.

'We search for the body, the body of a bad man, my friends and I.' The man's voice held a strange lilting quality to it. 'A body in the river. You understand?'

'I have not seen such a thing,' she said, tightening her grip on the basket. Strictly speaking she had told the truth. Lord Ravensworth was alive, she told the voice in her brain. There was truth and there was telling the whole story. 'I am looking for my charge, a young girl. Have you seen her? She ran off a little while ago, leaving me behind.'

'We have not seen any little girls, alive or dead,' the man intoned. His eyes were ice-cold and the pupils had contracted to pinpricks in a sea of red. He cracked his knuckles. His voice held a tone of sinister menace. A wave of cold went through Daisy. 'We are looking for a dead man. He stole something, something valuable, something that belongs to me and my brothers. There's a reward, you understand? A large reward.'

'I would not like to encounter a corpse. Or a thief.' Daisy gave an involuntary shudder and brought the basket closer to her.

'They are far from pleasant, yes.' The man's eyes appeared to glow red in the gloom. 'The things this man has done…'

Daisy willed her gaze not to go towards the hollow. She prayed that Lord Ravensworth would show sense. The last thing they needed was a confrontation. Lord Ravensworth might be able to hold his own in a fight the vast majority of the time, but not after being half-drowned in a river. 'Perhaps it is best that he died.'

'You would not have liked to encounter him alive. He has a bad reputation…particularly with the women.'

A shiver ran down Daisy's back at the man's leer. Had she misjudged Lord Ravensworth? She rejected the notion instantly. His grandfather had a sterling reputation and had spoken highly of his grandsons. And she knew from her time with the Flytes all about the Ravensworth fortune. Lord Ravensworth might have all the hallmarks of a rake, but he would have no need to steal.

She readjusted the basket on to her hip, forced her shoulders to relax. 'Thank you for warning me. I shall return to Gilsland with all due speed. Hopefully someone will have found my charge. I should not like her to encounter such a man.'

'My pleasure, ma'am.' The man touched two fingers to his cap. 'Should you find anything, anything at all, have someone send for Mr Sanjay.'

'Yes, I will do that…if I encounter a corpse. You might want to try the waterfall. Perhaps he went over and washed downstream. No one could survive that.'

The leader gave an ironic smile and called for his men to follow him, berating them for not discovering the body. The thick-set man aimed a kick at the dog. The dog avoided the blow with ease.

Daisy kept still, watching them, resisting the temptation to run back to where Lord Ravensworth lay. She heard a faint crackle of a twig, but kept watching where the men had gone.

What if they returned? What if they were speaking the truth and not Lord Ravensworth? What if they discovered she had helped him? Panic forced her throat to close and her palms became slick against the basket's handle.

Daisy shook her head, rejecting the notion. Whatever Lord Ravensworth had done, he did not deserve to be beaten and tossed in a river to drown.

'They have gone for now,' Lord Ravensworth said, coming out from hiding and brushing his trousers. From his fingertips, her much crushed bonnet dangled.

'That is a far from comforting thought.' She held the basket as a shield between them and resisted the urge to snatch the bonnet from his fingers.

'It is not meant to be one.' He gave an ironic smile. 'False comfort does more harm than good. But thank you for keeping me secret. Thank you for believing in me.'

'Were those men your attackers?'

He gave a careless shrug and handed her the bonnet. His warm hand brushed hers. Daisy concentrated on her hat rather than on the sensation that tingled up her arm. The bonnet had suffered and its brim showed signs of wear, but it proclaimed what she was and would always be—a respectable governess.

'They may have been,' he said finally. 'It was a dark night and I have a lump the size of a goose egg on my head. Only bits and flashes are in my memory.'

'His gaze made my flesh creep.' Another shudder ran through her. 'There was something about his eyes. Peculiar. Burning. I have never seen eyes like that before.'

'I saw only his boots. They were far too fine for his manner.' Lord Ravensworth put a warm hand on her shoulder and his breath tickled the back of her neck. 'You must concentrate on the pleasant things, and not the things that are designed to unnerve you.'

A small curl of heat twisted its way around her insides. Daisy struggled to maintain control. She would not give in to the misconception that because she was a governess, she was desperate for a man's attention. He was simply experienced in such matters and was attempting to distract her from her fear of the man. 'I had the situation under control.'

'You saved my life. Again.'

'Then do not throw it away unnecessarily.' She gave the basket a little swing. 'Are you coming, Lord Ravensworth? It is your hide they are after.'

'The spirit is willing, but my body is bruised.' His face went white with pain as he started to take a few steps. Daisy's heart clenched. Against her better judgement, she discovered she admired his courage and the way he treated his near drowning as the merest trifle.

It made a change from Mrs Blandish's dramas. 'The river was a bit rockier than I thought. Lying there in that hollow, all the aches and pains have started to come out.'

'You need a stout stick for support. And you should put the picnic blanket around your shoulders.'

'The blanket is an admirable suggestion, but there is no need for the stick. I will hobble, if I can hang on to your arm.'

Daisy's throat went dry. The thought of being near him again did strange things to her pulse. But to refuse would be to admit that she was attracted to him. 'If you wish…'

'I do wish.' His eyes deepened to rich golden amber. 'And maybe you can explain why you are choosing to believe me now.'

'What do you mean?' Her lips became full and ached with some unknown longing.

'Why did you protect me from those men? For all you know, I may be a scoundrel or a rogue.' His voice held silken lures and promises, making her want to lean towards him. But there was also a knowing glint in his eyes.

Daisy forced herself to concentrate on the way her boot still squelched every time she took a step. She had not been a governess for the past six years without learning how to keep her mind focussed on the things she should be focussed on.

'I take against men who carry cudgels and spit in front of ladies. It is a small quirk of mine.' She gave a small polite cough. 'And one should never kick a dog.'

He gave a resounding laugh. 'You have put me in my

place, Miss Milton. Here I thought it was my innate charm that convinced you.'

'Undoubtedly your high opinion of yourself will soon recover.' Daisy turned her face from him and concentrated on finding her footing. One of them at least believed she was immune to his charm. It was an important point. She would do her duty and then this adventure would be over. She had forgotten how singularly uncomfortable adventures could be. Instead of wishing for something to happen, she should have wanted her cotton-wool life to continue, where nothing more strenuous than working out the truth in Nella's latest tall tales was required.

He stopped suddenly, put his hands on her shoulders, looking deeply into her eyes. Her whole being quivered, but she did not pull away. Everything ceased to matter except the shape of his mouth. He leant forwards slightly as she lifted her lips.

A featherlight touch, little more than a butterfly's. Then a gradual sinking of his warm firm lips on to hers. Before she had time to consider the shape or the feel of his mouth, it had ended.

Startled, her hand flew to her mouth, exploring it. The same but somehow different, fuller and pleasantly aching.

'Miss Milton, as you can observe, I keep my promises. Your reputation will be protected and you will have a new pair of gloves.'

'And who will protect me from you?' She tilted her head to one side.

His hands took the bonnet from her nerveless fingers, placing it on her head. He frowned slightly and with expert fingers straightened it and tied the bow. 'There, quite the governess again and impervious to anyone's attempt at charm.'

'I am always a governess. I will always be a governess.' Daisy stepped away from the warmth of his body. 'It is my vocation as well as my career.'

'Or is it the shield you hide behind?'

Chapter Four

'The hotel is just up this slope. You see—all the danger has passed,' Daisy said as they reached a well-trodden pathway. 'You are safe now.'

'Am I?' A tiny smile played on his lips. 'It is pleasant to know. Slightly disheartening though. I had not planned on being safe just yet.'

'You know what I mean.'

'You react well to teasing, Miss Milton. I would have thought governessing had drummed it out of you, made you into a drab creature who matched her clothes. I suspect underneath there beats a passionate heart.'

'I suspect we should keep on walking.'

'As you wish.'

Daisy concentrated on taking steady calming breaths and maintaining a dignified silence. She tried to think about the men they had encountered, rather than her passionate heart. Had they returned to the clearing? Had they discovered that two people had been there, instead of just her?

Several times during the journey back to the hotel's grounds, she had started to turn around, convinced the men were about to reappear. But Lord Ravensworth had trudged relentlessly onwards, refusing to let her stop.

In a way, it was easier because every time they paused, her thoughts drifted back to the kiss he had bestowed. When she was a girl, she had often dreamt of her first proper kiss. Then it had been all orange blossoms and sweet-scented myrtle. She had never considered that it might have been from an injured man under a sun-dappled oak as they hurried for their lives. For luck, he had said. And she wished it had been for something more.

'I believe I know this path. It leads down to the popping stone and the kissing bush,' Lord Ravensworth said.

'I am surprised you know where that is. You do not look like the marrying kind.' Daisy made her voice light. The popping stone was one of the main attractions in Gilsland Spa as Sir Walter Scott had famously asked his wife to marry him there. Miss Blandish had been after Lord Edward to take her for a stroll in that direction, but so far he had resisted.

'It pays to be wary. But kissing is always in season.' Lord Ravensworth removed his arm from her shoulders for the first time since they started out from the oak. 'I can find my way to the hotel now.'

'I am quite happy to walk you to the hotel and explain the situation. My employer is an active member of the hotel's circulating library and the innkeeper knows me.'

'You have done enough. Your part has come to an end.' Lord Ravensworth inclined his head.

He was dismissing her. A lump of disappointment grew in Daisy's throat. The connection with him she had felt only a few moments before had been a trick of circumstance, an illusion.

'If you are certain…' Daisy straightened her shoulders, and gripped the handle of the basket tighter, holding it against her body. For her, she could not get the touch out of her mind. For him, it had been the merest brush of lips. 'You are quite right—I have no wish to expose myself to scandal. Imagine if Nella's tongue got the better of her…'

'And what happened to Christian duty?'

'You are deliberately being provoking.'

'A little.' His features relaxed into a heart-stopping smile. 'Your eyes flash when you are angry. They reveal the passion that your employers have not been able to extinguish. I wanted to see you as Daisy Milton, my saviour, rather than as Miss Milton, the governess, for one last time.'

'You are wrong. I have always been like this.' Daisy firmly turned her thoughts away from passionate eyes and towards the state of her gloves and the hours she would have to spend mending the rents in the gown. Luckily, she knew how to sew a fine seam, and the black stuff could be repaired.

'I have no wish to deprive you of the blanket the next time you go on an expedition.' He took the woollen picnic blanket from his shoulders. 'Shall I put it in the basket for you?'

'No, I am perfectly capable of arranging my things.' She took the blanket from him and placed it in the basket.

His face became inscrutable, the haughty face of a viscount again. 'I know you are capable.'

'Then it is goodbye and good luck, Lord Ravensworth.' Daisy held out her hand.

'Next time I need the perfect governess…I will know who to call.' He bent over her hand and kissed it as if they were at a ball, rather than standing in a glade. 'Miss Milton, you should work on a come-hither look. You will find that honey catches more flies, even when you are a governess.'

'I doubt you will have cause for such a glance.' Daisy gave her fiercest glare, the one that sent Nella running to hide in a corner, in an attempt to hide her confusion. 'You do not appear to be the marrying sort.'

'Men do not have to be married to require a governess, Miss Milton.'

'This is goodbye for ever, Lord Ravensworth.' Daisy turned on her heel and fled.

'Not for always, Miss Milton,' Adam said softly, watching the way her skirt swirled about her ankles. But Miss Milton's step remained resolute and her back stern.

The necklace had to be retrieved. It was another mistake. He should have insisted on carrying the basket for her. It was safe for now in the lining, but he would have to get it back. He frowned, annoyed at the slip. Miss Milton had distracted him with the provoking way her white teeth caught her full bottom lip. No, he decided it was only the after-effects of the drugged beer and the dunking in the river. The next time he encountered her, things would be different.

He began to climb up towards the hotel, his muscles

screaming if he put a foot wrong. And he wished that he had been less hasty in dismissing Miss Milton.

'Ravensworth? Is that you crashing through the borders?' a well-bred masculine voice called out. 'My God, you are alive.'

Adam started. The last time he had heard those drawling nasal tones was over a hand of cards at White's in London a month ago, just before he had set off for his business in Scotland. He straightened his shoulders, arranged his face into his more normal arrogance. 'Heritage, what are you doing here? A bit far from your usual haunts of St James's and Piccadilly.'

'Looking for you.' Heritage rounded a boulder and stood. His black frock coat was impeccably tailored and his stock was just that fraction higher than was physically comfortable. He took a handkerchief from his pocket and wiped his pale forehead, pushing a white blonde lock to one side.

'Why?' Adam's body tensed, ready to spring. Heritage should be far from here. 'Surely you have not come from London expressly for that purpose?'

'I have been taking the waters, here in Gilsland.' Heritage waved a vague hand. 'I have a great-uncle who might be persuaded to name me as his heir. It seemed worth a trip, and anyway, London has been duller than dull ever since the king became ill. And now that he is dead, everyone must observe the correct mourning period. No balls, no opera and the gaming tables are distinctly on the thin side.'

Adam forced his hands to stay at his side as the pain in his head grew. Heritage's words explained everything and nothing.

'I was speaking about you the other night at table. India came up and I remembered your fabled luck. What did go on at the hill station? We all thought you were a goner when you insisted on going back up with such a small company to root out that nest of thieves. They were operating under the very nose of his Majesty's officers. And I remembered how they said their treasure was cursed as was anyone who touched it; they ended up dead and you had that necklace as proof. But you came back victorious. Made myself a pretty packet. Never bet against a Ravensworth, I said that day, and I stand by it. Still, here you are alive.'

'That is ancient history, Heritage.' Adam's head pounded. He thought he had left the thuggee and their curses behind seven years ago. The necklace was cursed, but not in the way it was whispered. It reminded him of the heart he had lost. But the thuggee were no more. All of them had been brought to justice. Heritage had been in charge of ensuring the hanging of the surviving thuggee was carried out. 'Why were you searching for me?'

Heritage hesitated for a fraction too long. 'Your carriage was discovered earlier. We feared the worse.'

'I will survive.' Adam gave a careful shrug, despite his muscles screaming in protest. 'My clothes have seen better days and my boots are gone. My valet will be ready to commit murder about the boots. He had just perfected his blacking technique of that particular pair. And having survived one attempt on my life, I have no wish to risk another.'

'That's the spirit.' Heritage clapped him on the shoulder. 'What happened? How did you end up here?

Your carriage was found abandoned a few miles from here.'

'We were attacked after we left Brampton. After my time in India, I can sleep anywhere, and I wanted to return to Newcastle. The carriage was stopped and surrounded. I escaped, rather than submitting.'

'The carriage was found abandoned on the Brampton road. Someone had set about it, but a farmer spotted the wreckage when he was taking his cows to pasture. He came to the hotel while I happened to be speaking to the innkeeper. I went along to help and recognised the carriage straight off. The one body was far too portly to be you and so we have been searching. The whole village turned out.'

Adam regarded Heritage. Perhaps the story was true. The men on the riverbank could have been innocent searchers, but somehow he doubted it. However, he would content himself with surviving and plotting his revenge. 'How was my coachman killed?'

'Strangled.' Heritage paused. His face turned grave. 'Strangled with a yellow scarf, knotted in one corner with a coin. They found it wrapped around his neck.'

Adam stilled, ice creeping down his spine. He had hoped the memory was caused by the drugged beer, but apparently not. The group of thuggee that he had routed had favoured strangulation with a vivid yellow scarf. They had had their sacred grove, dedicated to their demon goddess. There were times when he was playing cards in White's or drinking at Brooks's that he considered the whole episode to be some sort of fantastic fable out of the *Arabian Nights*. Unfortunately, it would appear that his enemy also knew of the tale.

'That is not possible, Heritage. This is England. All of them were brought to justice. The ones who were alive after the attack swung for murder.'

'The scarf was there. I saw it with my own eyes. Bright yellow, you know that peculiar nasty shade that sends chills down your spine. It made me wonder if somehow I had conjured them up what with my story about your exploits to my great-uncle.'

Pain seared through Adam's head. Heritage looked positively shaken by the scarf. 'Coincidence.'

'You may be right, but it made a shiver run down my spine all the same.' Heritage pulled at his cuffs. 'How many besides you are left from the battle? I can think of nary a single man.'

'Curses are for the superstitious, weak minded and gullible.' Adam shut out the memory of Kamala's soft voice telling him to be careful as he pocketed the necklace. He had laughed at her fears and had gently kissed her neck. Later, after the battle when she had told him that she was leaving, he had wondered. But the necklace was a symbol of his folly, nothing more. 'I put my faith in reason. But I will grant you that the entire operation was planned, down to the smallest detail. Somebody wants me to think of India and the events there.'

Heritage rocked back on his heels. 'Was there anyone else with you?'

'With me?' Adam's vision swam as wave after wave of tiredness and pain hit him. His body needed rest and food. 'I travelled alone. I wanted to get back to the delights of London.'

'I thought I heard voices earlier. A woman's voice.'

Adam put a hand to his head. The pulsating headache grew to a crescendo and his vision turned dark at the edges, driving all the thoughts from his brain. But he struggled to focus. Miss Milton had a good reputation. He did not need Heritage to destroy it through misplaced gossip and innuendo. 'I met a woman who had been picnicking with her charge. She helped me out of the river. She took a tremendous risk, but she left me to continue on.'

'And her name is? Who is this paragon of virtue? We go back a long way, Ravensworth.' Heritage's face took on a foxlike expression as it slid in and out of focus.

Adam redoubled his efforts. What had happened to Kamala all those years ago was not going to happen to Miss Milton. He would protect her. He would save her life.

'It really does not matter, Heritage. She was a governess of the most exasperating sort. A nobody of little consequence. Leave it there.'

'Miss Milton, Miss Milton, you are back!' Nella's tear-stained face greeted Daisy when she reached the schoolroom at the Blandishes' rented house.

'Of course I returned, Prunella.'

'Is the man…dead?'

Daisy wrinkled her nose. How much did Nella need to know? Certainly nothing about her attraction to the man, or the fact that she suspected he might be a rake. 'He is alive.'

'Oh, how wonderful!' Nella clapped her hands.

Daisy busied herself with removing her gloves and

bonnet. Everything in the pristine schoolroom was just as she had left it—the papers stacked neatly and the ink bottle full. A small fire glowed in the grate. Nothing to say that her adventure had even happened.

'The situation was resolved speedily. He is recovering at Shaw's. No thanks to any help you sent.'

'I know. I utterly failed you, Miss Milton. You put me to the test and I proved unworthy.' Nella gave a series of rapid sniffs. 'I betrayed you and your trust.'

'How did you betray me?' Daisy asked quietly, refusing to allow her mind to speculate. Calmness and fortitude were a governess's watchwords. Never show surprise whatever your charge might do. 'Surely you did as I requested and informed the innkeeper about the injured man.'

'I never got the chance. Mama sent me to my room for telling fibs.' Nella's bottom lip trembled. 'She threatened to paddle me with a hairbrush. Called it a Banbury story of a cock and bull.'

'For what? You did tell her that I needed aid. That a man was seriously injured?'

'I told her that you were with a naked man and needed someone to assist you in your endeavour.'

'You did what!' Daisy was unable to stop her mouth from falling open. A great black hole opened up inside her. She had little doubt that Nella had injected a bit of colour into the tale. But to twist the story in that particular fashion! She could well imagine what Mrs Blandish would have thought. Hopefully Mrs Blandish would recollect that her references were of the highest order and that she had never been involved with impropriety in her life. Her fists clenched, but she resisted the temptation to shake Nella. 'Lord Ravensworth was clothed.'

'I had to say something to get their attention. They were outside the hotel, on the terrace overlooking the riverbank. Susan was complaining about Lord Edward's absence and Mama was busy gossiping with Mrs Gough, the vicar's wife, and another lady. I tried and tried. No one noticed. I simply had to do something dramatic.' Nella played with the tie of her pinafore. 'I thought they would understand, but then Susan started screaming and demanding smelling salts. Mama had the severest look on her face and Mrs Gough, well, she puffed herself up like a wet hen. The squawking was frightful.'

Daisy's lungs collapsed against her chest. The scene and its outcome were simply too dreadful to contemplate and all too vivid in her imaginings. Nella had to be exaggerating…again. Daisy gazed up at the crack in the ceiling, regaining some semblance of composure. 'You can see why it is important to tell the truth, Nella. A man's life depended on the truth.'

'But I did tell the truth.' Nella gave a mournful sniff. 'And Mama always says that a man without a jacket, waistcoat and cravat is undressed. You agreed. I remembered that. And undressed is another way of saying naked. So I wasn't lying despite what you say.'

Daisy twisted the black stuff of her gown around her fingers. Governesses never engaged in shouting matches with their students. Governesses always maintained rigid self-control. 'I said might as well be undressed and we were speaking about formal dress at a ball.'

'Oh.' Nella's eyes grew round. 'I do beg your pardon.'

Daisy walked over to where the basin of water stood and splashed water on her wrists, restoring some equilibrium. How much damage had Nella done with her embellishment? 'Lord Ravensworth, third Viscount Ravensworth, is the grandson of Lord Charles Ravensworth, the second Viscount Ravensworth.'

'But why was he—?' Nella stopped, raised herself up on her tiptoes and rocked back and forth. 'I have heard of Viscount Ravensworth. He is worth a tremendous fortune and unmarried. I am certain he was mentioned in the scandal sheets recently. His name appears quite regularly. He goes to all the best parties. Women keep throwing themselves at him or something.'

'How do you know this, Nella?'

'I know where Mama keeps her secret store of newspapers, which she reads when she thinks no one is looking. One must be up to date on all of society's news.'

'Never mind who Lord Ravensworth is.' Daisy wished she could sit down with a tisane to drink and a cold cloth over her eyes. Less than a minute with Nella and everything was beginning to spin out of control again. Her worst fear was confirmed. Lord Ravensworth was a notorious rake of the highest order.

'I would like to meet a man who has made courtesans swoon.'

'You have caused a bit of mischief, young lady.' Daisy cleared her throat and gave Nella what she hoped was a suitably quelling look. 'Hopefully you will have learnt a lesson. Luckily, the situation was resolved and

I did not delay at the riverbank, waiting for help that never came. And ladies should not worry about what courtesans do.'

Nella gave a slight nod before sniffing loudly and scrubbing her eyes. 'Mama wants to see you as soon as you appear. You know I did love you as a governess, Miss Milton. You have been much better than my seven other governesses. Even better than Mademoiselle Le Claire.'

Daisy closed her eyes and leant back against the wall. Nella's word echoed round and round in her brain like some ghostly chant. Ice stabbed at her heart. She had done nothing wrong, but Nella's quick tongue had put her position in danger. Her position and her reputation.

She could not afford to be without a reference. Not with a score of other women vying for each place. She had worked hard to achieve her success and the salary it commanded. She might not earn the same as a top-drawer finishing governess, but she did well enough to allow Felicity and Kammie some small measure of freedom. And after her stint with the Blandishes was complete, finally she would perhaps have enough in savings to open a proper school in the little village of Hinckley, one which could take a charity pupil or two. Felicity knew of a house that they could rent.

Silently, Daisy counted up her current savings. Meagre, although it should see her through until she could secure another position, but the dream of being with Felicity and Kammie would have to be postponed yet again. Panicking never solved anything and there was a slim chance that Nella was wrong. Her cases had not greeted her at the door as Louisa Sibson's had when her affair with Jonathon Ponsby-Smythe had been discovered. She might yet keep the job.

Yes. Nella was up to her attention-seeking tricks. The tension eased out of Daisy's neck and shoulders. She would be the mistress of the situation. Mrs Blandish would have to take action about Nella.

Daisy grabbed a cloth, went over to the basin and wet it. 'Scrub your face and stop feeling sorry for yourself, Nella. You were the one who was caught out.'

'But…'

'Prunella Blandish, telling tales can get you in trouble. I trust you will remember this lesson and there will be no need to repeat it.' Daisy shook out the folds of her gown. The mud splatters and rents made it impossible for her to wear the gown in public. She would have to take the time to change. And she would wear her grey gown and her Indian brooch, the one her brother had sent her just before he had died. It would set the right tone for a sober and responsible governess, one who could not possibly have shared a kiss with a rake of the first order.

'Where are you going?'

'To see your mother and inform her of the truth. You will have to write out a hundred lines for me.'

Nella screwed up her nose and made a gagging sound.

'In your best handwriting, Nella.'

'And what do I have to write?' Nella gave a winning smile. 'How much I love my governess?'

'Telling tales leads to mischief. It will give you something to do rather than sitting here, feeling sorry for yourself. Remember I am still your governess.'

Nella's lips curved upwards. 'I will do that.'

Daisy resisted the urge to smile back or show any sign of softening. Without discipline, Nella would not learn. And that was what she was here for—to be a governess and not to be anything else at all.

Chapter Five

At the drawing-room door, Daisy smoothed the skirt of her grey gown and kept her head high. The brooch at her throat and the light shawl over her shoulders completed the outfit. The absolute picture of a sober hardworking governess, rather than the bedraggled waif she had glimpsed in the mirror earlier, and definitely not someone whom a man would ever embrace.

After entering the room in a dignified manner, Daisy made a brief curtsy to the assembled throng of women. Her curtsy was neither too deep nor perfunctory, but precisely at the correct height.

Mrs Blandish was enthroned at the other end of the room, a silver teapot at her side. The remains of two cakes littered her plate and several crumbs had spilt down her ample bosom. Her glance turned ice cold as Daisy rose from the curtsy.

Silently Daisy went over her savings once again. Whatever happened, she refused to crawl or beg. She would rather starve. If she could leave with dignity and a civil reference, another position would be relatively easy to secure. Five other families had been after her services. She had chosen the Blandishes because the salary was more than the others.

'Ah, Miss Milton, I see you have returned.' Mrs Blandish's purple turban twitched. She set her tea cup down with a distinct clank. The naturally high colour became higher still. 'How good of you to come and find me. I trust my daughter gave you the correct message.'

'She passed it along, Mrs Blandish.' Daisy inclined her head. Calm, collected, professional were the words she lived by. Mrs Blandish for all her airs and graces was the granddaughter of a fishmonger. 'Without embellishment, or so Nella informs me. I believe you were at pains to explain the situation to her.'

'Good. My daughter seems sadly prone to exaggeration since she has come under your care. Not a day goes by without some sort of incident. Today's little episode was the worst by some way.'

Daisy's neck muscles tightened, but she choked back a quick retort. Nothing would be solved by antagonising Mrs Blandish in front of the assembled crowd.

'I am endeavouring to curb the tendency, Mrs Blandish. It would be helpful if she was not encouraged.' Daisy kept her tones measured. Surely Mrs Blandish had to see the sheer nonsense of Nella's allegation. 'Her words are often the subject of much conjecture and gossip, rather than being treated as fantastical imaginings.'

'Fantastical imaginings. Hmm, you do have a point.' Mrs Blandish took an overly dainty sip from her tea cup. 'I wish to reach the end of this coil.'

'Coil? Which particular coil of Nella's are you re-
ferring to?' The back of Daisy's neck prickled. Silently
she offered up a prayer that Mrs Blandish had seen
through Nella's stratagem and had decided to do
nothing.

'Are you or are you not permitting my daughter to
consort with men of unsavoury reputations? Have you
thought what it could do to Miss Blandish's chances
with Lord Edward, if the news gets out that my governess allows my youngest daughter to consort with
unknown men? She permits her to wander about the
countryside on her own. Goodness knows what sort of
ruffians might lurk in the undergrowth.'

Daisy's hand clutched the brooch for an instant and
drew strength from it. She had survived these sorts of
interviews before. She needed to keep her temper and
answer the accusations in a calm manner. It was one of
the reasons why she had taken the time and trouble to
change and redo her hair. Image mattered. She clung
to the thought that she had done nothing wrong and that
logic would rule the day. She was an experienced
governess rather than a novice.

'I sent Nella to get help. I understand that she was
not believed. This was unfortunate. A gentleman's life
was in danger.'

Miss Blandish made a little moue with her mouth.
'She blurted out some foolish tale about you being
in an embrace with a naked man. Mama wished to
save your blushes, but you have forced my hand. I
refuse to stand by and see Mama abused in such a
fashion.'

The rest of the company gave a tittering laugh.

Daisy stood, keeping her face blank and her back ramrod straight. 'My blushes, Mrs Blandish?'

'We took you on and paid your high wage, Miss Milton, given that your references were of an excellent quality.' Mrs Blandish gave a tight cough. 'It simply does not seem to me that this is how well-bred ladies act. I count on you, Miss Milton, to shield my daughter from life's unpleasantries. One day, Nella will have to take her place in society.'

Daisy counted to ten, and then ten again. She forced her shoulders down and her head up. 'Will you allow me to tell my side of the story?'

Mrs Blandish held up her finger. 'Was the man without clothes?'

'The gentleman in question was without his jacket and waistcoat. He retained his shirt and trousers.'

'Indeed, and how did you come to discover this person of unknown origin?'

The sheer awfulness of having to stand there with Mrs Blandish's gaze becoming more and more narrow swept over Daisy. She was innocent. She had saved Lord Ravensworth's life. But this woman, the grand-daughter of a fishmonger, dared to judge and repri-mand her without listening to the full facts. And there was little she could say in her defence without jeopar-dising her position. They must never discover that Lord Ravensworth had brushed his lips against hers.

'If you will allow me to explain…in private.'

'You do leave me with little choice, Miss Milton.' Mrs Blandish's turban quivered so violently that it threatened to slip off her head.

Daisy's stomach clenched. She had misread the

situation. She would be dismissed without a reference. Silently she offered up a prayer. 'All I did was my duty, Mrs Blandish.'

The door crashed open.

'Forgive the intrusion, my dear ladies!'

'Lord Edward, how good of you to join us.' Mrs Blandish immediately became all smiles as Miss Blandish hurriedly bit her lips and pinched her pale cheeks. 'I trust you have discovered your friend, and he has suffered no lasting injury.'

'My friend has been found. He is resting at present.' Lord Edward made a flourishing gesture. 'It is a weight off my mind.'

'Do please stop and have a cup of tea with us.' Miss Blandish gave a rather unattractive snorting laugh, batted her lashes and began to simper. 'You must have time, if your friend is otherwise occupied. We are all agog to hear what happened.'

'Miss Milton, you may retire.' Mrs Blandish waved her fan, signalling to the footman for another cup. 'I will accede to your request to discuss the matter in private, after my guests depart.'

'As you wish…' Daisy made the barest of curtsies. Her mind raced. She would pack everything and leave instructions with the butler for her trunk to be sent on once she had secured lodgings. It was the only sensible course of action. Silently she cursed her decision to become a governess with the Blandishes. Six years of hard work gone because she had saved a man's life. 'I will go and see if Nella has finished her lines.'

'You set Nella's lines? How clever of you.' Miss Blandish clapped her hands. She fluttered her lashes at

Lord Edward. 'My sister does need discipline. You know what she is like, Lord Edward. Always telling the most outlandish stories about me.'

Daisy fought against the temptation to make a cutting remark. Such a thing was beneath her.

'Forgive me, ma'am, but I believe your governess is the lady I am searching for. She cannot leave yet.' Lord Edward turned towards Daisy. His swept-back blonde hair gave him the appearance of the consummate gentleman, but there was something hungry in his eyes, something that remind her of the searchers on the riverbank. Daisy blinked and the look was gone. 'Tales of your heroism have reached my ears and I have come to offer my heartfelt appreciation. If our new queen possesses one-tenth of Miss Milton's bravery, I predict we are on the brink of a truly momentous age.'

Daisy stared at Lord Edward. There could be no doubting who his friend was. Between Lord Ravensworth and Nella, soon she would not have a shred of her reputation left. What had Lord Ravensworth told his friend?

'Her heroism? Her bravery?' Miss Blandish squeaked; her tiny mouth opened and closed like a cod's.

'Pray tell, Lord Edward, what has my governess done that is deserving of such praise?'

'She rescued my dear friend, Adam Ravensworth, the third Viscount Ravensworth.'

'Mama, a viscount, a proper eligible viscount, here in Gilsland,' Miss Blandish said in a hoarse whisper.

'But what happened? Why did he go missing?' Mrs Blandish gestured with her fan. 'I had no idea Viscount

Ravensworth was in Gilsland Spa. He has yet to
register at the circulating library.'

'He had been attacked and escaped by diving into the
River Irthing. He was more dead than alive when your
governess found him.' Lord Edward gave his head a
slow shake. 'Whatever is this country coming to when
people are attacked in their own carriages?'

The gathered throng let out gasps of astonishment
and murmurs of condemnation against the thieves as
the tale continued. Finally, following Lord Edward's
recounting of the tale, they broke out in a round of
applause. One or two of the ladies sighed.

'I salute you, Miss Milton.' He captured her hand
and raised it to his cold lips. Daisy fought the urge to
snatch it away.

'You should have said something, Miss Milton,'
Mrs Blandish said. 'I had no idea that you were
rescuing a friend of Lord Edward's and a viscount at
that. It puts the matter into an entirely different com-
plexion. How very resourceful of you.'

'Nella was sent with a message, but unfortunately her
vivid imagination embroidered the details. Hopefully
soon she will learn to keep her embroidery to her needlework.'

'Embroider. Needlework. That is very good, Miss
Milton. Lord Ravensworth never said that you had a wit.'

'Yes, Miss Milton is such a clever governess,' Miss
Blandish said, fluttering her lashes.

Daisy kept her voice even and her face bland as her
insides churned. Now that Lord Edward had proclaimed her a heroine, her position in the household
was secure. 'How is Lord Ravensworth?'

'His usual charming self.' Lord Edward gave a languid wave, but his eyes narrowed. 'How did you come to find him, Miss Milton?'

Miss Blandish tapped Lord Edward on the arm with her fan. 'It was my sister who found him. Nella said that quite clearly. Miss Milton, it was too bad of you not to tell Nella the man in question was a friend of Lord Edward's and a viscount in his own right. If I had realised that, I would have endeavoured to run all the way there myself and assist you in the rescue.'

'How noble of you, my dear Miss Blandish,' Lord Edward said. 'Perhaps I might be permitted to take you on a stroll tomorrow morning and we can discuss it in greater detail.'

Miss Blandish hid her face behind her fan and gave her simpering assent.

'I have never believed that the worthiness of being rescued was dependent on one's forebears.' Daisy squared her shoulders and kept her gaze on the bookcase. The particular pair deserved each other.

'But surely you knew he was a friend of Lord Edward's? It was cruel of you not to say. I…I have been concerned for him.'

'We did not discuss such things. We had more important matters to attend to.'

'More than a friend, a companion in arms. We served in India together. One of the King's regiments, rather than one of John Company's. You understand the difference.' Lord Edward bowed low. He smiled, showing too many teeth. 'It was worry for my friend that drove me to miss this tea party. Am I forgiven or am I to be cast out into utter darkness?'

Miss Blandish's cheeks coloured and she stretched out her hand. 'You are forgiven, Lord Edward. I am only grateful that our governess was able to assist your friend.'

'I believe, Mrs Blandish, that my presence here is unnecessary,' Daisy said, turning away from the pair. She had no doubt that the banns would be posted in due course. But by the time the wedding did happen, Daisy planned to be opening her school. There would be no need to wonder if she would happen upon Lord Ravensworth. 'Nella must be kept to her task or she will begin daydreaming out of the window and who knows what will happen then.'

Mrs Blandish tapped a finger against her tea cup. 'I have merely expressed my concern about my younger daughter's distressing habit of embroidering without recourse to needle or thread. You remain a most welcome addition to our family. After all, you clearly have the knack of rescuing the right sort of person.'

Daisy concentrated on taking deep breaths and not giving into her temper. It would be easy to give up her job, but that would be cutting her own throat. She had other people to think about besides herself. She had little doubt that the next post would bring yet another plea from her sister for more money. It would not do them any good if she was out of work. A governess without a reference had a difficult time keeping a roof over her head. She would be gracious in victory.

'Besmirching a lady's reputation for pleasure is an unsavoury pastime, Miss Blandish,' Daisy said, looking the woman directly in the eye. 'I make no accusation, but simply comment. I trust I may return to my charge now. Hopefully next time, when she requests urgent help, her pleas will be listened to.'

Daisy swept from the room. In the hall, she put a trembling hand on the wall. All the anger and the injustice drained from her, leaving her flat and deflated. She gave a weak smile. Here this morning she had been thinking about the job and its pleasant prospects. Now, Lord Ravensworth had managed to turn it all on its head and she couldn't wait to leave. The door clicked behind her.

'Well played in there, Miss Milton.' Lord Edward blocked her way. His face assumed a foxlike expression and his eyes suddenly appeared crafty, reminding her again of the man on the river bank. She blinked and the expression was gone. 'It is even more fortunate that I found you before anything amiss happened. I too know what Miss Prunella can be like. And I am gratified that you discovered Ravensworth and managed to bring him back here.'

'I am grateful to you, sir,' Daisy kept her voice polite, but her nerves were on alert. Why had he followed her out into the corridor? 'Mrs Blandish leapt to certain unfortunate conclusions. However, I would have performed the same task if Lord Ravensworth had been a penniless tramp. People are owed the common courtesy of life.'

'The parable of the Good Samaritan is your byword. Truly admirable, Miss Milton.' He put his hand against the wall and moved closer.

'If you wish…' Daisy ducked under his arm and regained the space between them. Lord Edward had never shown her the slightest interest before and she sincerely hoped Lord Ravensworth had not told him about the kiss he had bestowed. The last thing a governess needed was to attract the wrong sort of male attention. 'I am sure that Miss Blandish is pining for your company and Nella will have written about seven and a half lines. Her present occupation will be daydreaming. She needs a steady hand.'

His laughter rang out, but he remained, blocking her way. 'I am merely grateful that you discovered my friend and had the good sense to escort him to the hotel. But I am puzzled as to why you abandoned him before you reached the hotel. Did he behave inappropriately?'

'Lord Ravensworth appeared determined to make his own way to the hotel.'

'I am not chiding you, but seeking to determine his route.' Lord Edward held up his hand, but his eyes were cold. 'I am trying to ascertain if he dropped anything along it. I understand the thieves were unsuccessful.'

'He was wearing his signet ring when I left him, but I am not aware of any other valuables.'

'Thank you for that.' Lord Edward's face became more foxlike in its intensity. 'I will remember to check for the ring. Now was there anything else he mentioned? His pocket watch? Anything at all, no matter how trivial. I am anxious to apprehend the thieves.'

Daisy gave her head a quick shake. 'Lord Ravensworth is the best person to speak with about such things. He knows what was within his pockets.'

His gaze travelled slowly down her form, making her feel like an object rather than a person. 'Lord Ravensworth is not nearly as pleasant looking as you,

Miss Milton. It is a wonder that we have not had the opportunity to speak before now. Your perception and wit provide a beacon in an otherwise dull world.'

Daisy pressed her fingertips together. The last thing she wanted was a talking to from Mrs Blandish about the follies of engaging a single man in conversation. And Lord Edward was most definitely Miss Blandish's property, although she remained at a loss as to what could interest Miss Blandish beyond his title. She knew the rules of being a governess and she would keep them. 'My charge awaits, Lord Edward.'

'I believe I have a proposition for you.'

Daisy's eyes flew to his face. Lord Ravensworth must have said something about the kiss! It was the only explanation, and now Lord Edward... Daisy gritted her teeth. She wished she had left him on the river bank. 'You mistake me, sir. I am no lightskirt.'

'Not that sort. A thousand apologies.' Lord Edward's tone became even more oily. 'Lord Ravensworth will be distressed to learn that your rescue of him has caused you any moments of difficulty. He will order me to fetch you. I merely sought to save us both trouble.'

'Lord Ravensworth issuing orders?' Daisy raised her eyebrows. 'Why does that not surprise me?'

'I believe the proper word is invitation.' Lord Edward made a low bow, but his eyes twinkled slightly and a lock of hair fell over his forehead. 'Yes, an invitation from both of us. You will do me the honour of allowing me to escort you to him so we can both put his mind at ease.'

'Surely he is in bed with the doctor in attendance.'

'Alas, no. He refuses.' Lord Edward shook his head mournfully.

'Lord Ravensworth is an arrogant man.' Daisy cast her eyes heavenwards. 'He should pay attention to his doctor.'

'Please do me this one favour and make Ravensworth listen to the doctor. You succeeded in rescuing him and he will heed your words.'

Daisy tapped her foot. 'No one can make Lord Ravensworth do anything.'

'I fear you have not seen him at his best. He is generally considered to be an amusing companion. The ladies fall at his feet. In India on a hill station—'

'My brother worked for the East India Company and was posted to a hill station for a time,' Daisy said quietly. 'I know about the things that happen in India. England has different customs.'

'Your brother?' Lord Edward's mouth dropped open. 'I had no idea that you had any connection at all to India.'

'Tom, Tom Milton. He has been dead for nearly six years.' Daisy's hands straightened her skirts. 'He caught a fever and died. Perhaps you might remember him—he had different-coloured eyes, one was brown and the other green.'

'Fever happens to many poor souls. India's air seems to make you sick. When I think of all the men who have died…not to mention the children…' He gave a dramatic sigh and shook his head. 'I cannot recall meeting such a man, but if he was your brother, I feel certain that he would have been a sterling fellow. Did he give you that pretty brooch?'

'His last present. I consider it my good-luck charm.'

Daisy tried to keep her voice from choking. There was no point in explaining about her brother and his life. 'I appreciate your concern, but I must get back to Nella. No doubt her mind will have come up with some highly coloured end for me.'

'But you will go to see Lord Ravensworth.'

'When I have the time…' Was it her imagination that Lord Edward had taken yet another step closer? She glanced at the drawing-room door and willed it to open. Surely Mrs Blandish must have a sixth sense about these things. It was beneath her dignity to race up the stairs. 'Do give him my regards.'

'Miss Milton, Miss Milton.' Mrs Blandish waddled out from the library, her turban slipping slightly over one ear. Daisy felt the tension ease from her shoulders. 'I fear you may have taken offence at my elder daughter's rash remarks.'

'Offence? I feel certain you are mistaken, Mrs Blandish,' Daisy said, tilting her head. She would stay out her contract and no more. She would start a school and it would be a success. If she said it enough times, perhaps she would believe it.

Mrs Blandish dabbed her handkerchief to her eyes. 'Nella is so very fond of you. It is a mother's concern that tempers my words. I am at my wit's end with that child. So much consternation and bother.'

'I was explaining to Miss Milton that she must help me out with Lord Ravensworth. He refuses to obey the doctor until he knows she is safe. He fears that somehow he has put her in danger.' Lord Edward's mouth twisted up into a smile. 'And yet, she states she must see to Miss Nella's lines. Surely, you can spare her for a little while.'

Mrs Blandish stopped. 'Shall I send some calf's-foot jelly to the viscount? I have several jars of it, in case my nerves start acting up. Miss Milton can bring it on my behalf.'

'What a splendid idea, Mrs Blandish.' Lord Edward rubbed his hands together. 'What say you, Miss Milton?'

'What can I say? It appears my life is being arranged.'

'Miss Milton, when you are ready to depart, you will find me taking tea with the ladies.'

Daisy juggled the calf's-foot jelly along with her parasol as she waited for Lord Edward to open the door at Shaw's. Her one bonnet was beyond simple repair, the brim hopelessly crushed, and no amount of ribbon or flowers would hide the stains. And she had not had time to empty her basket of its paints.

She resisted the temptation to redo her hair, but had allowed a mass of ringlets to form on her temple. She hated the way her heart quickened at the thought of seeing Lord Ravensworth again. If she was not careful, she would begin blushing and sighing. She could only hope the infatuation would die when she saw him in his natural habitat.

'Miss Milton, may I assure you that Lord Ravensworth's charm is legendary.' Despite the jocularity of Lord Edward's tone, his eyes were glacier pinpricks.

'He was perfectly agreeable the first time we met…under the circumstances.' Daisy closed the parasol with a snap. 'I dare say being attacked and then nearly drowning would try the patience of a saint.'

'You need not parry words with me, Miss Milton. I am aware of Ravensworth's faults. He can be trying. I only wish we knew why he was attacked. And for what purpose.'

'I will keep that under consideration.'

Daisy moved further away from Lord Edward. She disliked his cold hands as they had guided her across the green. There was something odd in the way he kept sweating, but seemed to have such cold hands.

She shook her head slightly, banishing the thought. Lord Edward had a sterling reputation and his family were very well known. He had not behaved in any way that lacked propriety. But something eluded her. Before today, his eyes had slid over her completely and now he watched her like a cat watches a mouse. What had she done?

'Indeed.' Lord Edward's eyes gleamed. 'I will send for a cup of refreshment and you can explain the precise circumstances of the rescue. Perhaps we should adjourn to a private parlour…'

'My journey is to see Lord Ravensworth.' Daisy tightened her grip on the parasol. Private parlour indeed! She had been trapped in a ruse. After her dismissal, Louisa Sibson had tearfully confided about how Jonathon Ponsby-Smythe had trapped her in similar circumstances. The *naïveté* of it all.

Had Lord Ravensworth even requested to see her or had Lord Edward simply used it as a pretext?

Normally, she was more attuned to the undercurrents. Her very reputation depended on it.

'I have no complaints to make of his behaviour. Lord Ravensworth was a perfect gentleman during the rescue.'

'Miss Milton lies. I was the very devil and refute any suggestion otherwise.' Lord Ravensworth's authoritative voice resounded at the end of the hall. 'She has seen me at my worst and has lived to tell the tale. This woman will believe no pretty fable, Heritage, about my civility or charm. She is made of sterner material. Thank God.'

Daisy turned towards the sound and saw Lord Ravensworth lounging against the banister. His stubble had gone and his hair was neatly swept back. He had changed and was now wearing a coat, shirt and cream-coloured trousers, the very model of a British aristocrat.

The jar of calf's-foot jelly grew slippery in her hands, but she clung to it much as a dying man clings to a spar. Lord Ravensworth was even more dangerous fully dressed than when she had discovered him on the river-bank.

Lord Edward drew down his mouth. 'Ravensworth, I had thought you would follow the doctor's instructions and rest.'

'How can I rest when I know my attackers remain unaccounted for?' He gave an elegant shrug, but Daisy saw the white about his lips and knew the effort it must cost him to stay upright. 'It suited me to speak to the parish constable in a public room, rather than in my suite.'

'You see what I must contend with, Miss Milton,' Lord Edward said to Daisy in an undertone. 'If I let him, he would not give me or indeed any of the staff a moment's peace. The doctor was firm on the matter. Sleep is the best medicine.'

'Then you die. I have had quite enough of dying for

one day, Heritage. I may have spent time in a river, but my hearing remains as acute as ever,' Lord Ravensworth said, sounding far more like the man she had first encountered than the man who had kissed her. 'You forgot to bring your basket, Miss Milton. I had not thought to see a governess without her basket. I should think there must be a statute or a law about it. Are you a governess without a basket?'

'My basket?' Daisy stared at him. What sort of game was he playing now? 'It is at the Blandishes, full of paints and brushes. Ready to be cleaned out by my charge.'

'A pity—you could have used it to carry whatever revolting concoction it is that you are balancing in your hands.' Lord Ravensworth gestured imperiously with his hand.

'Calf's-foot jelly. It is good for invalids,' Daisy replied, lifting her chin slightly. She tightened her grip on her parasol and wished she had thought to hide the calf's-foot jelly in a bush. The smell was truly stomach-churning. Hastily she put it down on a table.

'For what? For making them ill?' Lord Ravensworth put a hand to his head. 'I have devotedly prayed that I might be spared from the misguided ministrations of do-gooding females. It appears that my prayers have gone unheeded. You should be resting from your labours, but instead you bring lashings of calf's-foot jelly.'

'Ravensworth, you should consider the feelings of your friends,' Lord Edward said.

'I was not aware you were friends with Lord Edward Heritage, Miss Milton.' Lord Ravensworth's eyes became hard lumps of amber.

'Lord Edward is friends with my employer.'

'How very convenient. It saves me the trouble of finding you and your basket next time I have need of a governess. Which I don't at present.' Lord Ravensworth pushed off from the banister and started forwards. Daisy put out her hands to steady him as he stumbled down two steps. He glowered at her and she allowed them to drop to her side.

'Miss Milton is safe.' Lord Edward gestured towards Daisy. 'You were agitated about the governess being safe, Ravensworth. A little bit of detective work and here she is. Gilsland is not a large village and there are limited numbers of governesses.'

Lord Ravensworth's face became blacker and more thunderous with every breath he took. 'I had not asked you, Heritage, to interfere in my affairs.'

'Has the blow to your head entirely destroyed your sense of manners, Ravensworth? You asked about her.'

Daisy attempted to ignore the sudden sinking of her stomach. Lord Edward had blatantly lied. Lord Ravensworth had not asked for her. He had no desire to continue the acquaintance. She would retain her dignity and he would never guess how deeply his remarks had wounded her. 'Perhaps I should depart and return at a more opportune time.'

Lord Ravensworth kept his gaze fixed on Lord Edward. 'My sense of propriety is as acute as it ever was. I merely enquired why you felt compelled to bring Miss Milton here. At this time.'

'To get you to rest, obviously,' Daisy said in exasperation. 'He mistakenly thought I might have some influence.'

'I can take care of myself.'

'Ravensworth, be reasonable.' Lord Edward held out his hands in supplication, his eyes sliding from one to the other, but never resting. 'Who knows what might have happened if I had not intervened? Her charge had apparently given a highly inflammatory story about you two embracing when you were naked.'

'It is an intriguing suggestion.' Lord Ravensworth's gaze travelled slowly down her form and then back up again, far more slowly this time. Daisy wished the floor would open and swallow her up. Or that she could go back and start the day again. 'But alas, that was not possible. You are very bad for me, Miss Milton. I discover that I have developed a conscience.'

'Nella is given to exaggeration.' Daisy clung to the parasol. She would ignore the blatant invitation in his eyes. Why was it that her prayers were never answered? 'My charge merely wished to enliven proceedings. Unfortunately, Nella's tall tale ensured no rescue party was sent.'

'It is to be regretted,' Lord Ravensworth murmured and his eyes deepened to caramel as if he too remembered the kiss they had shared.

Daisy straightened her shoulders as the air crackled between the two men. 'If you will excuse me, gentlemen, I will need to return to Nella.'

'The girl who nearly caused you to be dismissed?' Lord Ravensworth raised an eyebrow and his lips twisted into an ironic smile. 'Yes, I can see why you might need to see her.'

Daisy inclined her head, keeping her annoyed expression from view. The man was truly insupportable.

He had not wished to see her, despite Lord Edward's polite fable. He probably would have been quite content to see her dismissed without a good reference. It irked that her heart had leapt at the chance.

'Thanks to Lord Edward, Mrs Blandish is now aware of the precise circumstances.'

'You are now the heroine of the hour, instead of merely being an evil influence on her daughter,' Lord Ravensworth observed.

'You do have a way with words, Lord Ravensworth, but, yes.'

'Speaking my mind is one of the privileges of my rank, Miss Milton.'

'I suspect you would speak it even if you had been born a pauper.'

'You are definitely a bad influence, Miss Milton, for I cannot tell a lie with you in earshot. Guilty as charged.' A dimple flashed in his cheek, transforming his face, making it heart-stoppingly handsome. 'But now that you have arrived bearing…gifts, I have a job offer to make.'

'I am already in employment,' Daisy replied carefully as her mouth grew dry. A notorious rake offering honest employment? He must assume that she was completely naïve. She knew the sort of offers rakes made. It was why she took pains with her dress—to show that she was a governess, first, last and foremost.

'The doctor informs me that I will need a nurse for a few months while I recuperate. I can think of no one better,' Lord Ravensworth said and his voice became like heavy silk sliding over her skin. 'You know of my faults and your conversation is more amusing than most. Should you wish the position, it is yours. I will pay half as much again as your present employer.'

'Lord Ravensworth!' Daisy stared at him in astonishment. If she went to work for him, she might as well forget about ever being a governess in England again. She could well imagine how the interviews would go if he gave her a reference. The slight tutting and then the news the post had been filled. 'You are unmarried!'

'Double what Mrs Blandish is paying you. You drive a hard bargain.' His eyes were molten gold with flecks of amber, eyes that Daisy knew she'd dream about for months to come, eyes that silently urged her to say— yes. 'It should be more than sufficient to make you swallow your principles about being employed by an unmarried man.'

'Without my principles, I am nothing.' Daisy clasped her hands in front of her and concentrated on breathing rather than on his velvet voice. 'I am a governess, not a nurse. There is a great deal of difference. Therefore, I must refuse, Lord Ravensworth, and urge you to seek a suitable person for your needs.'

His eyes widened with surprise. Daisy wondered if any woman had ever told Lord Ravensworth no before.

'Surely you cannot enjoy looking after children,' he said. 'Schoolrooms are worse than prisons. You are alone most of the time without friends or companions beyond ungrateful wretches who do not want you to be there in the first place.'

The retort died on her lips. Had her loathing of her current job shown that clearly on the journey to the hotel? Normally she enjoyed teaching her pupils, if they were receptive. Nella was a challenge, but one which she was determined to conquer.

'I would have hardly become a governess if I hated children.'

'You love reading poetry over and over again until the very lines that fired your blood becomes as dull as ditch water.'

'Poetry is far from dull. With the greatest respect, Lord Ravensworth, you are a philistine.'

'Did I say poetry is dull?' A tiny smile played on his features. 'Merely the repetition. And children by their very nature are philistines. Deny that if you will. I therefore am like a child in need of instruction.'

Daisy gritted her teeth and longed to wipe the smug expression from his face. 'And this is leading where?'

'I thought you would have relished the opportunity to reform me. And turn me into someone who is not a philistine.'

'You, Lord Ravensworth, would be my worst nightmare.'

Lord Ravensworth stopped, one finger in the air as he searched for a quick riposte and appeared to reject several without speaking.

Daisy inclined her head. 'The point is mine, Lord Ravensworth.'

'Wonderful.' Lord Edward's voice rang out. 'Miss Milton has you there, Ravensworth. A rapier-sharp wit indeed. You neglected to mention that facet of your rescuer. I see she is a jewel that I overlooked. Perhaps I can persuade her to come to London.'

'Miss Milton has many talents, but I doubt she would make best use of them in London,' Lord Ravensworth remarked, regarding her with an unfathomable expression.

'They should be put to better use,' Lord Edward said, clearing his throat. 'The younger Miss Blandish is an acquired taste.'

'You saved my life this morning, Miss Milton. I take that into consideration. You have had a busy day and are no doubt fatigued,' Lord Ravensworth pronounced, waving his hand. 'The position will remain open until you have time to properly consider my offer and its consequences for your future.'

'Is my life in danger?' Daisy shook her head. Arrogance, pure arrogance. As if she was some sort of empty-headed female who jumped simply because he said to in a low seductive voice. Become a nurse indeed! It was one step away from being his mistress. A warm tingle went down her spine. Was that what he intended? A sudden vision of his limbs entwined with hers entered her head, refusing to leave. Her cheeks flamed. How would Felicity and Kammie cope if she became a fallen woman?

'Your life is in danger of being kept in aspic.' Lord Ravensworth's honeyed voice curled around her insides, enticed her to do his bidding. 'I can free you from that, Miss Milton.'

'We must agree to differ, then.' Daisy clung to her sanity with her fingernails. Something deep inside her wanted to say, yes, yes, and to grab life with both hands, but she knew it was madness. She had responsibilities, but she was beholden to no man. Felicity's dreadful marriage had shown her what men could be like. 'I am no prisoner in the schoolroom.'

'Your name is connected with my rescue, Miss Milton.'

'I fear your fall has affected your brain, Lord Ravensworth. Lord Edward explained the situation to the Blandishes and all is well.' She drew a deep breath and regained control of her thoughts. 'I regret that I must refuse your kind offer and you must look elsewhere for a nurse.'

Lord Ravensworth's brow darkened and his eyes shot fire, but Daisy found it impossible to stare anywhere except at his mouth. The memory of it on hers assaulted her, made her lips ache. 'And the offer remains open.'

'I will keep that under consideration.' Daisy lifted her parasol. Her life was going to return to normal. She knew her goals and she would keep to them. Lord Ravensworth would not distract her. She belonged to no man. Never would. And yet a pang shot through her. These would be the last words she spoke to him. 'Good day to both you *gentlemen*.'

'Miss Milton, I look forward to making Mrs Blandish's acquaintance.' He paused and his whole being radiated mischief. 'And that of her very charming daughter.'

Chapter Six

'Why did you bring Miss Milton here, Heritage?' Adam stood in the centre of his sitting room at Shaw's. The interview had gone badly. But Miss Milton had not seen the last of him. Refuse his job offer, indeed! He'd attend to that.

The necklace was the difficulty. All it would have taken was a slight flick of his wrist to remove it from the basket when they had parted, but he had forgotten. He had been too intent on trying not to kiss her again. And now Heritage had made the situation worse.

After their recent confrontation, he could hardly ask Miss Milton for her basket or explain what was in it. No doubt she would return the necklace when she found it. Miss Milton was that sort of person. However, the prospect filled him with no cheer. Whoever wanted it was prepared to kill for it, and the necklace needed to reappear at the time of his choosing and not before.

Adam rolled his shoulders, noting how they protested. There was something else that nagged him.

Heritage was not known for being altruistic. Why had he gone in search of Miss Milton? And why bring her as if she was some sort of trophy? He hated that his mind was proving sluggish.

Adam's fingers probed the lump on his head. This was all about the mistakes he had made and one day his mistakes would kill him.

'I never asked to see her,' Adam continued. 'You have complicated matters.'

'You very nearly ruined a governess without even kissing her.' Heritage gave a braying laugh. 'It was a close-run thing. A few more moments and her cases would have been piled at the door. And prickly Miss Milton would have been gone for good.'

'But why did you think I should care about her future?' Adam undid his stock with impatient fingers. Heritage made a good point. He had made a fundamental error when he had left Miss Milton. He had forgotten about her charge and, instead of protecting her, had very nearly doomed her. Heritage was correct. He should have insisted on having Miss Milton accompany him to the hotel; such a little thing with nearly such disastrous consequences for the woman.

'You expressed a desire to make sure she was safe.' Heritage gave a languid shrug. 'You clutched at the doctor's arm and demanded to know that the governess had been unharmed and unmolested.'

'I have no memory of that.'

'You have a lump the size of a goose egg on your head. Stands to reason.'

Adam frowned. 'Did Miss Milton make any comment about my health on your return journey?'

'She thinks you are overdoing it. She saw no reason for an escort either. She was at a loss as to why you should insist on one.' Heritage widened his eyes and settled into a chair in Adam's suite of rooms. He reached out and took an apple from the fruit basket that the innkeeper had provided.

'If Miss Milton is going to make remarks about my health, then she softens. In time, she will accept my offer.'

'Was it bona fide?'

'What do you take me for? A cad? I never joke about job offers to governesses.' Adam shrugged out of his frock coat. 'Tell me about the Blandishes. After all, it was the daughter who alerted Miss Milton to me. Perhaps you should have brought the child as well. I am concerned about the child's welfare.'

Heritage gave an involuntary shudder. 'Ghastly upstarts, particularly the mother, but possessed of rather a large fortune in funds and coal. We shall have to see what transpires from that quarter. Getting a wife with her own fortune would go a long way towards convincing my great-uncle that I intend to settle down.'

Adam lowered his body gingerly down on to the sofa. His muscles groaned slightly, but eventually relaxed into the cushions. He stifled a yawn and prepared his mind for another recital of Heritage's woes. Even in India, Heritage had been obsessed with Heritage. 'Your great-uncle will understand the necessity of having the appropriate wife, one with accomplishments and who will be at ease in society.'

'Oh, the elder Miss Blandish is presentable enough, if one likes that sort of thing. All blonde with too many teeth.' A smug smile played on Heritage's face. 'She desires the cachet of an earl's son. We both know what we are on about. There is little real feeling on either side. As long as she has a title, she will not ask too many questions.'

Adam listened with half an ear. He had little desire to hear of Heritage's matrimonial pursuits. But the necessity of a wealthy bride did not surprise him; Heritage's reputation was that of someone who enjoyed the high life without wishing to pay for it. 'One does what one must.'

'I wish I had paid more attention to the governess before now, though.' Heritage twirled the apple core. 'Never even thought to learn her name. She was simply Miss Nella's governess.'

'Why?' Adam sat up, every nerve suddenly awake and his pain forgotten. Last year, Heritage had achieved a certain notoriety for seducing servant girls. Not that he thought Miss Milton would allow him the liberties, but…she ought to be protected from men like Heritage, and himself, if he was being truthful. Adam knew he'd be bad for her. Women like her deserved marriage to staid sensible men, not to be involved with rakes who had no intention of marrying. 'Trust me on this—it is never good form to seduce the governess of your intended's younger sister.'

'Miss Milton's brother was in India. Tom Milton, or I suppose Thomas Milton. You might remember him, a factor from the East India Company.'

All the air left Adam's lungs as Heritage's words slammed into him. Thomas Milton. Tom to his friends. Tom Milton, who was in the end twice the man Adam ever could have been and was far more worthy of Kamala's love. He should have asked or at least suspected once Miss Milton had given her name. But it was a common enough name. Miss Daisy Milton was Tom Milton's sister. And he owed Tom a debt that he could never repay.

'I know the man you mean. He was at the hill station with me.'

Adam half-closed his eyes and Tom's face rose in front of him. He had had the same determined chin and eyes as Miss Milton. Not a warning, his apparition on the riverbank, but a reminder of a past failure. Had fate given him a second chance? He rolled his eyes upwards. Would fate ever be that generous? He had spent seven years regretting his actions. He could clearly remember the maharajah's sword at his throat, thinking it was his last moment on earth when Milton had appeared, dishevelled but resolute. Milton had dispatched the maharajah with several blows. Then calmly, as if they were at some club, Milton had bent and retrieved a small pouch of jewels from the maharajah's belt, explaining that he differed with the maharajah's notions of hospitality. Adam forced the door of his memory closed. 'He was useful in a tight spot. I always considered that he should have been a soldier, rather than a bean counter.'

Heritage bit into another apple, greedily devouring it. 'He died of brain fever, according to Miss Milton. Shortly after his wife died. Probably lost the will to live.'

Milton's wife. Kamala. She could have been his, if he had not been foolish and arrogant. Adam winced. Even now the wound to his soul was not fully healed.

He remembered how, with a bloodied hand and a steely gaze, Tom had plucked the necklace from Kamala and handed it to Adam. And Adam had known in a blaze of honesty what he had done. How he had sacrificed Kamala for false wealth. He should have grabbed her and run that first morning when the monkeys had chattered all about them. Or when she had confessed about the child she carried, his child. But the knowledge of Adam's love for her had come all too late. By the time he had returned, Milton had saved her and had won her.

'It was a waste of a life,' Adam said quietly.

'Ah, I remember now. I heard he's the one who plucked a king's ransom in uncut rubies from the maharajah's corpse. I wonder whatever happened to them.' Heritage closed his eyes. 'I can remember those Indian fellows, the ones I had to guard, cursing his name and swearing vengeance from beyond the grave. The leader was the worse, a regular mad dog with his snarling about revenge and the need for blood.'

Adam closed his eyes and cursed. He had made another mistake. The basket was now very dangerous indeed if the wrong people discovered the connection. If it was the thuggee that were after him, then they would seek vengeance for what her brother had done. And would they believe that no governess could possess a fortune in jewels?

'Have you ever seen a governess dripping in jewels?'

'Certainly not working for the Blandishes.' Heritage tapped his fingers together. 'On second thoughts, the story was wrong. Milton must have resigned for other reasons. Wasn't his new wife a dancing girl? The authorities must have objected to him going native.'

'Sometimes—it is the only explanation.' Adam forced a short laugh and closed his eyes. This time, instead of Tom or Kamala's ghostly features, he saw Miss Milton's upturned face with her lips slightly parted after he had kissed her. He opened his eyes and stared directly at Heritage. 'Hopefully you will keep silent. Miss Milton might be disturbed to learn from others that I knew her brother and neglected to mention the connection. Allow me to tell her in my own fashion.'

Heritage leant back and smiled. 'You know me—silent as the grave on the subject. But did Milton have the stomach for the fight? I had always thought these factors were a bit lacking…'

Adam bit back the words that bubbled to the surface about Milton's heroism and sacrifice. Those were for Miss Milton. He wanted to tell the story in his own way. It was perhaps wrong of him, but he wanted Miss Milton to think the best of him. 'The man was Miss Milton's brother.'

'I never said he was a coward.' Heritage tossed the apple core in the air, caught it with one hand. 'Miss Milton would be quite pretty if she did not wear such hideous clothes and such fierce expressions.'

'Never really noticed. We were busy discussing other things. Like getting me here alive.' A piece of his mind nagged at him, but drowsiness made thinking difficult.

'I say, wasn't Milton the one to pull that woman off the pyre?' Heritage's words jerked Adam awake. 'What was her name—Kam, Kammie something, Kamala? Wasn't she a courtesan or something to you?'

'Heritage, that was long ago and far away.' Adam put a finality into his voice. Heritage was far too interested in the events at the hill station all those years ago. 'The woman is dead.'

'But I understood—'

'It was a tale that was exaggerated many times over before it reached Bombay and Calcutta. Leave it in the past.'

'But interesting. Milton was brave as well, come to think of it. I doubt I would have done that—pulling a woman off a funeral pyre. Wonder if she had anything to do with the jewels.'

Adam pressed his fingers into his forehead. For now, he would assume Heritage's interest was pure curiosity and there was no evil intent. Heritage was a brother officer. Heritage had been the man in charge of the detail that had hanged the prisoners. It had been his task to make sure all the thuggee who remained were hanged. He could remember how bitterly Heritage had complained in the officers' mess about the task and the men under him, how it had prevented him from pursuing some Indian beauty that he had lost to another man.

'Right now all I want to think about is a soft bed and a dreamless sleep.' Adam wrinkled his nose. 'I dare say that I will have to take the laudanum the quack left.'

'You were never fond of opium.'

'Saw too many men's minds turn in India. I much prefer an honest glass of port.'

Heritage's pale cheeks coloured slightly and his eyes slid away from Adam. Adam smiled grimly. He had remembered correctly. Heritage had been fond of

opium back in India, preferring to spend the day
smoking away rather than seeing to his duties. There
was no harm in Heritage besides his being lazy, and
anyway. India had had its own set of problems.

'So they all say. Not all of us are as lucky as you
were on the hill station. They did say the treasure was
cursed, though. How many of you are left? Only you.'

Heritage's laugh echoed as the door closed. Adam
sat up, reached for his fountain pen and began to
make plans. Tentacles from the past were reaching
out. He refused to let them harm her, an innocent bystander. He owed it to Milton's memory and he owed
it to Miss Milton for saving his worthless hide. He
would find a way. He would keep Miss Prim and
Proper safe.

The familiar confines of the schoolroom greeted
Daisy when she returned to the Blandish household.
Perhaps they were a little dull, but they were safe and
a known quantity. She knew how to be a governess and
what was expected of her. And if she started to become
emotionally involved with her charges, she departed.
It was the best way.

Daisy picked up Nella's blotched writing-
exercise paper. Nella for once had completed the
task. At the end, she wrote: *I love my governess,
Miss Milton, very much and have no wish to get her
in trouble.* Daisy's heart contracted. It would hurt
more than most times when she left Nella. Maybe
this once, she would break her rule and keep in
touch with the child. It would be interesting to see
how she turned out.

'Miss Milton. Miss Milton, you must tell me all about Lord Ravensworth. Susan wants to know. She quizzed me for such a long time after you left with Lord Edward.' Nella rushed in with her hair ribbon askew. 'And Susan never notices me, except to scold!'

'There is nothing to tell. Lord Ravensworth is a highly respectable man. He is with his friends and his other carriage and his valet will arrive shortly.'

'Why is no one ever friends with unrespectable men? Why is the world made of rules and regulations?'

'Because anarchy is not the way the world works.' Daisy ran her finger along the edge of the schoolroom's table. Order and peace. Her adventure was over. She had made the correct choice for everyone. 'Have you emptied the basket from our excursion?'

'Do I have to? We, you and I, have been invited down to supper.' Nella gave a twirl. 'Imagine, supper like a grown lady! I wish to wear my blue dress, the one that matches my eyes. Some day I will be the toast of seven regiments.'

'Can lady explorers be toasts of regiments?'

Nella screwed up her nose, considering. 'Lady explorers can do anything they want to. I promise to empty the basket first thing…'

'First thing in the morning, then. I want to show you how to correctly clean the brushes.'

'Miss Milton?'

'Hmm…' Daisy glanced up from the lines to see Nella still standing in the centre of the room, hands behind her back, swaying on her tiptoes.

'Shall I find the scandal sheets? I am positive Lord Ravensworth is the gentleman who seduced a marquis's wife at a ball last year. Or was it that he had a duchess running after him all over Paris? It can be so hard to puzzle out the names.'

'Nella!' Daisy gave her fierce glare, but Nella merely raised her eyebrows. Daisy tapped her finger against the table. The scandal sheets would be just the thing to cure her. Her place was in the security of the schoolroom, and not in the blazing ballrooms of society. 'Very well, you may bring them. Then we shall try to determine if you are exaggerating.'

'You are the best, Miss Milton.' Nella gave her a quick hug and raced away.

Daisy shook her head and began to tidy the room. Everything in its place. Neat. Orderly. Like her life.

Two days and a pile of unsatisfactory scandal sheets later, Daisy turned the handle of the schoolroom's door. Papers littered the floor. Her new bottle of ink was turned over, the ink pooling beneath the table, like some great spreading evil, staining everything it touched. Chaos and confusion reigned everywhere. She shook her head and started to pick up the nearest pile of papers. Nella had gone too far this time.

A faint noise made her turn her head towards the window. In the shadows, the figure of a man loomed. She screamed and started for the door.

Something cold touched her neck, tightening. Daisy jabbed back with her elbows and connected with flesh. With every ounce of strength, she fought against the tightening pressure about her neck, twisting first one and then the other. As the world started to turn black, Daisy made one last try, kicking as well as jabbing and suddenly the pressure on her neck was gone. She was free.

Daisy fled the room, slamming the door behind her. As she reached the corridor, her legs gave out. She slumped against the wall and willed her heart to stop pounding. Like a mouse under the gaze of a snake, she watched the handle of the schoolroom door. Would it turn? Would her attacker pursue her? Would she have the strength to run?

'Is there a problem, Miss Milton?' Lord Ravensworth's velvet voice resounded in the corridor. Daisy put a hand to her forehead and tried to blot out the sight and the imagined sound of Lord Ravensworth. Things like this did not happen to her. She forced her lungs to meet her stays and wished that she had not tied them quite as tightly.

'Is there a problem, Miss Milton?' Lord Ravensworth repeated, this time nearer, clearer and definitely not a trick of her mind. 'Miss Milton, answer me! Now! Are you unharmed?'

'Perfectly fine!'

'You appear less than fine. You look as if you have seen a ghost. I doubt you are a woman usually given to exercising her lungs in that manner.'

She turned and saw that he was standing at the top of the stairs, a concerned expression on his brow. Her heart skipped a beat. How long had it been since someone had cared about her as a person, rather than as a governess? She knew Felicity did, but she had Kammie to look after.

Daisy hated the way her eyes roamed over him, taking in the black frock coat, immaculately tied neckcloth and the figure-hugging cream trousers. She searched for signs of his injury, but he appeared to be moving with a grace and elegance as if the other day was of no consequence. His hair flopped over his forehead, giving him a slightly roguish appearance. The infamous Lord Ra—from the scandal sheets.

'Miss Milton, are you entirely yourself? You screamed earlier. And now you appear to be struck dumb.'

Daisy attempted to secure an errant lock behind her ear and smooth her skirt. If she willed it, the fright would recede and her common sense would re-assert itself. No one was in that room.

'How…how did you know it was me?'

'You have a distinctive screech.' He raised an eyebrow as his gaze travelled down her form. His lips curved up into a smile. 'You appear uninjured. Were you practising for the next time you discover someone lying beside the river?'

Daisy pinched the bridge of her nose. Absurdly she wished that she had worn something that brought colour to her eyes rather than her grey gown. She quickly banished the thought. Lord Ravensworth probably ate women like her for breakfast. She managed a weak smile and turned her gaze forcibly from his amber one. She raised her chin and used her best governess voice. 'Thank you for your concern, Lord Ravensworth, but my fright is over. You may go and pay your respects to Mrs Blandish. Undoubtedly her calf's-foot jelly aided in your recovery.'

He remained standing in the corridor. If anything, his stance became more solid and unyielding. 'I discount exercising your lungs, Miss Milton.'

'The schoolroom was disturbed. Papers were thrown about. I had left it neat and tidy before I went down to breakfast. Something got wound around my neck.' Daisy put a hand to her head. Surely there had to be the logical explanation. Who would attack her in broad daylight? 'I overreacted. The wind caught something and it became wrapped around my neck. I panicked.'

'The air has been still.' The words were quiet but firm and allowed for no dissent. 'Are they in there?'

Daisy regarded the unmoving door handle. 'I am a neat and tidy person, Lord Ravensworth, not a stupid one. I freed myself, rushed out of the room and slammed the door. No one followed me.'

'Common sense is one of your virtues. You have already convinced me of that.' A smile tugged at his mouth, transforming it. 'Help has arrived, Miss Milton.'

'Have I? Has it?' Daisy hated the way her voice became breathless and soft, as if she was some helpless female. Resolutely she cleared her throat. 'I feel I can take charge of the situation now. It is my schoolroom. You may go and greet Mrs Blandish.'

'Allow me to discover what is going on in your room. Then you may take me to your employer. And we can explain together.'

Daisy hesitated. She hated to think what would be said if it was discovered that Lord Ravensworth had been alone with her, but the imperious look he gave her made her swallow her objection.

'I would welcome your assistance as it will be the quickest way to be rid of you.'

Adam watched the tiny pulse in Miss Milton's neck. She appeared to have recovered from her earlier fright. Silently he prayed that she was right, that it was simply a misplaced shawl. 'Shall we end the mystery then?'

Miss Milton gave the tiniest of nods. 'You are not to worry about me, Lord Ravensworth, I am quite recovered.'

Adam threw open the door. A cool breeze blew from the open window, stirring the papers. A bottle of ink dripped a blue-black puddle on to the carpet. He silently cursed as a quick glance did not reveal the basket. Miss Milton was safe, but the necklace?

He crossed the room in a few quick strides and closed the window with a resounding bang. The room overlooked a narrow porch. The thief must have exited that way. It would have had to have been someone desperate to chance being seen in broad daylight. There again, the attack on his carriage had been audacious. But he had his answer. The thief was after the necklace and not Miss Milton. For once, his feelings of impending doom were wrong.

'There is no one here, Miss Milton. And I do fancy you are a far tidier person than this.'

He forced a light laugh and waited for her to retort with a clever phrase or two and be the strong woman she had been on the riverbank.

But Miss Milton stood, poised in the doorway, her hand clutching her throat, unmoving like a marble statue. Several tendrils had escaped from her hairstyle and framed her face in ringlets, making her appear far younger than when he had first seen her, younger and more vulnerable. Her frightened eyes looked past him.

Adam tried again, stepping over the upturned trunk and piles of ink-stained paper. 'No one is here, Miss Milton. You are quite safe. No one wishes to harm you.'

She lifted a hand and pointed to the table where a yellow scarf with a single knotted end lay discarded, draped over a doll's neck. An inarticulate cry emerged from her throat and she averted her face.

Adam froze. The easy words died on his lips. And if he undid the knot? Would he find the coin? How much of the ritual did these thieves remember? The time for treating Miss Milton's sensibilities softly had ended. She was in danger.

'Get it out of here, please get it out.' Her voice rose. 'That thing was around my neck. Cutting off my breath. Someone wanted to kill me.'

'To frighten. Not to kill. The men who used to use these things were experts. If they wanted you dead, you would be.'

'Why does that not fill me with comfort?'

'I thought that as a governess you would prefer the truth. I stand corrected.' Adam forced his voice to sound light as he picked up the offending object and threw it on the coal fire. It hissed and twisted like a snake before collapsing into ash. He would act, but first he had to have all the facts. If he frightened her, he would get nothing. Right now, he needed facts. 'Can you see if anything is missing? Your basket?'

Miss Milton blinked and the terrified expression in her eyes lessened. 'Nella has my basket. She wanted to gather flowers. We emptied out the paints last night. I never think she does a very good job, but she assured me she had taken everything out.'

Adam's neck muscles relaxed. Nella had the basket. He forced air into his lungs. No one could know that he had secreted the necklace there. It was in the lining, rather than lying amongst the jumble of paints and books, safe and in the hands of a child. This was a warning, rather than an attempt to kill. Miss Milton was alive...for the moment.

'It is an oblivious thing to go missing.'

'I am sorry, Lord Ravensworth. I simply cannot see a thief, traipsing from room to room like a housewife on market day. The thieves in London must be very different from the thieves in Cumberland or, for that matter, Warwickshire.' Daisy gave her head a little shake, sending more curls tumbling about her face. Her tongue flicked over her lips, turning them cherry ripe, tempting him. Adam smiled inwardly. Seduction might be the answer. She would have to yield then, but the first move would have to come from her.

'Do you have any idea why anyone would come into this room? Why anyone would want to harm you?'

Daisy remained in the doorway, her hands clasped together, but something flickered in her eyes. 'The scarf reminds me of a tale my brother told. In India, various men he knew were sent dolls with yellow scarves about their neck. Later they died. There again, my brother probably just liked to tell tales. You know what boys are like. He enjoyed frightening Felicity and me. The letter equivalent of putting spiders down our backs.'

Adam met her green-grey gaze. How much should he tell her now? Could he begin by confessing that he owed Milton his life? Would she understand then?

Would she forgive him for what he had to do? 'He was a brave man and a good one. I wept when I heard he had died. He and his family.'

'Did you? You knew him too?' Daisy looked at Lord Ravensworth's intent face. She wrapped her arms about her middle and tried to stop shivering. Lord Ravensworth was being kind, the same sort of kindness that he would extend to any woman. 'Lord Edward did not remember him beyond that they had served together. There again, I doubt that Lord Edward sees anyone who is not the same rank as him.'

'I believe you have correctly assessed the situation.'

'I am getting worse than Nella for letting my tongue run away with me. Lord Edward is your friend.'

'Remind me to tell you some time about the attack on the hill station. Your brother was a hero. He pulled a woman off a funeral pyre. They escaped and then he turned around. He came back to the hill station and fought with my men and me until the maharajah was defeated.' His fingers brushed her cheek. In spite of everything she knew about his reputation and all the promises she had made after reading the scandal sheets, Daisy's heart started to beat faster. 'Those men, the thuggee, are all dead, Daisy. But does anyone have any reason to harm you? Trust in me. This was a warning, nothing more.'

A warning. Tom had warned in his last letter about the thuggee, and the grudge they bore him. And that he thought she would be strong enough to keep his treasure safe. But the only treasure he had sent was his daughter, and no one could be after Kammie. 'There is no reason why anyone could wish me harm. I am a governess, just a governess. It is so cold in here, so very cold.'

'I understand.'

It was the single word. He understood. Daisy wrapped her arms about her waist again. It seemed incredible, but he understood. She was not alone and that somehow made it worse. An uncontrollable sob escaped her body. She took a half-step towards him, towards comfort and safety. 'I…I…'

'I am so sorry, Daisy. This should never have happened to you.' His strong arms went around her and held her, pushing her head against his chest. She breathed in. The citrus scent he wore invaded her being, calming her. She allowed her head to rest a moment longer, listening to the steady thump of heart. His hands moved gently down her back, sending tiny tingles of fire throughout her being.

She swallowed hard. Daisy knew she had to move away from him, but her feet seemed to be rooted to the ground. She glanced up into his smouldering golden-brown eyes, intending to tell him that he had no need to apologise, he hadn't done anything wrong.

All thought of speech fled.

His mouth descended on hers, claiming her. Gone was the gentle kiss of the other day. This was hard, possessive, insistent and filled her with a deep abiding warmth that drove away the all-pervading cold.

Her hair came free, tumbling about her shoulders, but she refused to care. Her world had shrunk to his mouth, his lips, and his hands stroking her hair.

Her back arched towards him, seeking his heat and strength. Instantly, he shifted, pulling her tighter against him. An inarticulate noise came from her throat as his lips blazed a trail across her cheekbones, her temple and throat, soothing her and blocking out all memory of the hideous scarf.

'It is all right. I have you,' his voice rumbled in her ear. 'Nothing and no one will hurt you while I am here. Trust me to look after you and to keep you from harm.'

'I…I…'

His mouth covered hers, blocking out speech, all thought. The only thing she knew was the pressure of his lips against hers, the way his hands felt on her back—safety and something more.

Her hand curled around his neck, burying itself in his thick hair.

His tongue traced the outline of her lips, demanded entrance once again. Her mouth parted, tasting him, as his arms drew tighter around her.

The nature of the kiss changed, deepened, asked rather than took.

A wild surge of heat went through her, blocking out all sensibilities. This was nothing like his goodbye in the trees. This kiss had hunger and something else, something that called to the inner reaches of her soul. His hands gripped her shoulders, pulled her closer, prevented her from leaving, even had she wanted to give into that tiny warning voice that whispered about a governess's reputation.

'Miss Milton, I have collected lots and lots of flowers this time. Oh, my! Oh, my! Oh, my!'

Chapter Seven

Daisy turned in Lord Ravensworth's arms and saw Nella standing there, her mouth opening and closing like a cod fish's as she held the basket up over her head.

Before Daisy could utter a word of protest or move away from Lord Ravensworth, Nella dropped the basket with a crash and ran down the corridor.

The delphiniums fell into the ink puddle and became stained blue-black. Such a pretty flower to be ruined like that, Daisy thought abstractly. Ruined—the word reverberated in her soul.

'Nella!' she called in a throaty voice that did not sound like her own. But the only answer was Nella's footsteps resounding down the stairs, each step another nail in the coffin of her reputation.

Daisy knew she might have withstood the earlier squall, but not today's tempest. She had no excuse. Her lips ached where Lord Ravensworth had touched them. His arm remained curled about her waist, holding her to his body.

Holding out her hand towards the door, Daisy tried again. 'Nella, come back! I can explain. It is not what you think.'

From far away, she heard Nella calling to her mother.

'Miss Milton, Daisy, we will have company shortly,' Lord Ravensworth murmured in her ear. 'We must decide what to do. What we are going to say.'

'What is there to be done? How can this ever be made right?'

She knew her hands should be searching for pins, straightening the mass of hair that tumbled about her shoulders, but all she wanted to do was to lay her head against his chest and have it all go away. She shook herself. It was that sort of action that had led to this mess.

Her mind kept going back and back to the same thing—she had been caught in a flagrant embrace with Lord Ravensworth, a man she barely knew, a man who had the reputation of a notorious rake. What was it that Nella had whispered—the most famous courtesans in Europe swooned after him?

She had kissed and pressed her body up against his for no good reason except that she had desired the sensation. Mrs Flyte had warned her of such behaviour and had predicted a bad end. And now, despite her years of caution, the prediction had come true. Her life was at an end.

'Everything is destroyed.'

'Be brave. A governess does not wilt. A governess is strong and fearless when faced with such things as spilled ink.'

Daisy moved away from the circle of his arms. This was about more than spilled ink. She knew it and he knew it. But he stood there, watching her with hard amber eyes, spouting platitudes about ink. No doubt for him, being caught embracing a governess was a minor incident, an inconvenience. His reputation would never suffer. But hers… She refused to allow her mind to go on such paths. 'Then I had best get to work cleaning up this inconvenience. You might wish to depart, Lord Ravensworth, if you don't want to get your boots dirty.'

She averted her face from his. She wanted him to stay. And the worst thing was that she wanted him to sweep her into his arms again and whisper that it would be all right, that he would be honourable. But he stood there, unyielding and silent.

Daisy took hold of a bit of blotting paper and knelt down. She wouldn't beg.

Behind her, Lord Ravensworth's footsteps resounded against the carpet. A bottle clinked against her basket as he moved it, but she did not look up. She stared resolutely at the ink puddle and the way it was spreading—blue-black, smearing and destroying everything in its path. Her skirt touched the puddle and even the grey wool turned blue-black. She uttered a loud oath.

'Is there a problem, Miss Milton? You appear distraught. Allow me.' He took the useless blotting paper from her stained fingers. 'It will not be as bad as you fear. Trust me. I know what is required in these situations.'

'You have already done enough, Lord Ravensworth.' Daisy stared resolutely at the ink stain, rather than at her seducer. 'Nella was here. She has gone to fetch her mother. Mrs Blandish will be appalled at the state of the room. Mrs Blandish is a great one for propriety...for a proper order to things.'

Daisy looked down at her trembling hand. She hated the way her throat closed every time she attempted to say the word—reputation. She should be screaming at him.

'Your basket is here with everything in its place. Nothing was taken from it. What is a governess without a basket?'

He brought the basket over to her and set it down. His arm brushed hers and sent fresh tingles through her. His whole being appeared relaxed as if what had just happened was of no consequence. If anything, his whole countenance appeared more relaxed. Daisy gritted her teeth, hating her attraction to him and the consequences of it. Two played this game.

'You are right. It should not take long to clean up this mess. Luckily the ink did not reach the hearth rug. It would be a great shame for that carpet to be utterly beyond repair.' A single tear slipped out and with angry fingers she wiped it away. 'For people for ever to point and to whisper about this incident and say what a silly ninny the governess was.'

A firm hand gripped her shoulder, turned her around. His face was dark and angry without the slightest hint of pity. 'The hearth rug be damned! You will have to do better than that, Miss Milton. It is *your* reputation that matters here. People will not draw their skirts back or look down their pointed noses at you. Not because of what happened in this room today.'

'You're wrong.' She put her hand to her head as a wave of weary resignation washed over her. 'It does not take much imagination to know what happens next. Mrs Blandish will dismiss me without a reference. But I will find a way to survive. I do have friends, Lord Ravensworth. You can stop worrying.'

Lord Ravensworth crossed his arms and his face became more remote than a statue's. A muscle twitched in his cheek; his nostrils flared as if he were attempting to control his temper. 'Will you attempt to wrap the shreds of shattered reputation about you, Daisy, and hope? You might survive, that is true, but somehow I doubt it. Few will believe your prim-and-proper act when Mrs Blandish's juicy tale gets about. The gossips will want to enjoy themselves at your expense. Where to next? The Continent? Or will you try your hand at a different profession?'

'That is an infamous suggestion!' Daisy balled her fists and longed to hit something hard. A courtesan! Her! Not on this earth! 'I would rather starve first. I am no short-heeled wench, Lord Ravensworth. How is that for answer?'

'I am offering you *protection*, Miss Milton. But it would be remiss of me not to point out the alternatives. You will be unable to carry on as a governess in Britain if Mrs Blandish wants to smear your reputation.'

'I believe I already know the alternative. No one stays a governess long without learning about the pitfalls. There are other places such as Italy and the Kingdom of Two Sicilies where they do not listen to local gossip.'

Daisy hated how her voice caught. Italy. Louisa

Sibson had found employment there after the Jonathon Ponsby-Smythe débâcle. But Louisa's letters always spoke of the longing to return home. Daisy's heart plunged. And what would Felicity do if she was in Italy? Would she bring Kammie out? Could they live there? The annuity barely covered Felicity's living expenses and Felicity was so insistent that Kammie be brought up as a proper English girl, despite her illness.

'Italy is full of ruins and artists. You wouldn't like it.' Lord Ravensworth dismissed the idea with a snap of his fingers. 'And you forget—we are both caught in this coil.'

Daisy sat back on her heels. 'It may surprise you, Lord Ravensworth, but I am not in the market for an illicit relationship, even after this. I would rather die than betray my principles. And how would you know if I would like Italy or not?'

He swung away from her like he was attempting to control his temper.

She stood, but discovered her legs had turned to jelly. She staggered a few steps to her chair, sank down and put her face in her hands, rather than see the look of scorn on his face.

'I have been very naïve and stupid, Lord Ravensworth. Arguing with you about the merits of where I should next search for employment will not make it any easier. Please go. I decline your infamous offer of becoming your mistress. Your honour must therefore be satisfied. Go, you stubborn man.'

The mantelpiece clock ticked loudly and she peeped through her fingers at him and immediately wished she hadn't. He was standing there with an indulgent expression on his face.

'You are very pleasant to argue with.' His eyes flickered with a strange light, promising pleasure in their depths, a subtle shift. 'A refreshing change from the mealy-mouthed women who think no further than the latest trinket or bonnet.'

Her hands itched to smooth the errant lock of hair from his forehead. She wanted to hate him, but there was something about the way his smile transformed his features… His eyes burnt with warm fire. Daisy gripped the arms of the chair until her knuckles shone white. Thoughts like those were going to guarantee the destruction of her dreams and everyone she held dear.

'Why do you remain here, Lord Ravensworth?' she asked, to break the silence that was beginning to press down on her soul. 'Why have you not taken to your heels and fled? Most men would have. We have fallen out of all civility, you and I.'

'For once in my misbegotten life, I am attempting to do the correct thing, Miss Milton, and to save your life.' He stood, glowering. A tiny pulse beat at the base of his throat and his hair still retained the imprints of her palm. 'You are being wilfully blind, Daisy Milton.' He slapped his fist against his hand. 'I intend to marry you. There will be no martyred governess today.'

She stared at him in astonishment. The room spun slightly and then righted itself. The infamous Lord Ravensworth had proposed marriage. Proposal? It sounded more like a declaration of intent, an order. She had to have heard him wrong. Men like him walked away from governesses and left them begging on streets, penniless and pregnant. Wasn't that what everyone warned her of?

'Is this some sort of joke? A jape that you can then boast about to your friends? Viscounts marry débutantes with perfect pedigrees and well-endowed marriage settlements.' She fluffed out her skirt. 'I am hardly what you would call a catch—well and truly on the shelf with no dowry or family connection.'

'Marriage has never been a joking matter for me, Miss Milton.' The flame in his eyes had become cold and hard. 'I came here today to make sure you were safe. And you will be safe after you marry me.'

'Your immersion in the river must have affected your senses. Are you suffering from a fever? Delusions?' Daisy gripped the edge of the chair. What reason did Lord Ravensworth have for offering for her? There had to be an alternative reason, something she knew little about. There was no pretence of love. Daisy tried to think. There were many practical reasons why most women would grasp the opportunity with both hands, but she had always wanted to marry for love and because she had great regard for her husband. She had seen other governesses marry men simply because it was a way to escape, only to end up far worse off. And this would be no easy match. He was demanding and stubborn. 'You are a stranger to me. We do not have finer feelings for one another.'

'It is what engagements are for.' The dimple flashed in and out of his cheek as if she had tumbled headlong into his trap. 'A long engagement, if you wish, but we will marry, Miss Milton, and I will have you in my bed as my wife.'

Daisy sat completely still. Her fingers pinched her hand hard. She was awake. This was not some strange waking dream. Yesterday, she had thought marriage and such things were not for her and now a man, a man with a fortune, was offering, a serious offer. But acceptance was out of the question. She had always vowed that she would marry a man who understood her need for independence and who would let her have some measure of freedom. With Lord Ravensworth, compromise was not an option. He was the sort to rule his own house. And she had seen where that could lead with Felicity's marriage.

She lifted her chin, gazing directly into the shifting amber of his eyes. 'It is my life, Lord Ravensworth. We merely shared a kiss.'

He put his hands on either side of the chair, pinning her there. 'Must I destroy your reputation entirely, Miss Milton?'

His face loomed closer. She could see the place where his hair caressed his collar, and the way it curled about his ears as well as the curve of his sensuous mouth. The warm place in her middle ignited, blazing once again. Despite the danger, her body longed for his touch. She gripped the arms of the chair tighter, fighting against the growing warmth inside her and the temptation to simply lift her mouth.

'But why? Are you seeking to ruin me? What have I done to you except to help you? I saved your life,' she whispered as the tingling started again in her insides.

'Are you always this difficult?' The small place where his valet had forgotten to shave him as closely was but inches from her, tempting her fingers as she remembered the rough silk of his face. 'Will I have to kiss you again? And this time, I will not stop for modesty's sake.'

'Miss Milton!' Mrs Blandish thundered from the doorway, her jowls slightly swaying. Daisy sat back with a start. Lord Ravensworth leisurely righted himself, tucking a stray tendril of hair behind her ear as he did so, as if they were already…lovers. Daisy's stomach somersaulted.

'Mrs Bland…Blandish.' Daisy stammered and wished her brain could think up something more intelligent, some way of explaining, but her wits appeared to have deserted her along with her sense of self-preservation. 'This may appear odd to you, but can I assure you that it is not what it looks like… Lord Ravensworth and I…'

Lord Ravensworth merely raised his eyebrow and his forefinger indicated her top three buttons were undone. She put her hand to her throat and fumbled with them, missed the buttonhole and tried again.

'It all depends on what Mrs Blandish thinks it looks like,' he said with a maddening smile.

Daisy gave up on the buttons, clasped her hands together, and prayed. 'Is there some difficulty, Mrs Blandish?'

'I came to teach my daughter a lesson and to call her bluff.' Mrs Blandish closed her eyes and adopted a pious expression. 'And what do I discover—you in a flagrant embrace with an unknown man? You have to have known my daughter spied you before. I gave you time, Miss Milton, as I did not want to lose you. And you persist in being here with this man.'

'We have not yet been introduced, Mrs Blandish. Adam Ravensworth, third Viscount Ravensworth, at your service.' Lord Ravensworth executed a precise bow, the sort one found in the best drawing rooms or on the dance floor. 'Pray forgive me for calling in this manner, but your gift of the calf's-foot jelly aided my recovery immeasurably. It is seldom that one encounters such Christian behaviour.'

'Lord Ravensworth?' Mrs Blandish went white and then red. 'My governess was embracing Lord Ravensworth? Why on earth would Lord Ravensworth embrace a governess?'

Adam regarded the turban mountain with the tiny mouth and piglike eyes. Any pretence towards beauty had long since vanished under the veneer of good living. However, he would accept her as an ally in this war with Miss Milton's sensibilities. Daisy would marry him. He would not permit whoever had attacked her to try again. The necklace had been waiting for him in its hiding place, and, God willing, Daisy Milton would never know the danger she had been in. Adam touched the necklace in his pocket and silently repeated the vow.

'I was a friend of Miss Milton's brother before his untimely demise. Miss Milton's father was known to my grandfather, Lord Charles Ravensworth.'

The tiny mouth smiled. 'You are a respected member of the *ton*, Lord Ravensworth. I feel certain we must have a number of acquaintances in common, besides my dear friend, Lord Edward. But I remain confused—were you seeking to give Miss Milton comfort? Has she suffered a bereavement?'

Adam fought against the temptation to punch the air. The woman had taken his lead. Daisy would have to agree to the marriage. It was a source of irritation that he had not considered the prospect before now. Miss Milton possessed all the qualities he desired in a wife—refinement, wit and an interesting mind. He might not love her, but love only existed in poetry. He would never treat her unkindly and his debt to her brother would be repaid.

'You are quite correct in pointing out the impropriety of the situation. The fault is mine.' Adam gave a slight wave of his hand. 'Miss Milton is about to do me the honour of accepting my proposal of marriage.'

'You are perhaps being over-sensible on this matter, Lord Ravensworth.' Mrs Blandish regarded him with a greedy expression, her hands moving like some ponderous trunk. 'My younger daughter is prone to exaggeration. I am willing to say that I saw nothing untoward when I arrived. My new butler was remiss. He should have escorted you to the garden where you belong.'

Adam clenched his jaw. Mrs Blandish was supposed to be his ally, and not Daisy's. The stupid woman. She was not going to ruin his rescue.

'And that is the truth,' Miss Milton said. 'Nella is prone towards exaggeration. I was simply feeling overwrought with the state of the schoolroom and screamed. Lord Ravensworth came to my rescue.'

Adam mouthed liar at her, but she resolutely ignored him.

'I know what I saw, Mama. His arms were around Miss Milton. He was *devouring* her.' The golden-haired girl came to stand beside her mother. Silently, Adam blessed her.

'Prunella!' her mother thundered.

'But it is true, Mama, every last word. He was positively eating her mouth and she had her hands entwined his hair.'

'More than twenty thousand per year and a title. Do you understand what is at stake, Prunella?' Mrs Blandish waved her fan very rapidly as her eyes blinked. 'You could do much better than Miss Milton, Lord Ravensworth. A man's reputation is very hard to endanger and a governess's is of no import.'

'Except to the governess.' Adam gave a tight smile. 'Have you considered Miss Milton's reputation? She is most definitely a lady.'

'Eh…what did you say?' Mrs Blandish's nostrils quivered and she turned a particular revolting shade of puce.

'Miss Milton has many admirable qualities.' Adam glared at the war elephant. For once in his life, he was offering to be a gentleman, and the creature was trying to put forward her own miserable daughter as a candidate. Here he had thought to make the creature his ally. 'Accomplished. Brave. And possessing more than a modicum of common sense. What more could a man ask for in a wife?'

Mrs Blandish made a small choking sound. 'I believe I might need a chair. Miss Milton, quick, get me a chair. Prunella, I want my smelling salts!'

'I greatly fear that between Lord Ravensworth's desire to amuse and Nella's penchant for exaggeration, I will be left without a shred of reputation, Mrs Blandish.' Miss Milton's eyebrows arched.

'I find nothing amusing in this situation, *Daisy*.' Adam lowered his voice to a purring caress.

Her lips parted for an instant, but then she blinked and the shutters came down her eyes. She drew herself to her full height. 'I did not give you leave to call me by my first name.'

'You gave me leave when I kissed you. You opened your mouth under mine.'

She snapped her mouth shut and her cheek flamed as Mrs Blandish gave a cry and fanned herself wildly.

'I was not myself,' Miss Milton whispered, twisting the fabric of her gown between her fingers.

'Would that you were not yourself more often, then.' Adam watched the tiny pulse at the base of her throat. Her skin had tasted of strawberries and sunshine, everything that was good about life.

He ignored the pulling of his shoulder. The back of his head buzzed, but he forced his mind to concentrate on the situation at hand, rather than his body's cravings. Miss Milton was in danger because of him and what had happened all those years ago in India. Kamala's warning as she had handed him the necklace had haunted his dreams last night. The thuggee never stopped until they reclaimed their own. He refused to stand on the sidelines and allow Miss Milton to join the parade of ghosts.

'I will leave you two then, since Lord Ravensworth appears intent on doing the proper thing.' Mrs Blandish's mouth turned down to a petulant pout. 'It is most enterprising of you, Miss Milton, to find a wealthy and titled suitor. I did not think you had it in you.'

'Mama, may I stay and watch? It looks like Miss Milton is ready to murder him,' a sing-song voice called from the doorway. 'Maybe Miss Milton will devour Lord Ravensworth. Can you imagine what Mrs Gough or some of the other ladies will say to this piece of intelligence? I shall be the very toast.'

'Nella! Unless you wish to exist on the edges of society, you will learn to curb your tongue!' her mother exclaimed and swept out of the room. Her footsteps echoed on the stairs.

Daisy looked directly at Nella, whose cheeks coloured but who remained rooted to the spot. 'Do you know anything about the disruption to the schoolroom, Nella? Did you scatter the papers or put the scarf about the doll's neck?'

Her eyes grew wide and she shook her head, the golden curls bobbing from side to side. 'I would never do anything like this. Do you know how long I spent drawing this map of Italy, and putting the rivers on? I suppose you will make me do it over again.'

Daisy knelt and put her face level to Nella's. 'Did you see anyone come up here? Has anyone been in here today?'

'Lord Edward came earlier to take Susan on a walk. He had to wait while the maid went and fetched another pair of gloves. He wanted to see the schoolroom. We had a pleasant conversation about how I found Lord Ravensworth. You were on your morning constitutional.'

Lord Edward. Daisy tapped her finger against her mouth and rejected the suggestion. It made no sense that he would be involved.

'Have they returned?'

'It was why I was waiting in the garden.' A sudden

smile crossed Nella's face. She rocked back on her heels. 'But I can't wait until I tell Susan! She will be pea-green with envy. Lord Ravensworth is far better looking than Lord Edward and I dare say worth quite considerably more.'

'Prunella, Lord Ravensworth's finances are no concern of yours!'

'Nella is correct,' Lord Ravensworth commented in a dry voice. 'And, Daisy, I insist on you using my first name—Adam—as we are now intimate.'

'I think you should go and see your mother, Prunella.' Daisy tapped her foot and looked sternly at the girl, ignoring Adam. After some hesitation, Nella gave a small curtsy and darted from the room.

Daisy's stomach knotted as Adam remained standing close to her with a smug expression on his face. She wanted to know the truth before she agreed to marriage. The indiscretion was far too small and insignificant and Mrs. Blandish had given him plenty of opportunity to release himself from it. No, Adam Ravensworth had another reason for wanting to marry her, something so far removed from desire that it scared her. But she needed time alone to think. She summoned all her energy and raised her chin, meeting his stare. 'Go away, Lord Ravensworth. Leave me in peace.'

He withdrew his gold watch from his waistcoat pocket.

'You have precisely one hour, Miss Milton.' He snapped his pocket watch shut. 'I will expect you to be properly dressed for a turn about the garden. We will discuss the precise terms of our engagement then.'

'And you refuse to take no for an answer.'

His mouth turned up in an ironic smile. 'How well you are beginning to know me.'

Chapter Eight

'You have had your hour of solitude and reflection, Miss Milton. Leave the rest of the cleaning for the maids. It is why Mrs Blandish pays them.'

'I must finish my task. It is one of my duties to keep the schoolroom tidy.' Daisy refused to turn around and look at Adam Ravensworth. If she turned around, she would stumble into his arms and lay her head against his reassuring chest. She had promised herself over and over again after finding the scrap of paper under the doll that it was precisely where she would not go. She was the strong one who stood squarely on her two feet. Always. 'Our discussion must be postponed.'

'Now.' His fingers drummed against his thigh.

'You are not my master. I will have no master.' Daisy kept her head up, ignoring the sudden jolt in her pulse.

'Are you issuing me a challenge? We know where that ended the last time.'

Daisy kept silent and calmly reached down, picking up the few remaining papers and putting them into a pile with Nella's old sketchbook. Behind her, she could feel his temper growing. She was playing with fire, but with each thing she put away, her own control returned. Until she knew she was safe from temptation and would not melt into his arms.

'Hopefully I have not kept you waiting, Lord Ravensworth,' she said when the last paper was picked up. She looked about the room, but there was nothing more she could legitimately use for delay and Adam Ravensworth remained, glowering at her from the doorway. She smiled her best smile. 'If you will now permit me to change my gown and fetch a bonnet, I will be happy to join you for a turn about the garden.'

'You have had your hour.' His eyes glittered with fire. 'If you insist on changing, I will invade your bedroom and we can conduct the interview—in or out of the bed.'

'You are awfully sure of yourself.' She crossed her arms and tapped her foot, but her breath came more quickly than she would have liked. 'Seduction never solves anything.'

'You have no idea what it solves.' He lifted an eyebrow. 'But you need to wait, Daisy. First the business of the engagement, and then the pleasure. Surely it is how a proper governess would want it.'

'I don't need…any protection. No one wants to harm me. How could they? I haven't done anything wrong. I am a governess, only a governess.' Daisy wrapped her arms about her waist and resolutely kept her gaze from the pile of papers.

'You stopped being a governess an hour ago when you accepted my offer of marriage.' He took a step forwards and his eyes glittered as his gaze raked her form. 'Now, which is it to be—the bedroom or the garden?'

The afternoon sun brushed Daisy's cheek and she drank in the cool air as she stepped outside into the garden. Mrs Blandish and the others had vanished. She glanced up at the windows of the schoolroom, silent and dark, and an unwanted shiver convulsed her.

'What other object did you find in the schoolroom?' Adam's hand grabbed her elbow. 'There is more to your reluctance than simply wishing me to vanish into thin air or to turn the clock back. Why do you find it necessary to be strong and brave? Confide in me, Daisy.'

'Am I that obvious?'

'Your hands were shaking when you piled up the papers.' He gave a half-smile. 'I rather fancied the promise of a kiss would distract you. There are hidden fires beneath that governess exterior. You are quite an intriguing find.'

'Whoever wrecked the room left a message—death to all those who aid the enemy.' Daisy shook her head. Seduction had no part in her life. She should have guessed that Lord Ravensworth meant to tease.

Adam's face offered little comfort. 'Someone wanted to frighten you badly. You must stay at the hotel where my people can look after you. Whoever it was means business, Daisy.'

'Yes, of course you are right. I need to make sure Nella is safe.' She tightened her shawl about her shoulders. Everything crashed down around her. She looked up at the brilliant blue sky and blinked away the hot tears.

Silently he handed her a handkerchief. She gave a trembling smile and attempted to pass it back, but he shook his head and pointed to her cheek. 'I never cry. Felicity, my sister, weeps, but not me. Remember, I am the governess. Governesses can't afford to weep.'

'Keep it. You may need it.' His fingers curled around hers. 'Viscountesses can afford to cry in a way that governesses can't. My late mother wept once a day. Twice on holidays.'

'This whole incident has sent my insides quivering like jelly.' She dabbed at her eyes and attempted a laugh. 'Silly of me. You would think after all the years I have been a governess, little tricks would cease to bother me. That is all it was—a trick. Nobody was injured. He let me go when I struggled the least bit. If he had intended on killing me, he would have done.'

She waited for him to agree with her, but he looked at her as he had looked at her on the first day when she had not believed him about the men. Then his brow darkened and the line of his jaw became more determined. Daisy was pleased she had resisted confiding in him earlier because then she'd have ended up in his arms. And he was as much a threat as her unknown assailant.

He put his hand over hers and life-giving warmth pulsed through her, urging her to give into her attraction and rest her head against his chest. Daisy quashed it. Their worlds were completely different. There was something more to his offer of marriage and a long engagement, some reason behind it that she couldn't quite fathom, but she doubted it would lead to the altar. It was not the now she was thinking about, but the future.

How could she bear it when he found someone more suited?

'I blame my arrogance,' he said. 'If I had even thought for an instant about your last name and questioned you, I would never have forced you to help me. I would have sent you on your way.'

Daisy withdrew her hand from his. What sort of women must he know? As if she would ever leave any creature in need. 'You are being far too kind, Adam. Far more than I deserve. I was determined to help you. Christian duty and all that.'

'You used my first name. We begin to move towards *civility*.' Adam stared down at her, his eyes crinkling at the corners.

'It is the shock,' she said in a quiet voice.

'Your brother would have approved of me marrying you.'

She twisted the handkerchief about her fingers. What did Adam owe her brother? 'Tom? He has been dead for years. He never cared who I would marry. He used to laugh and say I was destined for a prince, but that was just him, teasing.'

'Tom saved my life and he gave life to someone who was very dear to me. He would expect me to act like this.' His gaze travelled out to the gardens and she knew his mind had gone back seven years. He saw her brother and not her and that tore at her insides. 'He acted like this once. I fought a duel with the maharajah and lost. Tom skewered him for me.'

'My brother saved your life because it was the right

thing to do. I am far from some green girl who must be protected from tricksters. I have worked hard at being a governess for six years. I knew what I was doing when I kissed you. I knew the risks. You must not feel obligated.'

'I am being pragmatic.' His face became an arrogant mask, once again. 'I do not believe in romance or love. Marriage is something that has to be faced.'

'You make it sound like a business deal. Marriage should be…more.' Daisy regarded her hands. She had always considered that if she married, it would be for love and mutual regard. Without those ingredients, marriage could all too easily become a prison. She had seen Felicity's marriage and in at least three of the households where she had been a governess, the wife had been desperately unhappy. One had even died of an overdose of laudanum rather than face her husband's tyranny any more.

'When your brother died—'

'My brother died of a fever. The Company sent a letter.' She shook her head, and cut him off. 'A letter…with all of his things, all of his possessions. The story about the thuggee was a tale to frighten my sister and me. My nerves were on edge and I reacted badly. Now that I am out of the room, it seems clear. Someone for some reason is playing a practical joke.'

'What possessions?'

Daisy concentrated on refolding the handkerchief. How could she begin to explain about Kammie? Could she trust him when she did not know what game he was playing? What would he say if he knew about Kammie's illness? Would he react like Felicity's late husband and demand Kammie be put in an institution? Felicity would say she was a fool to even consider telling him before the marriage, that this was her chance to end all threat of institutions and doctors' bills. Daisy clasped her hands together. She would wait to explain about Kammie until she knew Adam better.

'Things. His books. A few objects. Does it really matter what he sent home?' Daisy forced her voice to sound firm. 'He died without becoming a nabob and that is the end of the matter. Do not invoke my brother again!'

Daisy started towards the house, hurrying away from the temptation. Adam would prove to be like Felicity's husband—domineering and dictatorial. She had seen what it had done to Felicity. And what it had cost her to stand up to Colin Fulton when Kammie had arrived and he had wanted to send the baby to the orphanage.

If Adam Ravensworth wanted something from her, he would have to ask her outright. He knew more about these people behind the attack than he had told her.

Adam stared at her retreating back, hating the dark twisted thing within him. He had lived with it for seven years, but now he wanted to be better. He wanted Daisy to think him worthy, but she was definitely hiding something from him. He had to discover it before the secret killed them both. The note she had found had rattled her. He had to give her a little information, something to ease her mind. He would have to take the risk that she could keep his dark secret.

'The man who ransacked the schoolroom and attacked you is searching for something, something that is connected with India,' Adam called. 'Who else will you put in danger? I am your only hope, Daisy. Trust me.'

Daisy paused. Her back remained stern and resolute.

He willed her to trust him. She didn't need to know about the necklace or the part he'd played yet. That confession could wait until later. Her fear was from another source. What had her brother sent home? Did it have anything to do with Kamala's last note, the one she had written as she lay dying?—*Trouvez félicité dans votre vie, cher Adam. Cherchez une petite fleur, une marguerite. La, c'est la vérité pour toi.* He had always assumed a little flower was her urging him to take a mistress, but it was possible the note had another meaning. It was possible that Milton had dictated the note. Had he heard rumours that some of the thuggee still lived and had sought to protect his sisters? Silently he cursed. He should have thought of the connection earlier. Marguerite was French for Daisy.

'Who else did your brother call a little flower? A marguerite? Who is Felicity? Verity? It is important, Daisy. It might be a clue, a clue I overlooked years ago. Your brother wanted to keep you safe. He wanted me to find you, Margaret. Tom called you by your real name— Margaret.'

She spun around, her skirt brushing the gravel path. 'How did you know Tom always used my real name? He never liked Daisy. I hate Margaret.'

'And your sister's name?'

'Felicity Fulton. She is Colin Fulton's widow.' Her eyes became fixated on a spot somewhere in the middle distance. 'But I know no one who has the *first* name of

Verity. Were you planning on protecting her as well? I thought there was a law against bigamy.'

'Why did your brother want me to seek you out? What did he send you and your sister from India?' Adam ignored the barb.

'Did he?' She arched a brow. 'It has taken you six years to come to this conclusion. And surely our meeting here is a startling coincidence.'

'I had forgotten about his love of codes when I first read the letter.' Adam willed her to accept the statement. She gave a small nod. 'Your brother and I hunted and destroyed a nest of thuggee. They were some of the worst of the worst and had amassed a huge treasure culled from their victims. This treasure vanished the night of the attack.'

'Did you take the treasure?'

'No.' Adam touched his pocket where Kamala's necklace now rested. Some day, when he knew she'd see the good in him, he'd tell her about the necklace and how he'd hidden it in her basket. 'People are always ready to assume things without looking towards the obvious—that I have an eye for an investment. Heritage said that there were rumours about your brother taking the treasure.'

He shrugged and waited, but her eyes did not even flicker.

'Tom would never take something like that! Just help himself! He was not that sort. He sent nothing like *that* home!'

The protestation was quick, almost too quick. Adam's eyes narrowed. Exactly what did Daisy know about her brother? He had a clear memory of the pouch that Milton had taken from the maharajah's body, but those jewels had been the maharajah's welcoming bribe. The maharajah had taken pride in knowing a man's weakness. 'I believe you, Daisy, but someone has started searching for the jewels again. I think that was why my carriage was attacked. Over the years, every single one of the men who was in the attack on the hill station has died.'

'In the same fashion? With yellow scarves?'

'Different ways. The last one wrote to me before his death, warning me about the thuggee-cursed jewels and how he regretted his share. But he suffered from malaria and I put it down to that.' Adam shook his head. 'I took sensible precautions, but even then it would appear that they were determined. The attack on my carriage was meticulously planned.'

'But why now? Tom has been dead for years. For six years.' Daisy tapped her finger against her mouth. 'And the attackers are not from the original gang?'

'Every last one of them danced on the end of a hangman's rope. Heritage was in charge of the men who did the hanging.'

'But who, then?'

'Someone who learnt the story and finds pleasure in murder.' Adam paused, tempted. His fingers touched the necklace again. The stones were cold against his palm. No, she wasn't ready to hear the aftermath of how he'd fought her brother. 'Tom trusted me to protect you, Daisy. I'm sure of that. Allow me to perform this small service.'

Daisy stood completely still, her shawl fluttering in the faint breeze. Adam willed her to understand what he was offering. Life.

'You may regret your offer, Lord Ravensworth.' She held out her hand.

He tightened his fingers around her palm, tugged, sent her tumbling towards him. He caught her and pulled her firmly against his chest. Her curves hit the hard planes of his chest. She looked up at him with storm clouds in her eyes.

'The name is Adam,' he whispered against her lips. 'Use it from now on.'

'Adam.' A sigh escaped her throat. She lifted her arms and her body melted against his, acquiescing. Their lips touched and melded.

He had won. He now had the chance to conquer the blackness of his soul. Fate had given him a second chance.

He put his hands on her shoulders and forced his body to move away from her while he retained some measure of self-control. His entire being wanted to ravage her mouth. The thought shook him to the core. He always kept his emotions carefully compartmentalised. Their engagement was based on necessity and not unbridled desire. The marriage would be pleasant. He had no room for love or other sentimental notions in his life.

'You will remove yourself and your belongings to Shaw's today. I will have them prepare a room for you.' He reached out and rubbed the back of his thumb along the outline of her lower lip. 'The note and the scarf did not magically appear. They killed my driver in pursuit of their so-called treasure and he had taken their coin. Do you want to stand in their way, on your own? Would you put the Blandishes in danger? Nella?'

FREE BOOKS OFFER

To get you started, we'll send you
2 FREE books and a FREE gift

There's no catch, everything is **FREE**

Accepting your 2 **FREE** books and **FREE** mystery gift
places you under no obligation to buy anything.

Be part of the Mills & Boon® Book Club™ and receive your favourite
Series books up to 2 months before they are in the shops and delivered
straight to your door. Plus, enjoy a wide range of **EXCLUSIVE** benefits!

- Best new women's fiction – delivered right to
  your door with FREE P&P

- Avoid disappointment – get your books up to
  2 months before they are in the shops

- No contract – no obligation to buy

2 **FREE** books
and a
FREE gift

We hope that after receiving your free books you'll
want to remain a member. But the choice is yours.
So why not give us a go? You'll be glad you did!

Visit **millsandboon.co.uk** to stay up to date
with offers and to sign-up for our newsletter

H0EIA

Mrs/Miss/Ms/Mr   Initials

BLOCK CAPITALS PLEASE

Surname

Address

Postcode

Email

The Mills & Boon® Book Club™ – Here's how it works:

Accepting your free books places you under no obligation to buy anything. You may keep the books and gift and return the despatch note marked "cancel". If we do not hear from you, about a month later we'll send you 4 brand new books priced at £3.79* each. That is the complete price – there is no extra charge for post and packaging. You may cancel at any time, otherwise we will send you 4 stories a month which you may purchase or return to us – the choice is yours.

*Terms and prices subject to change without notice.

MILLS & BOON®
Book Club

FREE BOOK OFFER
FREEPOST NAT 10298
RICHMOND
TW9 1BR

NO STAMP
NECESSARY
IF POSTED IN
THE U.K. OR N.I.

The colour drained from her face. 'And my family in Warwickshire? I have a sister and…a niece. Will you extend your protection to them? If these people think my brother sent home treasure, they could be in danger.'

Adam regarded the ground. It would be easy to offer comfort, but he couldn't lie to her. 'I am the target, Daisy, and not your sister. It is only after I am dead that they will turn their attention elsewhere. And, Daisy, I have no intention of dying of anything except old age.'

'How long do we remain there?'

'Until I know more. It is my turn to go on the hunt.' He tucked his thumbs into his waistcoat, fighting against the urge to take her in his arms and finish the job he had started in the schoolroom. But she was an English governess and not a courtesan. When he initi-ated her into the pleasures of the bed, he wanted to take his time.

Her long lashes swept over her grey-green eyes, hiding them. 'You leave me no option. I must fall in with your wishes.'

'Often, it is the best way.'

Daisy's footsteps echoed in the tiny room with an iron bedstead and bare hooks for hanging her clothes. Few traces of Daisy's brief occupation remained. Only her brush-and-comb set, and then she'd be packed away. Her life as a governess would have ended.

Daisy's hand curled around a little box, a gift that Tom had sent when he had known that his final illness was fatal. His last present to her. The note he had sent had been so cryptic that she had thought there must be more to it or that part of it was lost. She had tried and tried to work it out, but had given up when Kammie had been deposited on their doorstep by the vicar's wife returning from India with her three young ones. Tom's meaning had become suddenly crystal clear.

It was simply a clever rattle, a ruse for Tom to write about Kammie without actually mentioning the baby. Felicity agreed with her that his superiors must not have approved of his association with a local woman. The box now bore Kamala's teeth marks where she had chewed a corner when she was little.

What would the attacker do when he discovered that the only treasure her brother had sent home was a half-English baby? And one who suffered from falling sickness?

Daisy's hands touched her lips. Adam had decreed that he would marry her, but she would not allow him to decree where Kammie would go. It wasn't as if Kammie was related to him. He would have to understand that certain things were not negotiable. Kammie stayed with Felicity in Warwickshire where she was happy.

'Miss Milton, is it true then?' Nella's small voice sounded in the hall, recalling her to the present. Hurriedly she placed the box in her satchel.

'True about what?' she called out, smoothing her skirts.

'That you are leaving. Today. In a few moments. Susan is to look after me until we find another governess. I overheard Lord Ravensworth telling Mama and then Susan started bleating.' A single tear trickled down Nella's face as she barged into the room. 'I would never have told Mama about you and Lord Ravensworth if I had thought that I would lose you.'

Daisy raised an eyebrow and Nella had the grace to blush. 'You knew quite well what you were doing, Prunella.'

Nella hung her head. 'I am sorry, Miss Milton. It was—'

Daisy held up her hand, cutting off Nella's self-serving apology. 'Next time, think, Prunella, and consider others besides yourself. Gossip has the power to destroy lives.'

'Couldn't you stay as my governess?' Nella held up her hands in an overly theatrical way. 'Perhaps Lord Ravensworth could court Susan and then everything would be forgotten. Mama seems to think that the situation could be salvaged. Mama is quite astute on such matters. You cannot be in love. You just met a few days ago.'

'It is for the best, Nella. Your mama would regret keeping me. Once one is labelled a wanton by the mistress of the establishment, it is impossible to be a governess in the household.' Daisy kept her head up. Her hands were numb with cold. Even now Mrs Blandish was angling, but there again it was how society thought.

'But Mama says that men must be allowed their little pleasures.'

'Lord Ravensworth is different from most men. He seems to possess a surfeit of honour despite being *your* notorious rake.' Daisy gave Nella a hard look. 'Against your mother's advice, he made a marriage offer.'

'The scandal sheets were wrong about him. How disappointing.'

'It should be a lesson to you not to believe everything you read in such papers.'

'Before I left them all downstairs, Lord Ravensworth said that I had done very well. He gave me sixpence. See.'

Daisy froze, her hand tightening around the little box so that the markings dug into her hand, branding it. 'You had done well? What do you mean?'

'I met him earlier. Introduced myself. He told me to be sure to come up to the schoolroom.'

Daisy pursed her lips and absorbed the knowledge. Her entire being went first flaming hot and then ice cold. It had been planned. She had fallen completely into his trap of expert seduction.

'Are you exaggerating again, Nella?' She pinned Nella with her fiercest gaze. 'I do not have time for your lies today. I want the truth!'

Slowly Nella shook her head. Then she went beet red and scraped her foot along the floorboards. 'Maybe a little. I did meet him and he did tell me to be sure to find you wherever you were hidden and bring you down to the garden.'

'With your next governess, tell the truth.' Daisy struggled to breathe deep calming breaths.

'Surely you could stay with me until you get married. Venetia Penny's governess did when she married the curate. Venetia went to the wedding and everyone made a fuss of her.'

'Lord Ravensworth wants to get to know me better and believes that it will be beneficial if I cease to be governess.' Daisy gritted her teeth. She hated that Adam's reasoning was correct. 'It is in everyone's best interest.'

Nella's answer was to fling her arms about Daisy's middle and sob. 'But what if my new governess is horrid?'

Daisy patted Nella's back. Nella would calm in a few moments after she left. She knew that. Nella was resilient. She hated to think how much she would miss the girl. 'You can write to me. I will look forward to your letters. And I shall remain in Gilsland while Lord Ravensworth recovers from his ordeal.'

Nella stopped crying. 'What a wonderful idea. I have always wanted a correspondent. And if you go to one of the balls that the Shaw's is famous for, then you can tell me truly once and for all how Susan behaves.' She cupped her hand around her mouth. 'I am convinced that sometimes she lets her lace slip.'

Daisy disentangled Nella's arms. She hated that she had been sharp with Nella. All the girl wanted was attention from her mother. Nobody had forced Daisy into Adam's arms. She had gone there on her own. It was time she faced up to the consequences and found her own solution.

Adam regarded his immaculate room. Nothing appeared to have been searched. But then did they need to? Had someone searched while he lay there helpless? He had vague memories of Heritage searching through his pockets, but Heritage would never stoop that low.

The worst was the knowledge that without meaning to, he had led the assailant to Daisy. He did not want to think about what might have happened, had he not been there. Or if Daisy had kept silent? Or had failed to fight the attacker off?

His body remembered the way Daisy had felt against it. It was the right thing to marry her. They could have a practical but satisfying marriage, not one clouded by things like love. He doubted if romantic love even existed. It seemed to resemble a case of indigestion where the couple went around with soulful looks for a few months before deciding that they could not stand the sight of each other.

Thankfully he had been cured of such things years ago. Kamala had ensured that his heart was dead. He had not even known that he had loved her until she had fallen for Tom and told him she was going.

He poured himself a glass of port. It would be better if he did not see Daisy today and allowed her time to adjust. He would not be running away as Kamala had once accused him of, but acting to protect Daisy. Kamala. For such a long time, he had thought her accusation that his heart was made of ice and stone was right. It was when he had refused to hide her and the baby she carried. And then he had met Daisy. He wanted her to believe in the good in him.

'I hear you are to marry the governess?' Heritage burst into the room, his frock coat flapping and his hair flopping to one side as if he had run.

Adam raised his glass, swirling the ruby-red liquid. He did not bother to glance at his pocket watch. He had barely had time to take a single sip. 'Have you come to offer your felicitations?'

'To express my surprise and astonishment. A governess is an unusual choice for your countess.'

'We all must marry at some point.' Adam took another sip of his port. Heritage appeared positively put out.

'But the governess…she is, well…a governess. Take her as a mistress if you must, but wives should be made of different material—well endowed.'

'Be careful, Heritage, it is my future wife you are talking about.' Adam narrowed his gaze. 'I trust you will treat her with respect.'

'I will admit not to have paid close attention to Miss Milton before now. My eyes were much more entranced with Miss Blandish.' Heritage gave an insolent grin. 'And her fortune.'

'There should be more to a woman than her fortune.'

'It is as easy to love a woman with a fortune as a penniless one. We do not all possess your advantages, your almost preternatural way with money. Even at cards, you win more than you lose. If you were not my friend, Ravensworth, I would hate you.'

Heritage's face took on a hungry expression. Adam frowned. Heritage was after something, but what? Had he wanted to seduce Daisy? Or was it something worse? Adam dismissed the thought as unworthy. Heritage had no love for the thuggee. 'Know when to quit and always play by Hoyle.'

'That has always been my failing—I have trouble remembering the rules.' Heritage swept his hair back from his face and the expression vanished as if it had never been. 'When I see a thing, I must have it.'

Adam inclined his head, keeping his expression bland. 'I will try to remember that.'

'But why are you marrying her? Surely you could simply bed her? Start her on her career, as it were.'

Adam toyed with the stem of the glass, contemplating whether planting a fist in Heritage's face was worth the trouble. 'Let us say that I found Daisy intriguing. Her brother would have approved of the match, I am sure.'

Heritage went white. 'Of course, her brother. I had not thought. Did he often speak of his sister? Did he have just the one? Miss Blandish is infuriatingly vague on the matter. Far be it from me to warn you, but such women often have a parcel of relatives who need feeding.'

'I will take the chance.' Adam saluted Heritage with his glass. Nobody paid attention to Daisy. It was quite probable that the gang had no idea about her sister or her sister's daughter. He would keep it that way. Moving them up here would be a mistake. Once the gang were caught, he and Daisy could marry in War-wickshire. He would even investigate obtaining a lease on a property near where Mrs Fulton lived.

'I only sought to warn you, but I see you must be correct. After all, the family is known to you.' Heritage's throat bobbed. 'When will you marry?'

'That is up to my fiancée.' Adam leant back in his chair and crossed his legs. Something was bothering Heritage. He couldn't sit still, but kept moving about and glancing over his shoulder. 'Someone searched Daisy's room at the Blandishes and left a threatening note. I mean to keep her safe, Heritage. I owe her and her family my life. Marriage is a small price to pay for that.'

Heritage's hand trembled slightly, nearly dropping the decanter's topper. 'I heard some vague rumour about that as well. I dare say it was the younger sister. She is a sly thing, always watching me from underneath hooded eyes.'

'I found Miss Nella to be quite an amusing child and very quick to grasp the exact nature of the problem.' Adam rubbed the back of his neck and resolved to send Nella a small present. Her intervention had been fortuitous. 'To keep you from being ground down by the gossip mill, I will explain. Miss Milton will be removing herself to the Shaw's Hotel. I have instructed the innkeeper to prepare her a room.'

'You are determined for people to forget that she was a governess.' Heritage's laugh became squeaky. 'Or are you worried about something else?'

'Society has a remarkably short memory,' Adam shrugged and picked up his new cane. 'I merely want her to have the honour due to her as my fiancée.'

'It is strange that you were not so keen to marry her until you learnt of her connection to Tom Milton and the missing jewels.' Heritage stroked his chin.

'Her connection to Milton had little to do with it.' Adam kept his gaze level and saw Heritage's pale cheeks flush slightly. 'It had everything to do with my honour as a gentleman.'

'It appears you have developed a conscience. It will be the talk of St James's once I am back in London. The great Adam Ravensworth was overcome with sensibility. Is there any hope left?'

'She did save my life.' Adam tapped a finger against the table. Heritage had shown him one thing. Daisy needed to be outfitted correctly. He would not have people whispering behind her back.

'Speaking of the attack, your cane has been discovered in Carlisle. Someone handed it in and because a description had been circulated they knew it was yours.

The innkeeper or one of his staff asked me to say. Your valet, Webster, told me as well.' Heritage waved a vague hand.

Adam stared at Heritage for a long moment. It was not beyond the bounds of possibility that one of the gang had been greedy. And Carlisle would suit his purpose. It would prove a distraction, and Daisy would be perfectly safe with Webster to watch over her. But why did Heritage want him to go? Did he have any part in this affair? Adam shook his head. He was becoming worse than the young Miss Blandish for inventing things.

Chapter Nine

~~~~~~~~~~~~~~~~~~~

A distinct drizzle soaked Daisy's bonnet, obscuring her view of the gorge. She glanced over her shoulder. Adam's valet still shadowed her. Ever since she had arrived at Shaw's yesterday afternoon, every time she set foot out of her suite, Webster was there, waiting. Adam had disappeared off to Carlisle, leaving only a short note and her new unwanted bodyguard.

The annoying thing was that in the drizzle, he looked a bit like the man she had encountered on the river bank. What if Webster had had something to do with the attack? It had been known to happen before, a disgruntled servant deciding to dispose of his master. Daisy pulled the brim of her bonnet forwards. She was becoming worse than Nella.

'Mr Webster,' she called out.

'Yes, miss.' He was there within an instant. 'Is anything wrong? Would you like to return to the hotel? Have you had enough of the countryside?'

'If I promise not to throw myself down any cliffs or

take a sudden interest in the river, do you think I might be able to go for a quiet walk on my own? You appear to dislike the scenery.'

'The master gave his orders.' Webster looked down his thin nose. 'I value my wage. There are a lot of men who would be glad of the salary.'

'Then will you walk with me?'

'That wouldn't be right, miss. You know that.'

'It was only a possible solution.' Daisy sighed. She knew the fine demarcations between master and servant and had often sought to maintain her position, but just now, she wanted to talk. 'Very well, I will return to my suite.'

'It is for the best, miss. It is not a good walk, that one. When we were here last summer, I found it very tedious. Far too much "nature".'

'Why were you here last summer?'

'Railways, miss. Lord Ravensworth is involved in financing the Newcastle-to-Carlisle railway and there were problems. Lord Ravensworth thinks the railway will make Gilsland Spa into a holiday destination.'

'You don't approve.'

'I think folks should stay where they belong. It keeps everything tidy. They were right to site the railway at Rosehill rather than at the Spa.'

Daisy drew in a breath. 'And does Lord Ravensworth agree?'

'Lord Ravensworth is a law unto himself.'

'But you enjoy working for him.'

'Yes, miss, I do. His lordship is most at home in the lights of London. He will never live anywhere else, he says. And I agree wholeheartedly with the sentiment.

The day he moves to the countryside is the day I give my notice.' Webster looked pointedly back at the hotel. 'Are you going to go back? The gorge is…well…countryside.'

Daisy clung on to her temper. There was little point in taking out her ire on Webster. It was his master who needed to understand. She had looked after herself for six years and she could be trusted in a crisis, but she was no society hostess and London was another world.

'I'm satisfied that the cane is yours, Lord Ravensworth,' the Carlisle magistrate pronounced from his wing-backed chair. He gestured towards his clerk and the silver-topped cane was placed back in Adam's hands.

Adam took it. 'And the finder? What of him? Was he one of the gang?'

'Lord Chesterholm vouched for him. He is a simple farm worker who stumbled across the cane while digging ditches.'

Adam pressed his lips together. It was all very convenient. And this entire trip was an exercise in frustration. What was worse was that his mind kept wandering back to Daisy. He wanted to know what she was doing and what she was thinking. Hopefully she'd been sensible and stayed with Webster. He turned to leave.

'Ravensworth!' a deep voice called out.

'Ponsby-Smythe, what brings you north? I thought your family was in Warwickshire.'

'My great-uncle died and I inherited his estate as well his title. Had to change my name to Fanshawe, but then I get the lot.' Lord Chesterholm gave a wry smile.

'It kept the peace and for a few short months my late wife enjoyed the trappings as well as the title.'

'But how did your man find the cane?'

'My great-uncle tried to knock down all the Roman remains around his house, but I find them fascinating. I am determined to prove that it was actually Hadrian who built the wall. We were out digging in one of the mile castles when my man came across that cane. It could have lain in that ditch for years.'

'It is good that your man turned it in. There are many who would be tempted.'

'He's a good lad. Once he showed it to me, I recognised the crest. How could I forget the fencing lessons we took together at Angelo's? It was obvious to whom the cane belonged. And then I heard about the attack. Any leads?'

'It was a bad business. I had hoped finding this cane would provide one, but it has been a nearly wasted journey.'

'That's a shame.'

'Although I have been able to visit a modiste. I intend to marry the woman who saved me, but she needs a new wardrobe.'

'And who is this paragon of virtue?'

'A governess. Daisy Milton. I doubt you will have encountered her.'

'It rings a faint bell, but I don't think my stepmother ever employed her. It will come to me.' Chesterholm stopped and paled slightly. 'I know where I heard the name. She was poor Louisa's bluestocking friend.'

'Louisa?'

'A governess I once knew, but unfortunately she died in a curricle crash. I was too ill to attend the funeral. I never remembered a thing about her being in the carriage until Clarissa and my mother finally plucked up the courage between them to tell me.'

'I am sorry.'

'It was years ago. Never knew what I had until she was gone. It seemed only natural to marry Clarissa then.' Chesterholm's brow darkened. 'Are you sure your Miss Milton will like the clothes?'

'What woman would not? It is the same as outfitting a mistress. She will be in ecstasy.'

'Ravensworth, you have a lot to learn about wives. Miss Milton, if it is the same one, was a regular bluestocking. Far too fond of her poetry for my liking. Do give her my regards, though.'

'I will take that advice under consideration.' With that, Adam turned the conversation towards the exact location where the cane had been found and how it had been placed.

Daisy, dressed in her most severe grey gown, regarded Shaw's terraced gardens from her sitting-room window. The sunlight on the morning dew caused the whole scene to be lit like a jewel case.

Behind her, nearly every surface of the room was covered in boxes. Frothy lace and ribbons spilled on to the dressing table. A whole array of off-the-peg gowns occupied the sofa. Daisy had lost count of the petticoats, stays and other unmentionables, the dancing slippers and other dainty shoes, instead of her practical boots. All had arrived from Carlisle. All sent at

Lord Ravensworth's order without regard to what she might want.

The worst thing was that some of the gowns were ones she had sighed over in Miss Blandish's fashion magazines.

Her hand crumpled the paper and tossed it down to join the growing pile of spoilt letters. She had lost count of how many times she had attempted to write to Felicity since she had arrived at the Shaw's yesterday and how many times she had been unable to find the precise wording. She who had proclaimed loudest about her independence had sacrificed it all because of a fright over a half-remembered tale.

Her current predicament defied all explanation. No. It would be better to write the letter after she had informed Adam of her intention to jilt him at the earliest opportunity. Felicity was less likely to be concerned when presented with a *fait accompli*.

'I trust you find everything to your satisfaction. I regret that I was unable to be here when you arrived, but I had to chase up a lead. My cane was found in a ditch near Carlisle.' Adam lounged in the doorway, a faint smile on his face. His face was all planes and angles. 'Do say that you will forgive me.'

Daisy swallowed hard and tried not to think about his mouth. Or that they were alone in a hotel room. Or that her dreams last night had been full of him and how his lips had moved on her skin. Daisy clasped her hands in front of her and attempted to ignore the surge of heat that flooded through her.

'Lord Edward explained that you had business to attend to,' she replied carefully. 'He was most attentive.

He kept asking about my brother and his last days when we took tea in the parlour. He appears to think I was Tom's only living relation.'

'Did you disabuse him of the notion?' Adam's cane stopped swinging and his eyes narrowed.

'I want to keep my sister safe,' Daisy said. 'As it was a public place, I changed the subject.'

'Ah, yes. Your fabled common sense. It is good that I can depend on you to use it.' He came into the room, making it seem small.

'I rather thought you would have waited…' Daisy winced as she said the words. They sounded needy.

'Finding the men who attacked me is my first priority. Once the mystery is solved, we can begin to lead our lives again.'

Lead our lives again. The words echoed in her head. Would she ever be able to lead her life again, in the way she wanted to?

'Did you find anything worthwhile in Carlisle?' she asked.

He waved a dismissive hand. 'It came to nothing. But as I was fond of the cane, I am pleased to have recovered it.' He paused and his eyes glinted with mischief. 'I would have preferred to find my boots, though.'

'I suspect your boots are at the bottom of the Irthing. Webster agrees with me.'

'I met an old admirer of yours. Jonathon Fanshaw, Lord Chesterholm.' At her puzzled expression, he added. 'Until recently he was Ponsby-Smythe.'

'He is no friend of mine!' Indignation rose in Daisy's breast. 'He is a callous seducer. My friend Louisa was

forced to leave the country after he was finished with
her. She currently resides in the Kingdom of Two
Sicilies.'

'He thinks Louisa died in a curricle crash.'

'He is wrong!' Daisy went to her letter box, and
waved a piece of paper in the air. 'I received a letter from
her two days ago. She is in Sorrento with two ladies.
Ponsby-Smythe was a heartless seducer.'

'He remembers you with admiration. You and your
feminine charm.'

Daisy clasped her hands together and attempted to
control her racing pulse. Adam had discussed her with
Jonathon Ponsby-Smythe.

'I would expect your attackers are long gone from
here.' Daisy resolutely turned her gaze to the window
again. She had to keep the topic on sensible subjects.
'They must know you are looking for them if they
remain in the area.'

'Then who ransacked the schoolroom? And why?
Don't you want to know?'

Daisy swung around. His clothes fit him all too well
and there was an air of smug elegance about him.

'If I knew that, I would not be engaged to you.'
Daisy opted for a sharp answer, which only appeared
to amuse him more. She gestured towards where the
boxes overflowed with lace and half-finished gowns.
'And would not be faced with all this.'

'I wondered when you would mention your new
wardrobe.' His gaze raked her gown. 'It was brought
to my attention that your attire was lacking in certain
feminine attributes. And as I was in Carlisle, I went into
a bazaar and ordered a few items.'

'A few items! You have purchased an entire wardrobe, a wardrobe fit for…well…not fit for a governess.'

'The fiancée of a viscount must dress differently from a governess. The point is obvious.' He raised an eyebrow. 'I have braved a modiste's establishment before. Ladies' garments hold no fear.'

'What is right for a mistress…' Daisy put her hands on her hips. Been to a modiste's before. Of course he had. Undoubtedly with a simpering, perfumed and perfectly coiffured woman at his side breathlessly choosing the garments that he would later take off. She hated thinking about all the sophisticated women he had helped dress and undress. All these clothes did was to underline her inadequacies, the reasons why a marriage between them would fail.

'Humour me on this, Daisy.' He waved a hand towards the boxes. 'Do what you will with them, but you are to wear suitable clothes. And I could not decide on the gloves. I owe you a pair and so a selection of Hexham tans have been sent. A fiancée may accept a pair of gloves.'

'A pair of gloves, but not a wardrobe!'

'And here I thought all women loved to be spoilt.' A muscle jumped in his cheek. 'Most women would breathlessly say oh, Adam, thank you for thinking of me. Thank you for taking time out of your busy schedule.'

Daisy twisted her fingers into her gown's material. She longed to wipe the arrogant smile from his face. He had assumed that she would adore the clothes without even bothering to discover her tastes, treating her like some fancy pet. Throughout her years as a governess she had seen how women could be marginalised and reduced to mere ornaments, worrying about nothing more than shell pictures and pin cushions. She had always vowed that it would not happen to her.

Daisy straightened her skirt, making sure the folds of the gown fell evenly to the floor, the very picture of propriety.

Two could play games. He had not won. She would make him see her as a person rather than as a doll. 'I thank you for the gloves, but have no need of—'

'It is all about playing the part, Daisy. Try them on.' He paused. 'I have engaged a lady's maid for you. A cousin of the innkeeper's. She is reputed to have some skill with hair. She should arrive this morning. The innkeeper's daughter is rushed off her feet as it is. Hopefully, though, she helped you with dressing.'

'I am used to dressing on my own. My hairstyle is quite simple. I have never had a need for assistance.'

'Sometimes, we can all use the help.' He looked pointedly at the various undergarments.

Daisy wished she had drawn her hair tightly into her usual governess style, instead of giving into a whim and allowing a few ringlets at her temples. 'My hair! What is wrong with my hair?'

She waited, knowing that she sounded about Nella's age, but it was the principle. It was her hair and her life. He had to see that her opinions mattered.

'It is charming, but perhaps it could do with a few refinements.' He inclined his head. 'Both the haberdasher and the modiste gave me to understand that you would require a maid if you wore this Season's styles. Helpless as a babe.'

Daisy pressed her palms against her eyes. 'Are the clothes even the right size?'

'The maid is very nimble with her fingers, or so her uncle assures me. You both may spend the day going through the items, deciding how you wish to make them your own.'

Daisy stared at him, astonished. She was to have a maid, but no say about whom she employed. It reminded her so much of Felicity's marriage. Her husband had dominated and domineered and the only time Felicity had dared oppose him was when she had fought for Kammie.

'And if I choose to spend my time in another way?'

'Do not even think about trying to find these men. You have enough to do.' Adam's presence filled the room. She would only have to stretch out a hand to touch his frock coat. She twisted her fingers around the grey fabric of her gown. 'I wish my fiancée to show her vibrant personality, instead of seeming like a staid old maid. You have a part to play, Daisy.'

Play a part. Staid. The words washed over her like a cold bath. He wanted to control her life and leave nothing to chance. If she allowed it, she would become the same sort of pale insipid creature that Felicity had been before her husband had died. No man would rule her. She had made that vow years ago. Independence of mind and body. If she started compromising, all her brave words would mean nothing.

Daisy strode purposefully over to the writing desk. She had spent years teaching reluctant pupils their sums and the finer points of English history. She would get her own way in the end.

'You must allow me to pay for my room here. I am quite content to take a small backroom, perhaps one that a maid might use. And the maid… I believe I can stretch to her wages. I have no wish to disgrace you.' Silently she prayed that this charade would not have to go on long. Once the men were caught and captured, she would break the engagement. It would no longer be a necessity. It was quite the best solution. 'But I have no wish to become a kept woman.'

'No one would ever mistake you for a kept woman. There is something about you that screams—governess.' He leant forwards, his eyes gleaming. 'You will never be my mistress, but one day soon you will be my lover, Daisy.'

'Adam Ravensworth, there are certain proprieties!'

'You are back to using my last name. You must be very displeased with me or perhaps you wish me to kiss you again. Did you miss me that much?'

His hand touched the inside of her wrist. No more than a whisper, but it sent a warm pulse down her spine. Daisy resisted the urge to lean into the touch. One single touch and her body melted. She glanced up to the ceiling and strove for a calm outlook. She needed to regain control of this conversation. Immediately. Things needed to be said between them, boundaries established, and speaking about becoming his lover definitely crossed all sorts of boundaries.

'Lord Raven…' She paused and regained her composure. 'Adam, then, we must be sensible. I have no wish to be a prisoner. Nor to be beholden to you. It is no way to behave. I have my self-respect. I have worked long and hard for my independence.'

'You have rehearsed this speech, Daisy.' He settled himself into the wing back armchair, crossed his legs. 'And as no doubt you have spent a great deal of time and expended a considerable amount of energy on it, I will do you the courtesy of listening to it.'

'You are laughing at me, now.'

'Perish the thought.'

'Yesterday was a day of upsets.' Daisy clasped her hands in front of her. She tried to remember exactly how the speech went, the exact mannerisms she had planned to use and not to concentrate on the way his lips twitched or his eyes had turned golden. 'But that does not mean we must be irrevocably linked. I suspect through a misguided attempt—'

'Misguided. Surely you could have used a better word.' He made a temple with his long fingers. 'There is nothing misguided about my intentions towards you. But continue, Daisy, do. I am anxious to see where your speech leads.'

'Please pay attention without interrupting.' The urge to stamp her foot nearly overwhelmed Daisy. She had spent years being thought of as calm, cool and collected, but every time she came near to Adam, something inside her simmered to boiling point.

'You should never play chess, Daisy. You wear all your emotions on your face.' His eyes became sober. He leant forwards and lightly clasped his knee. 'You remain in grave danger. These men kill. Whoever is behind this has targeted you because of me. I refuse to allow it to happen. That is where the matter ends. Your life is far more important than some illusionary independence.'

'I wish to make my own decisions.'

'Once we are married, you will be able to run the house.'

Daisy pressed her fingertips against the bridge of her nose. 'It is not what I meant. These clothes…'

'Are yours. You may burn them for all I care.' Adam stood up. 'But then what will you have to wear? I have given instructions that your other garments are to be destroyed.'

'You would not dare.'

'Try me!' He took a step closer and his fingers flexed. 'Do you wish to be thought of as a governess or a woman?'

The air between them quivered. A sudden exhilaration filled Daisy—he would kiss her again. And it shocked her that she wanted him to. She could remember Louisa's whispered confidences about how pleasant things could be between a man and a woman, entirely the opposite view of her sister.

'I take your point. The governess must go,' she gasped out and her hands grabbed on to the desk for support. 'I will spend my time altering the clothes. But when I wish to take a break or walk about the grounds, I shall.'

The spell between them broke. He raised an eyebrow. 'I am happy to see you have decided to be sensible, Miss Milton. I fear your speech-making is at an end. We shall go on as I deem fit.'

He made a correct bow before closing the door with a distinct click.

Daisy waited for a heartbeat and then tossed a handful of clothes at the door. Underneath lay a slim volume of poetry. Keats. Her heart skipped a beat. He had remembered she liked poetry. He may have bought enough clothes to outfit any mistress, but he had also bought a present specifically for her.

She wanted to hate him, but found she was beginning to like being with him. And that would simply not do.

'Do you truly consider it safe to venture out without an escort?' Adam's sardonic voice greeted Daisy as she stepped out in the garden the next morning.

Daisy put her hands against the small of her back and arched slightly, easing the tension that had come with several hours of sewing. Two steps. She had only taken two steps out of doors and he was there. 'Are you trying to keep me a prisoner?'

'Merely seeking to keep you safe.' He folded his newspaper. 'Webster has lost his wager.'

'Which was?'

'That I would be reading the newspaper when he returned.' His eyes crinkled at corners. 'You should know I would never wager on a lady.'

'Polly went to see her aunt to ask about some ribbon. A breath of fresh air is all I require. We have been sewing all yesterday afternoon and well into this morning.' Daisy pasted a smile on her face as her mind raced. She had anticipated Webster with his complaints about the weather, not Adam and his hooded look. 'But as it happens, I am pleased to see you. I wanted to thank you for my gift.'

'And which gift was that?'

'The book of poetry. I have longed to read Keats properly.'

His face changed and became lit with enthusiasm. 'Have you read his "Bright Star" sonnet? It is one of my favourites.'

Daisy stared at him in surprise. He had read Keats. Her insides twisted. She was guilty of pre-judging. 'I thought you didn't like poetry.'

'No, I do not like poetry being rammed down children's throats. Poetry has its time and place. You should read the sonnet, Daisy. Then we can discuss it.' His eyes glinted with a smouldering gold. 'I look forward to discussing it with you.'

'I will. Later.' Daisy held out her hand. 'But now, I should like to take a turn about the garden.'

'As it happens, I have a moment of free time. Do you wish to walk down to the popping stone? We could have a look at the kissing bush and see if it lives up to its name. Or perhaps you would prefer a game of bowls.'

Daisy automatically straightened her bonnet. The kissing bush. That was one place she did not intend on visiting with him. She had made up her mind last night. They had to be platonic friends. It was the only way she would get through this charade. It had come to her in the middle of the night. But she had to find a way to get him to agree. A game of bowls might be the answer.

'Bowls, as we are already engaged. You have no need of Sir Walter Scott's proposal place.'

A smile tugged at the corner of his mouth. 'How well do you play?'

'I used to be quite keen as a girl. And my pupil before Nella—Sheila Davenport—loved her bowls. It was the only way I could get her to recite her times table.'

'Innovative.'

'Effective.' Daisy crossed her arms. 'So I would say I am an expert at the game. I plan on winning.'

'Despite Miss Davenport's propensity to play, I suspect that I will hold the advantage due to my misspent youth.'

'You are over-confident.'

'Perhaps, but it will be a good match.'

Daisy walked alongside Adam as he led the way to a pristine bowling green. The keeper allowed them to have a box of bowls and they soon began playing. From the way he bowled, Daisy could tell that Adam was naturally athletic and was extremely talented at the game.

'You play very well,' she said as the game grew to a close.

'I doubt you can do better than that,' Adam said as his ball stopped within a hair's breath of the smallest ball, the jack. 'We should have wagered on the outcome.'

'I thought you did not wager on a lady.'

'This would not have been wagering on a lady but with a lady. Remind me to show you the difference some time.'

Daisy touched her fingers to her mouth and eyed the distance between ball and jack. 'That is an easy shot.'

'If you do it, then I would say you are indeed an expert bowls player.'

'Shall we wager on that?' Daisy asked, and her nerves became coiled. This was the moment she had been waiting for. She could not lose.

'Done.'

Daisy waited for a moment, forcing her neck muscles to relax. It was about more than winning the shot, it was about making Adam see who she was. She rolled the ball and knocked Adam's ball out of the way. Adam gave a low whistle.

'Victory is mine.'

'What were we wagering for?' Adam dusted his fingers with his handkerchief. 'It is always best to define the terms before you begin. Shall we share a kiss?'

His forefinger traced the air above her mouth. Daisy forced her mind from the sudden ache. He would not distract her this time.

'Information. Why were you attacked? What jewels do you have?'

'Is that what you want?'

'I deserve to know the answer. These men want to kill me. I know it is why I have had Webster as a shadow.'

For a long heartbeat Adam stood unmoving, the morning sun touching his shoulders, making him look like some Roman god. She thought he was about to refuse, but then Adam withdrew a necklace from his breast pocket. The rubies and diamonds shone in the sunlight, making a dancing pattern on the green. A king's fortune, but deadly. A cold finger of ice passed through Daisy.

'They were after this. It belonged to a maharajah and supposedly is cursed.' He ran it through his fingers and the stones appeared to light with some hidden fire.

'How did you acquire it? After the battle?'

'After the battle, it was given to me in payment.'

Adam's mouth held a bitter twist. 'I keep it to remind myself that there are some things more precious than jewels.'

'What did you give for it?'

'My heart and soul.' A brief mocking laugh resounded over the bowling green. 'What else?'

Daisy regarded the shifting colours on the green. He had never said anything about love or emotions. Was this his way of telling her gently that there could never be any real feeling between them? 'A heart can shatter, but it mends. It becomes stronger.'

He held the stones up once again, covering her in their red fire. 'Perhaps you are right. Perhaps the cost was only a shattered heart. I bow to your governess expertise in this.'

'What is the curse?'

'For the righteous, the love of a lifetime, and for the wicked, death and destruction after a life without feeling.' He shrugged, but his eyes showed a shadow of pain, which Daisy longed to erase. Surely he couldn't believe that he had given up all chance of love in exchange for the necklace's cold beauty. 'I took a chance and lost.'

Daisy put her hand to her throat. 'I don't believe in curses.'

'It is what the men were after. It is what they believe in.' He gave a rueful smile. 'You will have to forgive me, but I hid it in your basket for a while, thinking you were an innocent bystander. But the men learnt about your brother and this is why—'

'You did what!' Daisy stared at him in astonishment. 'When?'

'Before we met the men on the bank, I took precautions. Daisy, I had fought them once, but I was in no fit state to fight them again.'

Daisy's stomach churned as she remembered the man's burning eyes. 'They could have taken that basket on the riverbank! That man, the one with the foreign accent. You allowed me to confront him.'

'How could I have stopped you?'

Daisy stared open mouthed at him. 'You casually put me in danger.'

Adam developed a sudden interest in the balls. 'Not intentionally. It was your choice to go after the basket. I have never claimed to be a saint, Daisy. Far from it. I was only able to retrieve the necklace after Nella dropped the basket in the schoolroom.'

'You should have told me about its existence before now.' Daisy put her hand on her hips as all manner of scenarios raced through her brain. He should never have done that. The ends did not justify the danger he had deliberately placed her and the Blandishes in. 'What if they had done something to Nella? She carried the basket around. You should have said something when Lord Edward brought me to the hotel. I would have returned it immediately to you.'

'Stop speculating, Daisy. All was well. I refused to take the risk in a public place such as a hotel lobby.' Adam's face became a cold arrogant mask as if he could not believe she would challenge his word.

'You are only telling me now because I won the wager.' Daisy struggled to maintain control of her temper. All she was to him was a pawn to be moved about in some elaborate game of chess.

'If you had been more attentive in clearing out the basket, perhaps you would have brought the stones to me, but you weren't. Luck was on our side. I dread to think what would have happened if your attacker had discovered them.'

'I am not sure we are on the same side. You lied to me!' Daisy ground her teeth. She longed to shake him until he understood the hurt coursing through her. 'You deliberately put me in danger. You played with my life without any consideration. How long was I to remain in blissful ignorance?'

A myriad of emotions flickered across his face, finally settling on remorse. A stab of triumph shot through Daisy. Maybe there was hope for him. Even in his arrogance, Adam knew he had made a serious error.

'I was planning on telling you when the time was right,' he said in a low voice. 'This seemed to be a good opportunity. But I want you to think well of me. You see, because of you I am developing a conscience. I can't undo the past, Daisy. I can only make the future better.'

'How did you get the necklace? And, Adam, I want the truth.'

'This was given to me as proof that the maharajah was in league with bandits. The woman felt a British officer might be able to stop the murders. I took it, but before I could organise a rescue, the maharajah acted. He was going to burn her on a funeral pyre. Your brother saved her, but when I tried to return the necklace, she told me to keep it as a reminder.'

'The woman was Kamala, Tom's wife,' Daisy said

with sudden insight. 'That is why you are so insistent about protecting me. They want to harm me because of my brother's actions.'

'How was I to know who your brother was? I cannot believe how our paths have crossed here in Gilsland. It is imperative to keep this necklace out of their hands.'

'I had told you my name.'

'Milton is a common enough name,' he said with maddening complacency.

'That is supposed to make me feel better? What else do you have planned for me? How do I fit into the scheme? Have you ever thought of me as a person rather than a pawn?'

'I think about you as person, Daisy. It was my weakness that I did not retrieve the necklace before you left me that day.' His voice dropped to seductive purr. 'I was far too intent on trying not to kiss you again to see if your lips really did taste of strawberries.'

Daisy crossed her arms over her breasts and attempted to ignore how they seemed to ache and grow under his gaze. He would not distract and control her that way. 'Am I to be the bait to lure them in? Is that why you kissed me? Why you seduced me so you could use the gang's desire to kill me for your own ends?'

'You are the one saying those words.' Adam shook his head. 'It takes more than a few kisses for a seduction. Seductions are far more involved. But despite your prim-and-proper exterior, Daisy, there is a passionate part of you that longs for it and the enjoyment it will bring.'

Daisy clasped her hands to her head, blotting out the

sound of his honey-laden voice. He was far too aware of his power over women. Whatever happened, some day Adam Ravensworth would see her as a person. He might not love her, but he would respect her integrity. Otherwise marriage became another term for slavery. 'You destroyed my reputation! And all I ever did was to save your life.'

'I am trying to save yours.' He reached out and his bare hand brushed her cheek. It was the lightest of touches, but enough to provoke a fiery response deep within her. She tightened her stomach and forced it to vanish. 'There is something between us, Daisy, do not try to deny it. I could have made you my mistress, but I made you my fiancée. Think about the difference.'

She stepped away from him and focused on the jack ball. She should turn her back on him and leave now for Warwickshire and Felicity. But she couldn't. The danger was real. The killers were out there.

Worse still, in the logical part of her mind, she understood in part why he hadn't trusted her. Would she have trusted him? The important thing was not her pride, but finding the culprits. Even so, she refused to tie herself to such a man for ever.

'I will be your fiancée because I gave my word, but after the culprits are caught, we will part. It is my price and you owe me. We will have a platonic relationship. No more seduction. Or whatever you call it.'

'And that is the price for your continued co-operation?' Adam's mouth quirked upwards as he allowed his hand to fall to his side. 'That is your demand? What happens if you insist?'

'I won't,' Daisy said far more confidently than she felt.

'Very well. No seduction until you insist. This should prove…interesting.'

'I am deadly serious.'

He raised an eyebrow. 'As am I.'

Daisy ignored the tiny pang in her heart. He had capitulated so easily. She wanted him to protest or take her in his arms. But instead he regarded her with hard speculative eyes, and a sardonic smile. The necklace hung from his fingertips, glinting in the sunlight, mocking her.

'I would like to wear the necklace at the ball tonight,' she said quickly, slamming the door on her misgivings. All he offered was kisses without meaning or heart.

'At the ball?'

'The Shaw's is having its first ball since the death of William IV. Everyone is sure to be there, including whoever is the mastermind behind these foul deeds, if you are correct in your assumptions.'

'One of his men will be there. You may count on that.'

'I wish to demonstrate to whoever is searching for it that it remains in your possession. The sooner they are caught, the sooner our association will end.' Daisy said the last words quickly, hoping against hope that he did not guess she meant the opposite. She enjoyed crossing wits with him. After each encounter she felt far more alive. Life had suddenly become more than simply existing and trying to cram unwanted knowledge into Nella or another child's head. She already dreaded the final parting, but it would not do to become dependent on him.

'And you have a gown that would be suitable for a viscount's fiancée?'

'Yes, of course, I have a serviceable gown for the occasion. Mrs Blandish liked to see Nella briefly presented at small dances.' Daisy fingered her throat, her mind working fast. Her old gown might do for a quick visit, but would it do for capturing everyone's attention? She could alter it in time for the dance. She knew she could. The neckline could easily be lowered and sleeves made more off the shoulder. It was two hours' work, three at most. 'It is the best way, Adam. I have no desire to remain here, waiting like an animal afraid to venture out. It is no life.'

'You are being very brave, Daisy, but it is utterly unnecessary.'

'Sometimes, one has to take risks.' Daisy wiped her hands on her gown. 'The sooner the plan succeeds, the sooner the time will come when I can be free of you and your interference in my life.'

Adam's fingers drummed against his thigh and she wondered if she had gone too far. He placed the necklace in the palm of her hand.

'As you wish, but you will keep out of danger. You are simply there to wear the necklace, and to provoke a response. Allow me to deal with the response.'

'Agreed.'

His mouth took on a sultry expression as he raised her fingers to his lips. 'I trust you are able to dance, Daisy. Do governesses waltz? Perhaps you need a private lesson.'

The statement hung in the air. Daisy ignored the sudden image of his hand on her waist, holding her as they twirled around the ballroom's floor. His only purpose would be to show off the necklace, rather than having his arm about her waist. They had agreed on it being platonic.

'I enjoy dancing.' She kept her shoulders down and her voice steady. 'Mrs Blandish insisted that both Nella and I be present when the dancing master gave Miss Blandish her private lesson, so that Nella could be up to the minute with her accomplishments. I am well aware of the finer points of the waltz as well as this Season's quadrilles.'

'I look forward to waltzing with such an accomplished dancer then.' Adam gave a half-smile, a smile that threatened to entwine itself around her insides and weaken her resolve. 'I do love a good waltz with a *willing* partner.'

'I will keep that sentiment in mind.' Daisy closed her hand around the necklace. The stones appeared to radiate a sudden warm glow. Looking at them, she could almost start believing in its curse. 'Sewing calls if I am to alter the ball gown in time.'

'If you decide against the idea…'

'Once made up, my mind keeps to the same course.'

A small smile touched his mouth but there was the faint glimmer of respect in his eyes. 'In short, you are stubborn.'

'We both desire the same result—a return to our respective lives as quickly as possible.' She forced her lips to turn upwards. Every single time she uttered the phrase, her heart protested. 'I will be ready at half past nine.'

'It is good to know that governesses are punctual as well as mule-headed.'

* * *

'I think my hair should be off my forehead, Polly,' Daisy said as the maid worked on the elaborate hair-style.

'Your face looks better with ringlets about it. It softens your features, like,' the maid declared, stepping back from her handiwork. 'Take a look, miss, before you decide.'

Daisy picked up the mirror and turned her face first one way and then the other. Reluctantly she had to admit that Polly was right. Her face did look younger with the curls. Over the course of a few hours, she had come to appreciate the stout North-umbrian with her ready smile and quick fingers. It had been an age since she had had anyone to discuss matters of dress and hair style with. Polly seemed to know instinctively what suited her face and figure.

With Polly's help, the ball gown had been rapidly altered. The neckline was now lower and in keeping with this Season's style. And instead of staid governess, she resembled one of the fashionables set for a society ball. Daisy fluffed out the top tier of her skirt.

'Is it possible to make the stays any tighter, Polly?'

'They are as tight as I can make them, miss.' The maid frowned, walked around Daisy, making small considering noises. 'Your waist is small enough. But perhaps you need to emphasise it more.'

'But how?'

'The rose-pink walking dress has a burgundy sash. It will be the work of a moment to transfer it. Aye. It is almost exactly the same colour as them there rubies.'

'That would be a good idea, even though strictly

speaking it should be just white as we are in mourning for the king. However…' Daisy hesitated. Against all common sense, she wanted to see Adam's look of surprised shock when he first glimpsed her, and the sash would be the final touch.

'And, miss, if I might be so bold, would you please consider taking me when you leave Gilsland?' Polly made a quick curtsy after she had fastened the sash. 'My uncle says that a fine lady like you would be needing a lady's maid permanent like and I'm right handy with the needle. I've always dreamed of seeing the world and the closest I have ever come was Hexham market on a wet Tuesday afternoon. My aunt says that shy bairns get naught and so I am asking.'

'I will keep the request under consideration, Polly.' Daisy forced her voice to be light. The worse thing was that if she did have a maid, she'd prefer to have one like Polly rather than a French lady's maid. She hated that Adam had chosen so well.

She would play the part of a fiancée to perfection and Adam would see… Daisy hated the sudden lump in her throat. He would see what? She had to keep her emotions out of it, just as she had kept her emotions out of her teaching. Adam wanted to use her.

Daisy pulled the sleeves of the gown slightly so that her shoulders rose above the cream froth of the lace. She gave the mirror one last glance and barely recognised the woman who stared back at her. The necklace appeared to have cast its glamour and transformed her into a fairy princess.

Daisy touched the now warm stones. A shiver went down her back. The stones seemed to be more alive than ever. What was Adam's story about the curse? Was she pure of heart or would her heart turn to stone? A shiver went through her, but instantly she straightened her backbone. She was an English governess, and English governess were unmoved by Indian superstition. It was stuff and nonsense.

The men who wanted to harm her were flesh and blood. They were after the necklace for its value on the open market, not for its meaning.

Chapter Ten

Festooned with garlands of evergreens and blazing with candles, the ballroom held an air of hushed excitement when Adam arrived at ten o'clock. Perhaps the décor with its slightly faded bouquet of painted flowers was not as fine as Almack's or another London venue, but it held a certain charm. And the standard of dancing could easily grace any fashionable ballroom.

Despite the king's funeral earlier in the month, everyone here appeared determined to enjoy the occasion. Women's dresses were a bit more sombre, and made from velvet rather than silk, but white shoulders rising from décolleté necklines remained.

Adam scanned the room for Daisy, who was no doubt hidden in the shadows or sitting forlornly against a wall. She had left a note pinned to the door—gone down to the ball as you were late. The irony of his deliberately giving her a few extra moments was not wasted on him. No woman had ever been punctual before. He had misjudged Daisy.

A trilling laugh sent a pulse down his spine and he slowly turned. A vibrant woman stood in the centre of a growing throng of soldiers. Daisy—but it was a Daisy he had not encountered before. He took back all his statements about her looking forever like a governess. This Daisy easily could grace the most elegant of drawing rooms. Her golden hair glowed in the candle-light of the chandelier, and her white dress showed her shoulders off to perfection. The blood-red sash made her waist look as if it was no more than a hand span. His fingers itched to try his hunch. Resolutely he forced his gaze upwards.

As promised, the necklace sparkled on her throat, but instead of overwhelming her as he had feared it might, it only enhanced her luminous beauty. The end-teardrop ruby nestled within the shadow of her breasts. Adam clenched his fists as a primitive urge to haul her away from the staring eyes filled him. He waited a breath and willed his shoulders to relax. That had been the point of Daisy wearing the necklace—to draw attention to it, except now he wished that the attention was a little more focused towards the necklace and little less on the swell of her bosom.

He advanced forwards, and touched her gloved hand. She smiled up at him and made her excuses to the soldiers, several of whom reminded her that she had promised them dances later in the evening. The primitive desire to separate heads from bodies swamped him as one or two raised her hand to their lips.

'Here I discover you,' he said in her ear, leading her into the nearly deserted portico. The cool night air rose up around them, allowing him to regain control of his emotions. 'I would have been willing to wager that you would still be doing your hair or finding an excuse to hesitate, but there was no answer to my knock. Was that wise?'

She tapped her fan against the elbow-length kid glove and her eyes danced with a secret pleasure. 'Being a governess means accurate time keeping. When it became quarter to the hour, I assumed that you had wanted us to meet in the foyer. Polly came down with me. She's seated in the withdrawing room.'

Adam allowed the remark to pass. She would learn that he was not a pupil of hers to be lectured, but her husband-to-be. And he looked forward to administering the lesson in seduction. She would insist on it before the night was out. He would remain in control and she would begin to understand the meaning of passion.

He glanced down at where her bosom rose amongst the ruffles. The lesson would be very pleasant indeed… for the both of them.

'You are wearing a fortune around your neck. I had thought we could have a brief conversation about the plans. Actions you might take if approached, or signals that you could send to me if you felt threatened.'

She raised her fan, hiding her expression. 'I had no wish to make a false step, particularly after we made our agreement.'

'And what agreement was that?'

The fan snapped shut, revealing her delectable frown. 'About our engagement and its boundaries. You will respect my wishes on the matter.'

'Nothing will happen that you do not wish. Nothing has.'

'Sometimes, you are far from a gentleman.'

Adam permitted a tiny smile to cross his face as Daisy quickly raised her fan again.

'I did warn you that I could be a devil,' he reminded her. 'You should have believed me on the riverbank.'

'What did you want to speak with me about?'

'A few useful remarks about what might be expected.' He placed his hand under her elbow and noticed how agreeably her skirts moved against his leg. 'Something to ease your way in society.'

'I have been in society before. It might not be as grand as London, but I do believe that I can behave in the approved manner without instruction.' She arched an eyebrow and gestured towards the ever-growing crowd in the ballroom. The efficient governess was back despite her attire. Adam's neck muscles relaxed slightly. The governess he could handle. The fairy creature was a more difficult proposition altogether. He wanted to take her back to her room and keep her there.

'Have you considered the hidden dangers? Have you thought about an escape route?'

'Shaw's ballroom is safe.' She demurely lowered her lashes, but the necklace twinkled back up at him, its fire shifting and glowing like a living thing. 'Otherwise why would you allow me to wear such a precious object?'

'Danger lurks everywhere. The entire countryside appears to be at the ball tonight.' Adam removed his gaze from her bosom and forced it to stay on her determined chin and dancing eyes. She knew the effect she was having on him and every other man in this room. Adam groaned. He should never have agreed to her terms. He longed to throw her over his shoulder, take her back to his room and claim what was his by right. But he managed to restrain the impulse.

'You are overreacting.'

'Have you heard any gossip?' he asked in an attempt to move his thoughts away from the sudden image of her long limbs wrapped around his as she wore nothing but the necklace.

'Mrs Blandish considers the necklace to be vulgar and in poor taste.'

'Has she said so?' Adam stared with surprise at where Mrs Blandish held court. A half-dozen women surrounded Mrs Blandish and they were all regarding Daisy with distinctly uncomfortable expressions as if the blossoming of a dowdy governess was entirely unexpected and unwelcome. 'Northern manners must be far more forthright than southern ones.'

'I saw it from the look in her eyes and the curl of her lips when she raised her lorgnette. Then she mouthed *vulgar* to Miss Blandish and tapped her nose. She can be the most frightful tabby.' Daisy shrugged a shoulder, revealing a bit more of the swell of her bosom. Adam hurriedly transferred his gaze to her heart-shaped face. 'She remains annoyed that you slipped away before she had time to fully consider your suitability. Had the jewels been on her daughter's neck, she'd have been praising their stylish cut and uniquely refined charm from here to London.'

'I'd never have allowed her to wear them,' Adam said with a frown. 'The daughter has little charm. Heritage thinks he will be in charge, but with such a woman, I would not like to place bets.'

Adam examined the way Daisy's ringlets kissed the back of her neck. It amazed him that he had hadn't properly appreciated the exact sheen of her hair and how it shone in the candlelight. He wanted to whisk her away from here and keep her locked in his own private harem. It had been a mistake to have her wear the necklace. It was not the thuggee he was worried about, but the other men. Once they were married, he would settle down to a quiet country life, or else he'd spend his entire time jealous of the demands on his wife's attention.

'Who are your suspects?' A frown appeared between her eyes. 'Everyone seems to be looking at me this evening. I am not certain if it is because of the necklace or...'

'That is a crude attempt at fishing for a compliment, Daisy. You need to learn finesse.' Adam put his hand on her waist and enjoyed the way she worried her bottom lip. 'Everyone is watching you because of the dress and the way your eyes sparkle.'

'And the necklace?'

'We will find out in time if your hunch is correct. Keep to well-lit places with lots of people about.'

'Are you my keeper?'

'I intend to be.'

Daisy halted and focused on the patterned floor rather than Adam's face. An insidious warmth had curled about her insides. His dark looks suited perfectly the formality of evening dress. Ever since she had spied him, her pulse had pounded loudly in her ears, giving a lie to her appeal for a platonic friendship. She tried to tell herself that it was the excitement of the adventure, but it also had to do with the prospect of crossing swords with the infuriating man. She had to remember that he was more than capable of using seduction for his own ends. She would hold him to his promise. Daisy's heart skipped a beat. He had promised, hadn't he? It bothered her that a significant portion of her hoped that he hadn't.

'I do possess a modicum of self-preservation.' She glanced up through a forest of lashes and smiled as sweetly as possible. 'The necklace is about my neck, not yours.'

'Then you should have waited for an escort, but, Miss Daisy Milton, I think you enjoy taking risks now that you are no longer a governess. In that dress, you would take your place amongst the reigning beauties. That is your second compliment of the evening.'

Daisy opened and closed her mouth several times before attempting a dignified silence.

The corner of his mouth twitched. 'When you are through behaving like a cod fish, shall we make our grand entrance at the ball?'

'I never behave like a cod fish.'

'Or maybe behaving like a woman who desires to be kissed. You do keep pursing your mouth up.'

The warmth inside her threatened to burst into flame. Daisy fingered her fan. A tiny action, but it gave her the time she needed to regain control and dowse the heat.

Daisy bit her lip, her heart sinking. She had thought that this was the perfect way to demonstrate her independence, but she had come out of it seeming younger than Nella. 'Next time, it would help if you informed me exactly where you wanted me?'

'Oh, I know where I want you.' His voice tickled her ear. 'The question is getting you there.'

Daisy focused on the dancers and tried to ignore the sudden image of his lips touching hers, his hands stroking her skin. 'I believe we should return to the ball and get this announcement over and done with. All eyes will be on us.'

'As my lady requires.'

The announcement of their engagement was short and the entire room applauded. Several of the elderly ladies lifted their lorgnettes to gain a better view and Daisy was distinctly pleased that she had spent time on the ball dress. She looked the part, even if on the inside she knew she was a fraud. It was pleasant for a few moments to dream that this could be real.

'And now, the time has come for the main event.' Adam's breath tickled her ear and sent her stomach into loops. 'Who is going to appear? If they are not already here.'

The main event. The words penetrated her haze and she came crashing down to earth, all her palaces in the clouds vanishing. She was only here because Adam needed her to be. She was simply a warm body. Any woman would have done.

He put his hand on the hollow of her back and steered her in the direction of an elderly man who closely resembled a fierce walrus. 'Lord Denning has been eyeing the necklace ever since he saw you. He has a great fondness for jewels of all sorts.'

'Lord Edward's uncle?' Daisy said. 'I have encountered him before. He is quite formidable. I do not think he altogether approves of Miss Blandish.' Daisy stopped and glanced up at the shadows in Adam's face. 'You cannot suspect him! He has a reputation of the utmost probity.'

'He interests me for a number of reasons. He has quizzed me about India and its legends before.'

Daisy took a deep breath and wished that she had not had the stays pulled quite so tight. 'Nella swore that Lord Denning ate little girls and spat them out. Her remarks caused much upset.'

'I begin to like Nella more and more.' His eyes crinkled at the corners. 'A pity that she is not here to enliven the proceedings.'

'Ah, Ravensworth, where have you been hiding this exquisite creature? She is quite the talk of the ball,' the elderly man's voice boomed out.

'She was under our noses all the time, Uncle. Miss Milton used to be the younger Blandish girl's governess,' Lord Edward said, appearing from behind a pillar. His evening clothes were spotless and perfectly complemented his blond hair. But it was a studied neatness and elegance, rather than an effortless one. 'You remember the Blandishes. The elder Miss Blandish...'

'I am well aware of Mrs Blandish and her offspring. And this woman is the governess who possessed more wits in her little finger than any of them had in their heads. She alone saw what a folly it was to give a young girl free reign.' Lord Denning banged his cane down on the floor with a resounding crash. Daisy winced.

'That is correct, Uncle. Ravensworth intends to marry her after they were...' Lord Edward gave a chilling laugh. Daisy quietly consigned Lord Edward to the coldest room in hell. There was no need for him to make such remarks.

Adam stiffened next to her. 'I was not aware that my affairs were the subject of common gossip, Heritage.'

'Gossip is the lifeblood of the spa, old thing, particularly when your fiancée emerges wearing such a ravishing…necklace.' A hungry expression crossed Lord Edward's face. Daisy shook her head. Lord Edward? It made a certain amount of sense, but he had been concerned for Adam's welfare and had joined in the search for him. And he had come to find her… except that Lord Ravensworth had never told him who she was.

'The talk will die in time. But it is a seven-day wonder, Daisy,' Adam said in an undertone. 'I am merely concerned with my bride-to-be being discomforted. All eyes are on her.'

'And that magnificent necklace. From the Indian subcontinent?' Lord Denning raised his quizzing glass again. 'There is something about the workmanship.'

'I brought it back from India and have always intended on giving it to my bride.'

Daisy glanced up at the gilt ceiling. His words made her seem even more like a fraud. He had saved the necklace and had no doubt intended it for some perfect English rose, but instead circumstances had forced them together. She did not want to think about the woman who would one day capture his heart and wear the necklace as a gift of love rather than as a trap.

The conversation ebbed and flowed around her as she fought against the tight misery in her chest.

'What impresses me is that you managed to discover the gold that was hidden underneath the governess garments,' Lord Edward said. 'She is truly a delicious beauty.'

Daisy glanced from Adam to Lord Edward and back again. What was between them? Lord Edward was his friend. He had been concerned the day Adam was attacked. She remembered him questioning her about the valuable thing Adam had lost. He knew about the necklace, and yet... Daisy wanted to go somewhere quiet and puzzle it out, but it was impossible to leave without creating a scene.

'I am perceptive. And I am very lucky that she rescued me. Who knows what might have happened on that riverbank without her quick thinking? I credit Miss Milton with no less a feat than bringing me back to life.'

Daisy ducked her head. Her cheeks flamed, despite knowing his words for a lie, and a provocation. 'I only did my Christian duty.'

'I knew a man who once swore that if one did not have to consider a fortune, a governess was the best place to look for a bride,' Lord Denning said, thumping his cane on the ground, and breaking the tension that had grown between the two men. 'With Miss Milton, I would say the opinion is aptly expressed. You are a lucky man, Ravensworth. You best hold tight to her or someone will snatch her away.'

'My sentiments exactly.' Adam's fingers tightened slightly on her elbow. His breath touched her ear, causing Daisy to forget all the promises she had made herself before coming down to the ball. This was all for show. She was immune to his touch. Immune. She repeated it over and over again, but somehow, her body kept forgetting.

'I had best go and greet Mrs Blandish. Miss Blandish has been waving frantically.'

Adam appeared surprised. 'If you must…'

'Yes, I must. You stay here and talk to Lord Denning.'

She walked away before he could protest.

'Will you do me the honour of the next quadrille, Miss Milton? The music is just starting,' Lord Edward asked, blocking her way back after she had had a rather tense conversation with Miss Blandish. 'To make amends for my boorish behaviour. My attempt at teasing Ravensworth has fallen flat. I should learn to think before I speak. I most humbly crave your pardon.'

Daisy glanced over her shoulder, but Adam appeared in deep conversation with another man. He had forgotten her once again. She had served his purpose. Daisy made a little curtsy. 'I would be honoured.'

'You must not mind my great-uncle,' Lord Edward said as they moved towards the dance floor. 'He delights in teasing me about the need for an heiress and ridicules my choice. I am afraid I react badly to teasing. It was beastly rude of me. I shall be desolate if Miss Blandish slips through my fingers.'

'Miss Blandish always has appeared fond of you,' Daisy said carefully.

'You do my poor heart good, Miss Milton.' Lord Edward glanced down at her. 'This is the first time we have had a chance to speak since your unfortunate engagement.'

'Unfortunate?'

'I have your interests at heart. Your brother and I were friends. Do you really think that he would approve of you marrying such a man as Ravensworth? They were rivals, you know.'

'Rivals?' Daisy forced the word from her mouth. She'd never considered it. 'You repeat ancient gossip, Lord Edward.'

'For a maharajah's mistress.' He smiled down at her as the first figure of the dance began. 'They say she even carried Ravensworth's child, and that was why he fought so hard to get back to the hill station—not to save her, but because he wanted to fight a duel with your brother.'

'Nothing about Adam Ravensworth shocks me,' Daisy replied carefully as her mind recoiled from the bile that dripped from Lord Edward's tongue. Kammie was Tom's daughter. It was all a tissue of lies, just as he had lied about Adam wanting to see her on that first day. 'I am merely grateful that he has seen fit to protect my reputation.'

'He will be doing it for his own purposes. Trust me on this, Miss Milton. He never has done anything except for himself. Take the necklace you wear about your neck. You should have it valued. It is paste. I will do it for you discreetly if you wish.'

'You appear awfully sure of that.' Daisy tightened her grip on her fan.

'It is a friendly warning. Everything is not always as it seems.' Lord Edward's eyes held a curious dead look. 'Think about my offer, Miss Milton. Always better to be safe than sorry.'

'I do not believe that will be necessary.' Daisy kept her gaze focused on the garland of pale blue flowers. Was Lord Edward somehow involved with the attackers? 'I trust Lord Ravensworth, and I do not believe it will form part of my marriage settlement in any case.'

'Trust and Adam Ravensworth are two words that do not sit easily together. The stories I could tell you.' He gave a high-pitched laugh. 'Has he told you of the necklace's curse?'

'Luckily, as a governess, I do not believe in curses.'

Lord Edward raised her gloved hand to his lips. His eyes showed an unexpected stab of pity. 'For your sake, Miss Milton, I hope you are right.'

Adam watched Daisy dance a variety of reels and quadrilles, absentmindedly answering questions and then hurriedly having to think up the correct explanation when the lady or gentleman frowned. Her skirts swirled slightly and revealed her shapely ankles. And she laughed up at something an elderly gentleman said, setting the whole room blaze with the eagerness in her face. It was hard to believe that this sparkling woman once seemed so pale and listless with the life drained out of her. He had been right to rescue her from the drudgery of the schoolroom.

It also made his task harder. He could not be sure if the men were watching her because they wanted the necklace or because they admired her form. Her form was enough to make any man forget his duty. Normally he liked men to admire his mistresses, but Daisy was different. Daisy was going to be his wife. He wanted to take her to some distant estate and keep her there.

It bothered him that Heritage seemed intent on speaking alone with Daisy. First he danced with her and then two more times he made sure that he was in the same set as her. Adam frowned. What was Heritage up to?

He shook his head. He was concentrating far too much on Daisy, and the way her skirts swirled, revealing a glimpse of her ankle for the discerning.

Adam frowned. All he knew was that he did not like the way Heritage had assumed control of the situation. Even Miss Blandish was standing at the side of the dance floor, tapping her foot.

As the next dance started, Adam pushed his way into the increasing throng of men who gathered about Daisy.

'My dance, I believe. I claim a fiancé's privilege.' He regarded Heritage with a pointed look.

A faint flush covered Heritage's cheeks. 'I was merely trying to do a friend's duty.'

Daisy's quick smile did not meet her eyes as the gathering throng moved away from her. 'If you wish…'

The waltz rose up around them, one of the newer Strauss waltzes. Adam put his hand on her slender waist. 'Now we shall discover if you can dance a waltz as well as you bowl.'

She closed her eyes and a dreamy smile crossed her lips as she savoured the tune. 'I adore waltzing. I dare say that you will be better than Nella. She always stepped on my toes.'

'Ah, but will you be able to let me lead?' He glanced down at her upturned face. Her eyes sparkled slightly and her lips were parted.

'I will endeavour to do my best.'

Adam steadily increased the pressure on Daisy's back, bringing her closer so that their limbs were moving in tandem. Her lavender scent rose and enveloped him. He breathed deeply and forged the moment into a memory.

'Waltzing seems to suit your mood. Once we leave here, you will be the toast of London.'

'Hardly the toast.' Daisy's stomach tightened. Leaving. Right now, she did not want this enchanted evening to end and Adam was already speaking about departing. It was his way of reminding her that their association would be short lived. Determinedly, she stepped forwards and found her way blocked by Adam's leg.

'It took you all of two turns about the dance floor before you forgot that you were not the one leading.'

'Once a governess, always a governess.' Daisy attempted to give a light unconcerned laugh and found she could only gasp in light pants. Her heart raced far too fast and her body appeared to want to move in time with his. Every portion of her remembered the kiss in the schoolroom and wanted it repeated. Each time they moved, her body tingled in awareness. But somehow, she had to keep to the bargain. It was better that way. 'We should speak. I have been trying to puzzle out who the mastermind might be.'

'Is that why you were quizzing Heritage?' he murmured against her ear. 'You went pale during the quadrille.'

'I thought he might have something to do with it.' Daisy stared over Adam's shoulder, wondering how she could tell him about her suspicions. How could she tell him without saying about the horrid things Lord Edward had implied? 'It is silly of me. Probably simply fancies and far too much punch. I shall have a sore head in the morning.'

'Heritage is harmless. He likes to pretend that he knows more than he does.' His hand about her waist tightened, pulling her closer against him. They circled the floor once more, this time slower. 'But underneath his bluster, he is sound.'

She bit her lip and then the words bubbled up within her. 'You are wrong about Edward Heritage. He mentioned the ruby necklace when he escorted me to the Shaw's Hotel for the first time.'

He swiftly steered them towards an open door, not going out through the French windows on to the crowded terrace, but instead going down a short dark passage and into a small beam-hung room that was set up for cards.

Heavy drapery provided a secluded nook and several unlit candles stood on the card table. At some point in the evening, the serious gamblers would retire here and play until the cock crowed, but at the moment a faint chill clung to the corners of the room and the only sound was the popping of the pine logs in the open fire.

Daisy tilted her head to one side and took steadying breaths. Adam was far too handsome in his evening clothes. His breeches revealed the muscles in his thighs and his calves were the sort that would never need padding. And she knew her breathlessness was not coming from her need to tell Adam about Lord Edward, but rather from Adam's nearness.

'We will be safe enough here to talk,' Adam said. 'No one should disturb us. This room won't be used for cards until much later in the evening. Now, what do you have in your head about Heritage?'

'I remembered it tonight. How he had gone on and on about you losing something valuable. But I didn't think any more of it until tonight.' Daisy curled her hand about the fan and ignored the place on the sofa. 'Lord Edward swears the jewels in my necklace are paste. He offered to have them valued for me. Discreetly.'

'Naturally.' A smile tugged at Adam's mouth.

'But he must be involved with the gang.'

'Edward Heritage is severely let in his pockets and wants to exchange the jewels.' Adam's lips became a thin white line. 'He would never be involved with the thuggee. He hated them with a passion.'

'But what if—?'

'I thought governesses avoided Minerva Press novels.' Adam held her hand and his eyes became serious. 'Listen to me, Daisy. Heritage does not have the brains to be behind this. Killing a brother officer is against his code.'

Daisy struggled to take a breath. Minerva Press novels indeed. He was implying that she was worse than Nella. The world spun slightly and she put a hand out towards the back of a chair. She missed and stumbled.

Adam's hand instantly reached out and steadied her.

'Your corset is far too tight. Sit and regain your composure.'

'Do you always speak so boldly?' Daisy sat on the

edge of the sofa. Immediately the pressure on her lungs eased and the room stopped spinning. But she became aware that they were alone in the room together and his eyes smouldered.

'You had no problems moving swiftly before, particularly in the wood. I am aware of ladies' undergarments and their peculiarities.' A dimple flashed in and out of his cheek. 'You will find it easier if you do not give into fashion. Your waist is slender enough.'

'Shall we speak of something else while I seek to regain my composure?' Daisy kept her back upright and concentrated on taking steadying breaths. Entering into a conversation about her undergarments was not going to happen. She was going to keep to the spirit of the bargain. Platonic friendship. 'Tell me about India.'

'What shall I tell you?' His eyes crinkled at the corners as if he knew why she wanted to change the subject.

'Describe the hill station where you met my brother. What was it like?'

'The first night, the roof of the guest house where I was staying shook with a clattering and scraping.'

'Rats?' Daisy fought to keep the disappointment from her voice. She had hoped Adam would speak about Tom, something to erase the bile of Edward Heritage's words.

'Monkeys. The next morning I looked out over the mist-covered scene with the mountains lit blue and saw them disappearing into the jungle. A whole troop of monkeys, each holding the other's tail. The last one turned around and bared his teeth at me.'

'What did you do?'

'I burst out laughing. Kam—' He hesitated for a heartbeat and a painful expression flickered across his face. Daisy's heart constricted and she wondered why the woman had been standing next to him. Had they passed the night together? 'Someone told me to hush as they were a lucky sight.'

'It sounds like a different world.'

His fingers brushed a ringlet from her shoulders. 'Far removed from England.'

His eyes took on an enigmatic look. She glanced up and saw his face looming above hers. If she tilted her mouth slightly, raised her chin, she would touch him. Her fingers tightened around the fan. She wanted to touch him.

Did that make her a loose woman like Mrs Flyte predicted she'd become? How could it be within a few short days that she had forgotten all her principles and rules? 'We need to return to the dance. I am quite recovered.'

'Listen.' He held up his hand and cocked his head to one side. 'Quickly now and no missish mewlings. There is not anywhere else.'

He put his hand around her arm and pushed her into the nook. The heavy curtain swayed as he pulled it around them, shielding them from view.

The doorknob clicked and Daisy forgot to breathe.

Chapter Eleven

Adam stood in the tiny alcove with Daisy's nose squashed up against his shoulder. He reached down and twitched her skirt in, looping the ruffles over his arm. Daisy wriggled, trying to put more space between them, but at the same time trying to stay hidden, and his body responded to her every movement. Adam slowly counted to ten. And willed her to stop moving. This was neither the time nor the place to begin the next assault on her virtue. He had not meant to tell Daisy about the morning after his first night with Kamala, when he felt as if all were right with the world and nothing could go wrong.

'They will not notice us. Your reputation is safe, if you keep still.'

'I am trying to.' She glanced up at him, her eyes becoming wide and dilated. Adam permitted himself a small stab of satisfaction. This little interlude would turn out as he had planned…eventually. 'Are they friend or foe?'

'Time will tell, but I should imagine they are intent on finding a place to be alone, rather than on investigating if they actually are.' He tightened his arm about her waist and noticed that this time, she remained still as footsteps resounded in the room and the door was slammed shut.

'I told you not to follow me,' Heritage said to his unseen companion. 'You were to leave me strictly alone here. The lies I have had to tell to Miss Blandish…'

'That is not my problem.' The foreign voice held a distinct tone of menace. 'Are they real? The entire countryside buzzes.'

'It is mine! I need the Blandish money! My debts…'

'You promised and I spared your life. You have partaken of the opium…you are one with us.'

Daisy sucked in her breath as the curtain gaped. The man standing in front of the curtain had been one of the searchers that first day. The tall thin one with burning eyes.

'No one told me about murder,' Lord Edward protested.

The man held up his hand with the blackbird tattoo gleaming in the fireplace. 'How long do you think you will be permitted to continue with your miserable existence without me? Do you think your friends will protect you once they know what you have done? Now is the necklace the real one or an expensive fake?'

'Real. Ravensworth is far too concerned about it.' Edward Heritage's braying laugh echoed off the library's walls. 'Give me some time. The Milton woman will trust me and my judgement. I have a way with women.'

'Time runs short. He seeks her death.'

Daisy fought against the urge to scream. She glanced up, expecting another reprimand, but Adam's face wore a shocked expression.

'You should give me more time. You did not even know about her until I discovered the connection. I am sure her brother sent her things. Things you desire. I have heard stories…'

'And this creature is the blonde devil's only relation. We asked you to discover this.'

Edward Heritage pulled his arm from the man's grip. 'Give me some respect.'

'Respect comes to those who have earned it.' The man blew on his fingernails. 'I thought you swore that you checked Ravensworth and he did not have the necklace. Where did he hide it?'

'What can I say? Perhaps the driver spoke and gave warning. Remember the valet travelled in another carriage.'

'We have a bargain. The necklace or your life.'

Adam's hand tightened about her waist. Daisy drank in his scent, steadying her nerves. She had innocently told Lord Edward who she was and he had betrayed this knowledge to the men who wanted to kill her.

'Seduction should not be rushed.' Lord Edward went white. 'Miss Milton is a ripe plum ready for the picking. It will give me the greatest pleasure to seduce one of Ravensworth's women. She will betray him for me. The other one did.'

Daisy's insides churned and it was only Adam's iron hands about her waist that restrained her. Seduction? Betray Adam? The man had another think coming.

'I will admit to not understanding the attractions of English women.' A cutting laugh filled the room, sending prickles down Daisy's spine. 'Next time, you deal directly with my brother.'

'No!' Lord Edward's voice rang out with desperation and he flopped down on the floor, grovelling. 'If I disappear, Ravensworth will know the game is up and you will never get the necklace. I am your last hope.'

'One last chance, but no opium until then.'

'I understand.'

Two sets of footsteps went out of the room. For a heartbeat, Daisy stood there, unable to quite take in all that she had heard.

Adam's arms instantly loosened and Daisy stumbled from his embrace. Away from Adam, the room seemed chilled as if it held the taint of the two men who had been in this room, the two men who had casually spoken of killing her and Adam.

She ran her hands up and down her arms.

'I owe you an apology, Daisy.' He came to stand beside her. 'Can you forgive me?'

'You believed that he had some integrity.'

'He was my brother officer. I thought we shared the same notions of honour. I made a mistake.'

'What do we do now? Contact the magistrates?'

'We wait until we have more information. Heritage comes from a powerful family. We need physical proof. Heritage hasn't actually done anything, except perhaps seduced a few women I was tired of. I want the leaders, not the pawns,' Adam said firmly. 'Thanks to your actions tonight, the cage has been rattled and the snakes are running for cover. I should never have agreed to your scheme of wearing the necklace, but it has worked.'

'Did you have a choice?'

A tiny smile touched Adam's lips before he inclined his head. 'You will be safe, Daisy. You keep bringing out the chivalrous knight in me. Heritage will not harm a hair on your head.'

'I am sure you would do the same for any woman.'

'Not any woman.' He reached out and traced the line of her jaw with featherlight fingers. 'Only you.'

But will you *be safe?* The words trembled on her lips but she held them back. When this was over, Adam would go from her life. It would never do for him to know she cared.

'Why did Lord Edward lie to that man about my brother sending me jewels?' Daisy crossed her arms and watched Adam poke the fire, sending an array of sparks shooting up the chimney.

'He wanted to buy time. Heritage is a selfish creature.' Adam's eyes turned pure gold in the fire-light. 'You will not have to worry about him again. I promise you. Your brother was brave and true.'

'People get what they deserve in life.' A fluttering started in her stomach. She stood, helpless, needing his touch to block out her fear.

'Do they?'

'Yes, they do,' she replied firmly and tried to think of all the reasons why they should return to the ball and not the one reason why she wanted to remain here. She wanted to dissolve the bargain. She wanted to feel his lips against hers. 'We should go.'

'Not yet. I have wanted to do this all evening. Ever

since your lips first challenged me across the room.'
With two steps, he had left the fire and stood in front
of her. 'I would go so far as to say that they insisted on
it.'

He lowered his mouth and captured hers, submerged
her lips in an unrelenting kiss of the sort her innermost
being longed for. His hand curled about her head,
buried itself in her hair. Her carefully pinned hairstyle
shifted and unravelled, but she did not care. It was
nothing compared to the way his mouth felt against
hers. He was right. She desired this.

His mouth moved down her neck, tasting and
nibbling, calling to the fluttering inside her, flaming it
and driving all thoughts of Lord Edward, the necklace
and the thieves from her mind. The only thing she
knew was the tremors of fire that seemed to spread
outwards from his touch.

His tongue traced a line along her shoulder, sending
a small pulse of warmth through her. She had thought
the ballroom close before, but here her skin was on fire.

Daisy brought her hands up, intending to push him
away, but found they refused to do her bidding. Her
body melted against his, and her hands became entangled in his hair.

He lifted his head and they both stood there. His eyes
were a deep rich amber in the firelight, glowing with a
smouldering flame. His hair bore the imprint of her
fingers.

'We should stop.' Her voice was hardly a breath.

'If you truly wish it…'

He ran a finger along the edge of her dress and her
breasts strained even more, arching towards his

questing fingers. A little moan escaped her lips as he cupped her breasts, holding them over the fabric. His thumb flicked the tip and her nipples became hardened points, rubbing against the corset, sending ripples of pleasure through her. She struggled to breathe as she realised that she wanted him to touch them with his mouth. The thought should have shocked her. She knew that, but all the thought did was to increase the ache inside her.

He lifted an eyebrow, captured her hand and gently tugged at the glove. One by one he released her fingers. Then he slowly bent his head, captured the littlest finger in his mouth and suckled while his hands once again roamed over her breast. A moan escaped the back of her throat.

Voices in the corridor shocked her back to reality. She stiffened. Her body was wedged between his thighs, the skirts of her ball gown ballooned about them. 'Adam, we must stop. This is highly improper.'

Adam's face instantly changed. His fingers restored order to her gown, making it seem like the passion they had shared had never happened. The very act was like ice water, reminding her that he was highly experienced in such matters and had always been in control where she had totally lost all sense of propriety.

'Enough, I think, to keep the nightmares from your dreams.'

'Is that what this was about? An elixir to make me forget?'

'Why not? Your kisses provide me with delicious dreams.'

She bent her head. An errant curl of hair fell over

her shoulder. She greatly feared that she looked like she felt—a woman who had abandoned herself to a kiss.

Only a few days ago, she had considered such a thing impossible and now it would seem that it had been merely the opportunity she lacked. She bit her lip and tried to keep the tide of red from washing up her face. 'What should I do? My hair. I have lost my glove. People will think me…'

With deft fingers, he twisted her hair back into place, before retrieving her glove from the floor. 'You will find that I can play lady's maid. It will serve for now. And you will return to your room. I will send Polly up.'

'You must think me wanton.'

'I think you are my fiancée.' He put a hand on her arm and his eyes became serious. 'I would like you to go back up to your room and stay there. Allow me to handle this other matter. It is nearly finished. Things are moving in the direction that I thought they would. You have played your part admirably. I have never met a woman like you before. Our marriage will be a good one.'

'Desire is no sound basis for marriage.' Daisy hated the way her voice became breathless and betrayed her.

'Desire is a very sound reason, my prim-and-proper governess. It adds spice to something that otherwise would be an extremely dull state of affairs.' His voice rumbled in her ear. 'Are you frightened? Is that it? I will never force you to do anything you do not want to do. We stop when you say stop.'

Daisy regarded the shifting flames of the fire. 'I thought we had agreed that this was an engagement in name only. To wait for the wedding.'

'My door is open to you, Daisy, if you wish to make that choice.' His hand cupped her cheek. 'It would be wrong of me to deny that I want you. And our bargain holds. A seduction is more than kisses.'

'Have you ever practised denial?' Daisy drew as deep a breath as her stays would permit.

'You met me kiss for kiss, Daisy.' He ran a hand down her arm. 'Nothing happens unless you desire it. You remain in charge and all you have to do is tell me to stop. Shall I never kiss you again, Daisy?'

He laced his fingers through hers, pulling her close. His hot breath touched her skin. She closed her eyes, savouring the moment. Her mind knew she should say the word but her lips refused to work. This close, and all she could think about was how his mouth tasted.

'Please, please stop,' she whispered with her last ounce of sanity and his hands let her go.

'You see, I have stopped at your command.' His hand touched her hair.

'The agreement… I will not hold you to the marriage once this is done,' Daisy said the words through lips which were on fire.

'I believe I know what I am on about.' He let her hand go and she stumbled back two steps. Her heart pounded far too loudly in her ears.

Daisy unhooked the necklace and placed it in his outstretched palm. The rubies glowed like drops of blood in his hand. Her neck now seemed somehow seemed far too light, as if it had become used to the necklace. She felt colder, like a great hollow was opening up inside her. Had she proved unworthy?

Daisy dismissed the thought. It was simply a collection of lifeless stones.

'I believe I will go straight to my room after all. You can do what you will with the necklace.'

She started to sweep out of the room, stubbed her toe on the doorframe and swore.

Adam's laughter echoed after her. She stopped and glanced back over her shoulder. The twinkles in his eyes had transformed his features, making him appear younger. Her heart flipped over and she struggled to breathe steadily.

'You do have the most charming way of speaking, Miss Milton.' He sketched a bow.

Daisy's heart swelled and the coldness went. The curse had no power, but she knew she was in grave danger of losing her heart to Adam.

Adam came down the back stairs after he had escorted Daisy to her room. Despite her protestations, he was under no illusions about the danger she faced. He had caused it and now it was up to him to end it. The corners of his mouth twitched as he remembered her indignation. At some point over the past few days, the necklace and what it represented had ceased to have any meaning, and his life had begun to revolve around Daisy. It worried and exhilarated him at the same time. He now understood what he had felt for Kamala had been a young man's fancy. It was not that he was incapable of love, it was that he had not met the right person to love. But with the knowledge came the fear. He wanted her to believe in him. He wanted her to see him as the man he intended to be.

The ball was drawing to an end and a variety of carriages had already left, including the Blandishes.

A darkened shape emerged from the shadows, moving with an awkward grace. 'Webster, is that you? How much ale have you had?'

'Master, you cannot expect me to go to the pub and nurse a single pint all night. A man must have a few pleasures in the countryside.'

'Have you heard anything from the servants? I am looking for a tall thin man with hollowed eyes. From his appearance, I would say that he is in service, rather than being one of the farmers. There will be a connection with Carlisle, but it is not important.'

His valet's eyes widened. 'All appears normal. How have you learnt so much, so quickly?'

'Heritage. You were right about him. There is something amiss and it is more than chasing skirts.' Adam squared his jaw. 'He will have to be neutralised.'

'You can always tell a man by his boot polish. There was something not right about the shine, if you see my meaning.'

'After all the time he spent chasing the thuggee, I never thought that he would help the enemy, but his desire for opium has overcome any scruples.' Adam pressed his fingertips together, considering. Heritage was untrustworthy but at least he was a known quantity.

Webster lowered his eyes. 'And your fiancée? What are you going to do about her when this is over? Are you really going to have a female in the household? I will have to consider my position.'

'You will have to learn to cope, Webster. Your polish recipe is far too valuable.' Adam paused, pulling at his cuffs. He must be truly smitten if he was about to extol Daisy's virtues to Webster. 'Daisy will be part of my life. I owe it to her brother.'

Adam gave Webster his orders and then strode into the card room in search of Heritage. Heritage sat alone, with a pack of cards at one elbow and a full decanter of port.

Heritage downed his glass of port with a shaking hand. 'Ravensworth. I had wondered where you and your bride-to-be had disappeared to. You must congratulate me. Miss Blandish has taken against my suit. She says that I paid far too much attention to your little governess this evening. Having a shrew for a wife is no good, not even one with the size of Miss Blandish's fortune. I have ended the relationship.'

'Daisy developed a headache.' Adam contented himself with flexing his fingers, rather than ripping Heritage's lying head from his shoulders. There were codes, and he would abide by them, but Heritage's days were numbered. He would see him blackballed from every club. His revenge would be subtle, but effective. 'But before she left, she told me a story, Heritage. You appear to think the necklace is a fake.'

'Women—you cannot trust them.' Heritage shook his head. 'She is probably laying the ground work for a theft at some later date. After all, her brother was only a factor in John Company. Blood will out, as they say.'

'I have overlooked things, Heritage, based on the time we spent together in India, but here we part.' Adam leant forwards and grabbed the lapels of Heritage's coat and pulled him close. 'Go near my fiancée, talk about her to anyone else in that fashion and I will destroy you.'

The colour drained from Heritage's miserable face. 'You have gone mad, Ravensworth.'

'You have no idea.' Adam put his face next to Heritage's and fixed him with his steely gaze so there could be no mistake. Heritage had to understand that their association was at an end. 'I want names, Heritage. Who are you working for? Was it you who bribed my coachman? Who gives the orders?'

Heritage flinched, but clamped his mouth shut.

'You try my patience, Heritage,' Adam said with a clenched jaw. 'Do you doubt my purpose? Who gave you the order to harm Daisy?'

Heritage swallowed as rivulets of sweat began to drip down his face. 'Sanbay or something. I owed him money. I never thought…'

'How do you contact them?'

Heritage's eyes looked everywhere but at Adam. And Adam knew that there was far more to it. He would have to let Heritage go and wait. 'I leave a note in the old oak tree. I know nothing more than that. I promise on my honour as a gentleman.'

'You lost your honour when you traded it for opium.'

Adam released Heritage in disgust as Heritage continued to bleat about his precious honour and sincerity. How he'd never done anything. How he'd been playing them at their game and how he'd intended on telling Adam once he knew for certain whose side Daisy was on.

'We are alike, you and I, Ravensworth,' Heritage finished. 'You have blood on your hands. All you ever wanted was that necklace. I know what truly happened up there. How you behaved.'

Adam slammed his fist down on the table, sending the decanter crashing to the floor and stopping Heritage's words. The sound of the crash brought Adam to his senses. Heritage was nothing to him, but once upon a time he had made sure all the thuggee were properly hanged. 'Leave. Get out of my sight.'

'Leave? But my great-uncle—'

'Go or I reveal to the world the opium eater that you are, Heritage.'

'Go?'

'Leave, get out of my sight.' Adam stepped away from him. Years ago, they had served together. It still counted for something. 'If I catch you around here tomorrow, you will be exposed.'

'Tonight? But my great-uncle!'

'Tonight. The next time we meet, it will be in hell.' Adam turned on his heel and walked from the room.

Chapter Twelve

Daisy pulled the shawl tighter about her shoulders. Somewhere behind her, Webster was following her. She had no doubt of it. But it did not matter, she wanted to be outside in the early morning, rather than in her suite with the walls pressing against her soul.

She should probably have been more prudent and waited for Adam to accompany her on the walk, but that was precisely the point. Every day she delayed, she knew it was another day when her heart became more entwined with Adam's. Her dreams had been full of his mouth and the way his hands caressed her skin.

She paused and lifted the green gingham skirt over a puddle. Polly had carefully packed away all her old clothes, leaving only the clothes Adam had provided. However, Daisy had to admit the green dress did something for her spirits, and she did prefer the green-trimmed straw bonnet to the one Adam had ruined.

As she had suspected, no one was moving about on

the hotel's grounds this morning. Everything was still and the dewdrops hung on the spider's webs.

The mist cleared slightly. Her shoulders relaxed a little. As she suspected, Webster followed her from a distance. At her look, he raised his hand with an object tightly clutched in his left fist, saluting her. She blinked and rubbed her eyes, but the figure had turned, becoming no more than a dark shadow. A distinct chill went through Daisy. Was it Webster? Or the other man?

'Miss Milton, Miss Milton, here I find you.' Nella crashed through the yew hedge, her pinafore askew and her straw hat falling off her head.

'Nella, what are you doing here? Is your sister with you?' Daisy heaved a sigh of relief. No more ghosts and mist-wrapped figures, but a flesh-and-blood girl badly in need of direction and assistance.

'There is a huge row going on at our house.' Nella scuffed her boot in the dirt. 'Susan demands our immediate departure. Apparently Lord Edward is insupportable. He refused to attend her properly during the dance. Mama is consoling her and everyone has forgotten me.'

Daisy tightened her hands about her reticule. The chaos, confusion and general upset were things she did not miss. Mrs Blandish would be searching for targets on which to vent her irritation. It was no wonder that Nella had escaped. 'It is a shame that proposed match fell through, but no doubt Miss Blandish will have many more admirers.'

'Lord Edward was kind to me after I told him about your box of jewels that your brother had sent you from India.'

'Nella, my brother only sent me a rattle.'

'Then I drew a picture of him for fun.' Nella pushed her straw bonnet back still further and screwed her nose up. 'It is wicked of me, I know, to show it to Susan and she laughed. But Lord Edward tore the picture up and called me a wicked girl.'

'Why did he do that? Tear up your drawing.'

'I saw him talking to this strange man and thought he would be a good likeness. So he was the fox and Lord Edward was the snake.'

Daisy shook her head. No proof of wrongdoing in Nella's story. 'Perhaps you made too much of the satire.'

'You mean like the time I drew Susan as a cat lounging by the fire? Or Mama as an Indian elephant.'

'What did the other man look like?' Daisy attempted to keep her voice calm. The last thing she wanted was for Nella to go off into one of her tales.

'He had these odd eyes—one green and the other brown. They were all bloodshot as well. I thought he looked like a corpse that had just risen from the grave. And I thought he might be the man who used to frighten Mademoiselle Le Claire and me last year. We would see him striding along with his black bag, sometimes full and sometimes empty. Once I was sure that I saw him carrying a dead man. *Mademoiselle* said that he would eat me up if I was bad. This one had an angry scar around his neck, as if he had been hanged.'

Daisy gritted her teeth. *Mademoiselle* had a lot to answer for, encouraging Nella's imagination to run along those lines. 'Are you sure that the men were the same?'

'I think so. They had the same marking on their hand—a bird or something. I drew a picture of it in my last but one drawing book. It is why I want to look at my old sketchbook. He used to live in this hut. One day while *Mademoiselle* slept, I went off and I saw him dragging a body out. But no one believed me.'

'Where was the hut? I am surprised you did not tell me about the story when we were out on our walks.' Daisy kept her voice casual. The last thing she wanted was to be involved in another of Nella's Banbury stories, but there was a real possibility of finding the gang and ending this once and for all, before anyone else became hurt.

'The one in the woods. You know, the woods I don't like to go into because of the ghosts.' Nella made a face. 'Anyway, I have misplaced the sketch pad and wondered if you had accidentally taken it?'

'I do not think I took anything of yours.'

Nella drew a line in the dirt, scuffing the toe of her boot. She held out a pile of letters tied with a thin black ribbon. 'Some of your things were muddled with mine and I just wondered.'

Daisy stared at the handwriting. She had forgotten about Tom's letters. She had taken them with her the last time she had returned from visiting Felicity as Felicity was going on and on about not having any storage space. She drew a steadying breath and here at last was the simple explanation for the scrap of paper under the doll. Something must have become dislodged in her pile of letters. No one was after her at that point.

The irony of it—agreeing to be married partly because of an old letter. Even as she thought it, her heart whispered that she was lying. She had agreed to be married because she had wanted to.

'I will have a look for your sketch book, Nella.'

'I had just hoped. I wanted to see if they were the same man, but now I will never know for certain.'

'When do you depart from Gilsland?' Daisy put her hand on Nella's shoulder. There was little point in worrying Nella about the attackers.

'Mama hopes Susan is being overly dramatic about Lord Edward. Do you know how Papa is going to rant when he realises that Susan could have married an earl's grandson but she threw it away by demanding that he dance attendance on her?'

'Susan did the right thing. It is better to end a marriage before it begins.' Daisy regarded the line of trees. Was there a hut hidden the woods? It seemed so odd that her own vision had been right in front of the woods. Perhaps she had seen one of the gang, this man that Nella had described. She gave a small smile. There was always a logical explanation, if she took the time and the trouble to discover it.

'Precisely, which is why I am going to be a lady explorer and never have to be concerned about such matters.'

'I hope you *will* be a lady explorer. Now, you must get back to your dear mama before she worries.' Daisy gave Nella her fierce governess look.

'You are the best governess ever, Miss Milton.' Nella raised up on her tiptoes and kissed Daisy's cheek. 'But I think you look much prettier in the green dress. And you should have heard Mama and Susan go on about your ball gown.'

'Idle flattery will get you everywhere, Nella. I will take a second look for the sketch book.'

Nella laughed and ran off, her bonnet bobbing behind her. Daisy sighed. It was such a joy to watch someone be carefree and not have to reprimand them.

With deft fingers she brushed a patch of dirt that Nella's fingers had left from her gown. Adam would have to know about the man and his strange tattoo. It could be the breakthrough that he was waiting for and a way for them to begin to rebuild their lives.

'I wanted to let you know that Lord Edward became angry a few days ago when Nella drew his picture,' Daisy blurted out when she discovered Adam breakfasting on the terrace. 'He was in deep conversation with a man who had two different-coloured eyes.'

Adam put down his coffee cup. His eyes appeared drawn and haggard as if he hadn't slept. 'Heritage has departed. He left this morning for London. He left a note. Apparently he and Miss Blandish quarrelled heavily and there was no reason for him to remain.'

'Lord Edward has left?' Daisy stared at him in dismay. 'I thought after last night that he intended staying. He was charged with recovering the necklace… The man's overwhelming sense of importance still astonishes me.'

A faint smile touched Adam's lips, but his eyes glowered. 'Heritage decided on reflection that he likes the world to think of him as a gentleman. I suspect he will be in London as soon as he possibly can. Your paths will not cross again.'

'How do you know this?'

'Webster carried his valise.' He held out a plate of toast and his eyes softened. 'Do sit down and have some. You look hungry. I understand you woke quite early and went for a walk.'

'I found it impossible to sleep and…' Daisy paused. She could hardly confess that dreams of him touching her body had driven her from her bed. 'The outside called to me. I am often in the habit of walking before breakfast.'

He lifted a brow and his hand paused momentarily on the toast. 'Do you always take such risks? You agreed…'

'Strictly speaking, I was not alone. I saw Webster in the distance and waved. Then Nella Blandish discovered me.'

He popped a piece of toast in his mouth, licking his fingers slowly, one by one, reminding her of the way he had suckled hers in the card room. 'Then I stand corrected. But you must take care.'

Daisy gave her head a shake and concentrated on the sugar bowl rather than on the way her insides seemed to be melting. 'Nella gave me some information. She thinks the man with strange eyes is the same one who lived in the hut last summer. She saw the bird tattoo when he was speaking to Lord Edward and it reminded her…'

Adam wiped his mouth with a napkin, his body becoming instantly alert. 'Which hut?'

'There is a stone hut in the centre of the woods near here. Nella always hated it and I thought it quite deserted. Nella tends to have…well…a vivid imagination. But after the ball, I am far from certain.'

'Vivid imaginations sometimes have a basis in fact.' He frowned and shuffled through a variety of papers. 'Did Nella tell you why she disliked the hut? Or is it indeed another of her tall tales?'

'Her governess last year apparently used a man with strange eyes to frighten Nella into good behaviour.' Daisy crossed her arms. He had gone from indulgent lover to investigator in the matter of a heartbeat. Her heart gave a pang at the eagerness of the change. 'Nella swears she saw this man drag a body from the hut last summer. But I suspect it is Nella's imagination at work again. *Mademoiselle* would have certainly informed Mrs Blandish.'

'Does she have a portrait of the man? Anything that might help?'

'I drew a map of the approximate location. Nella has always insisted that we keep away.' Daisy placed the rough sketch on the table and kept her voice as brisk as possible. 'She also gave me some letters I left behind, letters from Tom. I want to go through them in case he says anything of interest.'

'He won't have.' Adam dismissed the idea with a sweeping wave of his hand. 'This is about real people, Daisy. Here. Today. In the present. Someone is using the story to mask their identity. You aren't wearing your brooch.'

'I could not find it. Polly has straightened everything up and has followed your orders to box up my old clothes, rather than my request to leave them.'

'Naturally, as I pay her wages.'

Daisy forced down a quick retort. 'Nella told Lord Edward some tall tale about my box containing jewels, which is where that idea came from.' She nodded towards the sketch. 'Shall we investigate the hut?'

'*I* will arrange for it to be watched.' He glanced at the rough sketch before folding the sheet and placing it in his breast pocket. Then his face changed back towards his seductive one. 'I am impressed that you did not go and investigate yourself.'

'These are men who hurt people. Why should I risk danger to prove a point? There is a difference between taking the morning air in sight of the hotel and going off on some adventure.'

'Very wise,' he purred. And Daisy began to suspect that he was using her attraction towards him to divert her attention. 'You look tired. How long have you been awake?'

Her heart lurched and she knew that, despite everything, she was sliding inexorably down the slippery slope towards caring about him. She glanced up at the sky. Sliding? She had already slid. At some point over the past few days, seeing him had become indispensable to her well-being. 'I will be fine.'

'You should rest and that is an order. Balls and country dancing exhaust the unwary.'

'And you intend to order me about?'

'Only when you need it.' His hand touched hers, curling about it. 'Please, Daisy, you have circles under your eyes. I will look into Nella's story. And before you ask, I will let you know the moment I hear anything. Like you, I am well aware of the danger. I am not about to take stupid chances.'

Daisy undid the black ribbon holding her brother's letters together. The bold handwriting leapt out at her, sending a pang through her body. How much would she give for Tom's reassuring common sense now? What had he thought about Adam Ravensworth?

Sometimes in the past few days, it felt like she had entered a hall of mirrors where nothing was what it seemed. Adam Ravensworth was an enigma, able to change moods so quickly that she found it impossible to know what he was thinking. She wanted to trust him and believe in him, but did she dare confide in him about Kammie? Had Tom trusted him?

She glanced at the date and the place. Simply one of his letters from the hill station near Mysoorie where he had spent the summer. He had met a woman, someone he was certain that she would like, but there were complications. The maharajah as a gesture of goodwill had given him two puzzle boxes as a welcoming present, but Tom suspected that the maharajah knew more than he said about the opium trade and the thuggee and wanted to keep him on side. The chief servant to the maharajah, Sanjay, had dual-coloured eyes, just like him. Daisy put the letter down with a trembling hand. Adam was wrong. One of the thuggee had survived. It could be the only solution.

Daisy stopped and reread the words again about the puzzle box. Why had she missed it the first time? Had the box Tom sent her been one of the puzzle boxes? Hurrying over to the dressing table, she searched for the box, but it had disappeared.

A cold crept over Daisy. She knew she had brought the box with her from the Blandishes. It always sat on her dressing table. Had someone searched this room like they had searched the schoolroom?

She shook her head. There was no warning scarf. She had to stop seeing things that did not exist. Polly would have simply moved it when they were doing all the sewing yesterday. Logic and reason, not superstition and fantasy, should rule.

A soft knock sounded at the door. Daisy opened it and saw Adam standing there, eyes alight, neckcloth askew. She took a few steps backwards and allowed him in.

'The world has done Nella a disservice!' he proclaimed with a barely suppressed excitement in his voice. 'The hut exists and shows signs of recent occupation. Webster is watching it.'

'That is good news.' Daisy forced her lips to turn upwards, and her voice to sound light and unconcerned, but her insides churned. They had reached the end.

'When they return, Webster will send for me. It is nearly over, Daisy.' Adam stopped and his brow became creased. 'Something is wrong. I thought you were merely overly tired from the ball, but it is something else. Confide in me, Daisy. Your troubles are mine.'

Daisy walked to the desk and shuffled through the brittle letters. 'I am becoming worse than Nella. I have been rereading my brother's letters. He mentions a Sanjay who had dual-coloured eyes.'

'Sanjay was one of the chief murderers of the thuggee gang. I had forgotten about his eyes.'

'Then he could be the man who is behind this. The man I met on the riverbank told me to ask for a Mr Sanjay. They must be one and the same.'

'Impossible. Sanjay is a common enough name in India. Your brother's Sanjay survived the battle. I can remember him snarling, spitting and swearing his revenge all the way back to Bombay, but he was hanged. Heritage was not negligent in his duty then.'

'Nella said that the man she remembered had an angry red mark about his neck.'

'Nella likes to exaggerate. You have said so many times. Sanjay was without friends in the end. And even if he had survived, how would he have gone from India to Britain?' His finger lifted up her chin and his molten-caramel gaze searched her face. 'What else is troubling you from Tom's letters?'

'Tom mentioned receiving two puzzle boxes as a gift from the maharajah.'

'The maharajah always gave bribes to the Englishmen who visited his palace. He was very good at spying out our weaknesses.'

'Tom loved codes and the like, so he did not go far wrong.' It was on the tip of Daisy's tongue to ask what Adam's weakness was, but then she decided that she did not want to know. All she wanted was for him to continue to look at her in that way. 'Tom's box is missing.'

Instantly the colour of his eyes shifted, and became hardened amber. 'Has anything else gone?'

'I worry if they went through my things. Kammie is Tom's daughter and if—'

'Your niece is Tom's daughter?' Adam turned a sickly shade of green.

'Yes, she is named after her mother, Kamala. Did you know her?'

'Yes.' The word resounded in the suddenly still room. He turned away from her as his look of anguish increased. 'I wish you had told me about your niece's parentage. I had assumed...'

Daisy's stomach tightened. How much danger was Kammie in? 'It did not seem important at the time.'

He tilted his head to one side and there was something in the way he held his shoulders as if he were waiting. 'And you are certain that this child is your brother's?'

'He arranged her passage with his dying breath. She was his treasure. She has become ours.'

'I had always thought their child died.' He raised tortured eyes to her. 'It is good to know that she is so well looked after.'

Daisy nodded, attempting to understand his mood. Tom had saved his life once. 'I think Kamala and my brother were happy for the little time they had together. Kamala died giving birth, and the vicar's wife said that my brother lost the will to live without her.'

'Where is the child now? Is she healthy?' He took a step closer, and seemed to fill the room.

Daisy bit her lip, knowing she should explain about Kammie's falling sickness, and Felicity's fight to keep her out of an institution. People tended to react badly once they learnt of the illness. Once, an employer had dismissed her after learning about Kammie, afraid that somehow Daisy might contaminate her own children. Daisy needed Adam's help. Later, once everything was over, she decided. Maybe after Adam had met Kammie. After he'd seen her sunny face and heard her laughter, he'd understand. Felicity would approve of her decision.

'She is with my sister in Warwickshire. My sister lost her baby just before Kammie arrived. A vicar's wife who was returning to England brought her. It was providence. Felicity regained her strength and her purpose in life.'

'It is good that you are looking after her. Not everyone would have.' He ran a hand down her arm, sending warm tingles throughout her body. 'You were working as a governess to support them. It was very good of you, Daisy.'

'I am not good. The vicar's wife who travelled from India said that she was Tom's. I thought she must be the treasure that he wrote about,' Daisy whispered as her body began to lean towards his. She could stop him any time she wanted, but right now she wanted his touch. 'I thought maybe his letter might have a clue, but nothing. He sent the box, but it turned out to be a rattle. Only now I wonder…'

'A rattle?' His hand stopped, and hovered above her elbow.

'I could never open it, neither could Felicity. Hers we opened straight away. Four moves and the lid lifted. There had been a letter inside, giving Kammie's name, but nothing else.' Daisy pressed her lips together, remembering the howl of anguish from Felicity's husband and how he threatened to throw the box on the fire. No, unfortunately they were simply novelty rattles. Designed to provoke and tease, typical of Tom. 'Did you know Kamala well? Only sometimes, Kammie asks about her mother.'

'Well enough.' His hand dropped from her arm and the shutters came down in his eyes. 'She was brave and beautiful.'

A searing pang of jealousy went through Daisy. Adam had had feelings for Kamala. Had Kamala had anything to do with the necklace? Had she been the one to tell him of the curse? Daisy knew in that instant that she desired Adam and wanted him to look at her with eyes that smouldered. She didn't want to think about murderers or curses. She wanted to feel his touch and to pretend that it was only for her.

'You will have to tell Kammie when you meet her.' Daisy forced her voice to be light as she tried to banish the jealousy.

He hesitated for the briefest of seconds before answering, 'It was a lifetime ago, Daisy. There are other more important things like finding this gang of thieves.'

'When will we know if the trap worked?' Daisy swallowed hard. 'May I come with you? I don't want to stay here, waiting.'

'Nightfall, if Webster doesn't contact me first.' Adam leant and brushed a curl from her forehead. His thumb traced little circles on her forehead, making it difficult for Daisy to think straight. 'I can stay here for a little while if you are nervous that they might return. Webster will find me.'

'It is very kind of you but…you and I alone together? People might talk.'

A smile transformed his face. Daisy wondered how many nights she would dream of that smile. 'A word of advice—Miss Prim and Proper does not work when your hair is loose and your toes are peeking out from your gown. People will talk no matter what. Shall we give them something to talk about?'

'You…' Daisy grabbed her shawl and tightened it

about her shoulders. The atmosphere shifted in the room, becoming more intimate. 'I wanted to tell you about the letters.'

'And I am grateful.' His hand eased a lock of hair off her shoulder. The heat of him rose and surrounded her body, holding her. 'Very grateful indeed.'

The words died on her lips as his fingers gently tilted her face upwards. His lips traced a lazy line along her temple and cheeks before coming to feast on her mouth, a persuasive touch that called to something deep within her. Daisy's resolve weakened and she clung to his shoulders. His hard muscles moved under the shirt. Her forefinger touched the soft hair at the nape of his neck.

'Please,' she whispered, not knowing if she meant for him to continue or to stop. 'Please, this is wicked.'

'Wicked can be good.' His hand burnt through the thin lawn of her dress, imprinting itself on the curve of her waist.

Daisy put her hand to her head and moved away from him. His heart belonged to another. He had as good as told her that. And yet she craved his touch. Had she fallen that far?

Daisy tried to cling to her sanity and all the while his hand lightly stroked the hollow of her back, making it impossible to think rationally. Behind, her bed loomed large. 'Our agreement.'

'Who will know? Who will question? People already believe, Daisy.'

His mouth returned to hers, covered it, devoured it and blotting out all thought but the burgeoning warmth inside her that grew more insistent with each passing breath. Her body arched forwards, her soft curves meeting his hard planes. She wanted to stop thinking and simply to experience, erasing any thoughts about attackers or ghosts. She had ceased wanting to think, all she wanted to do was feel.

'I want to live. I do not want to end up dying, unloved,' Daisy whispered, giving voice to one of her deepest fears.

'You could never be that,' he murmured against her ear.

She wrapped her arm about his neck, pulled him close and reclaimed his lips.

His arms went about her and, without realising how it happened, she found herself by the bed.

'Softer than the floor, I think,' she said with a catch in her throat.

In the early afternoon sunlight, his throat was a strong golden colour. His amber gaze watched her, much as he had watched that first morning on the riverbank. He ran a finger down the side of her face. 'Why are you doing this, Daisy? Why are you seeking to seduce me?'

'Because…' Daisy searched her mind for the answer. 'Because I want to. Because I want to finish what we started in the card room.'

Her heart whispered another truth. She wanted to because she was falling in love with him. She wanted to have one perfect time to hold in her memory. It was as if somehow the kiss in the card room had opened a Pandora's Box, and she had no wish to go back to the narrow bed and frustrated dreams of a governess. If anything, her brother's letters had shown her how short life could be. And now, if Adam was right, this was nearly over and he'd go away.

'Is there anything else?'

'Do you need any more reasons?'

He moved his mouth down her neck and stopped where her gown fastened at her neck.

Slowly he undid several buttons until his hands skimmed the tops of her breasts. Her back arched as his fingers touched her erect nipples. The tiniest of touches caused them to tighten further. His hands encircled them. Then he brought his mouth to the thin fabric, wet it, and caused it to go translucent so that he could see the dusky rose underneath the white. She wriggled slightly and an aching need filled her.

He put his finger to his lips and brought it to hers. She put out her tongue and tasted it. He gave a very masculine smile under hooded eyes.

He bent his head and suckled her breast. A sudden jolt thrummed through her. No one had ever explained about this. How it could feel. How every bit of her became alive at his merest touch.

'You are overdressed.' His fingers finished the rest of the buttons and pushed the material aside, exposing her breast. His firm fingers cupped it as his mouth once again approached. His cool breath caressed the erect nipple, sending wave after wave of pulsating heat through her. Nothing in her life had ever prepared her for such a thing.

Her head thrashed on the pillow as her body craved release from the burning that threatened to consume her. Her body wanted something more. She moaned in the back of her throat as her body bucked upwards, seeking him and his mouth.

Then with one movement, he raised her dress, and her limbs were exposed to his gaze.

She moved her arms, hiding her nakedness.

'Stay still,' he said, his voice sliding over her skin. 'Allow me to see your creamy perfection.'

'I would like to see you as well.' She reached up with her palm and cupped his cheek, the stubble rough but soft. Her thumb stroked along the line of his jaw. His eyes flared. 'Please. I am undressed and you are… very…dressed.'

A frown developed between his eyes. 'You must be certain, Daisy. I won't be able to stop if my skin touches yours.'

Her hands tugged at his shirt, suddenly impatient. 'What are you trying to hide from me?'

'Nothing.' He closed his eyes and concentrated hard. 'If you wish to continue, then we will, Daisy, but I want no false protestations of modesty afterwards.'

'I understand.' Daisy raised herself on one elbow. Didn't he see that she had already made her choice? She wanted him. She wanted to be loved once.

He took off his shirt, throwing it to the ground. A living statue of male perfection. Daisy tentatively raised her hand and touched his warm flesh. The glow of the fire had turned it to gold. She followed his lead, and her fingers squeezed his nipples, and stroked the sprinkling of hair on his chest.

He gathered her to him. They lay together, skin touching skin. Between her hips she could feel his arousal straining against his trousers. Her fingers strayed to the waistband.

'If this is what you want…' His lips brushed her temple. 'I had planned it for our wedding night.'

'I want you now, Adam.' A momentary panic hit her.

She tried to remember the whispered conversations of years gone past about how a woman pleasured a man. It was not necessary for a woman to do anything, according to Felicity. She was supposed to lie very still. She screwed up her eyes tight, dug her fists into the bed clothes so that she was not tempted to touch him.

The teasing of her breasts stopped. Cautiously she opened an eye. He looked at her with passion-filled eyes. 'I prefer my women to be active participants. I want to give them pleasure. Relax and all will be well.'

She gave a brief nod as his lips nibbled at her bare shoulder and then slid down her torso, coming to rest near her belly button. Lazily, he drew circles, round and round, coming closer and closer until his finger dipped into her nest of curls.

A grasp was drawn from her throat and her body convulsed upwards as heat streaked through her.

'Pleasure is anything but wicked,' he said and rested his head against her stomach.

'Is that all?' she asked as the world returned to normal. Somehow, all he had done was to increase this burgeoning burning hunger. She raised a trembling hand and touched his bare chest again. This time she allowed her fingers to linger and to trail over his flat nipples. 'You remain dressed, Adam. I want to feel your skin against mine. Your trousers on the floor…please.'

'As my lady requests.'

He put his hand to his trousers, shedding them in an instant. The extent of his arousal became visible. Far larger than she had thought possible.

A ripple of power surged through her. She had done

this to him. She reached out her hand and touched it. Velvet smooth, but with an underlying strength. Her eyes flew to his face. He gave an encouraging nod, and she touched him again. Firmer. Longer. Enjoying the hot feel of him, she knew that all those who said that this was wrong had no idea. It felt so very right.

His hand covered hers, pulling it over her head. His mouth turned up in his special smile. 'No more now. We have serious business to attend to.'

He positioned himself between her thighs. One hand held her wrists while his other inched lower, sending stars shooting through her. He stopped and played in her nest of curls and then found her innermost spot. He stroked. His finger went inside her, caressing. Her body tightened about him as wave after wave of pleasure shot through her. She lifted her arms and held him tight. They were together, connected, and she wanted it to continue.

His lips nuzzled her ear. 'It will hurt for a moment, but then it will get better. I promise you that.'

His knees wedged her legs apart, and the tip of him nudged her, demanding entry.

Her eyes flew to his and saw the immense look of concentration. She felt the slight pain and then a quick ache. His mouth absorbed her cry, but her body opened and expanded, welcoming him.

For a long heartbeat, they lay there joined. She knew that she could not go back, but had no idea what to do next. Slowly he started move. Gently, and the storm inside her grew again, reaching a crescendo, until, with a cry, she collapsed against the pillows, spent. And she knew that this was what it was like to live.

Chapter Thirteen

Adam regarded the pale oval of Daisy's face. Her long hair flowed over the pillows. A stab of guilt coursed through him. He had seduced her, deliberately. What he had done was wicked. He knew that, but with Daisy standing there, looking at him with her big eyes and the stubborn set to her chin as she asked to go and hunt the thieves with him, the urge to be with her had been irresistible.

He hated not having the marriage ring on her finger before this had happened, but it did bind her to him. Irrevocably.

Now she could sleep. And when she woke, the danger would be over. And they could marry, live their lives in peace.

It had been a shock to learn that Kamala's child, *his* child, lived. He had been certain that she must have died with her parents. And then to learn that for all these years, Daisy had worked to keep this child alive. And soon they would be a proper family.

'Daisy,' he whispered against her temple. 'You sleep. There is no need for you to fight or get hurt.'

Adam glanced over at the window and saw the sun had moved and was just beginning to peek through the side of one of the curtains. He reached over and pulled his pocket watch from his waistcoat. Time had slipped through his fingers. He could no longer afford to wait for her to wake. He kissed her shoulder one last time. She gave a vague murmur and turned over, perfectly content in her sleep.

Reluctantly he eased his body from the bed and dressed. He frowned as he looked at his neckcloth. It was unlike Webster to have put out a neckcloth with a bit of fraying. He would have to have a word with him once this little episode was over. Simply because one was searching for an armed gang did not mean that one allowed one's standards to slip. He had felt certain that his manservant understood this.

Before leaving, he picked up Daisy's discarded petticoat and stays. He straightened up the room, leaving nothing except the sleeping figure in the bed to show that they had experienced passion. He refused to risk slipping her nightdress on and waking her. But the maid should not notice anything was amiss.

'I will look after you, Daisy Milton,' he said, looking at the slumbering figure. 'But when will you stop being so stubborn? Stay here and all will be well.'

His heart pained him. He was in danger of doing the one thing he had promised never to do and that was to fall in love again. Quickly, without giving himself time to change his mind, he reached for the book of Keats and turned to the 'Bright Star'. He picked up a pen and replaced a single word. Then he put the book by her pillow where she was certain to find it if she woke before he could return. Or if he failed to return.

He shook his head and dismissed the premonition as ridiculous. He would return and then he would say the words properly.

The slightest of clicks of the door caused Daisy to wake. Late afternoon sunlight peeked in through a crack in the drawn curtains. She blinked and reached out a hand. The covers of her bed were drawn tight around her, but underneath she was naked. She had never slept naked in her entire life.

With cautious fingers she examined her mouth. Bruised. She attempted to move and found she had aches in places that she had no business aching. She had hoped that it was some strange waking dream, but knew it was not.

Her face flooded with crimson heat. She had begged a man she was not married to, to make love to her. Why? Because she wanted to appreciate it? Because she wanted to demonstrate that she was something more than a prim-and-proper governess? The word still taunted her. All she knew was that she had fallen in love with him, a fact that he must never know. He had made love to her and had left before she woke. It frightened her.

She moved her hand and a book tumbled to the ground with a thump.

'Ah, you are awake, ma'am.' Polly's cheerful voice resounded in the room. She bustled in carrying a tray and closing the main door behind her with her foot.

Daisy swallowed hard, hating to think what it must look like. Had Polly met Adam in the corridor? What would have happened if she had come into the room where they lay entangled on the bed together? Then all hope of her retaining her independence would have gone.

Instantly she forgave Adam for leaving in the way that he did. He had shown far more sense than she appeared to possess. No one must suspect that they had been together.

She could see that her dress was neatly hung over a chair, and her petticoats, stockings and stays were placed nearby as if she had calmly taken them off, rather than discarding them in passion. He had considered her reputation and that counted for something.

She should be lying here covered in shame, and worrying about the possibility of children, but she could only think about how alive she felt.

'The excitement of the ball turned my sleeping habits upside down.' Daisy strove for a normal voice, but every muscle was poised to see Polly's disapproving stare. 'I woke, feeling refreshed and went for a walk. Then suddenly tiredness came in waves and I had to go back to sleep. I certainly do not plan to make a habit of it.'

'You should have rung, miss.' Polly bent down and put the book in a pile with the others. 'It is what I am here for. To help with the dressing and undressing.'

'Next time I will.' Daisy reached for her dressing gown and slipped it over her shoulders, covering some of the nakedness. 'Normally I never sleep in the afternoon. I cannot think what came over me.'

'My uncle's punch is renowned for its potency. He

has a few extra-special ingredients. It is no wonder that you had to return to bed, but you should have rung for help undressing. Those petticoats are going to be creased, piled like that.'

'It seemed easier this way.' Daisy attempted a placating smile and at a breath Polly seemed to be satisfied.

Polly motioned towards the tray. 'I have brought you some restorative chocolate. Webster, Lord Ravensworth's valet, suggested it.'

Webster and not Adam. Daisy's stomach churned. Had Adam said something to his valet when he returned? Instantly she rejected the thought. Adam's straightening of her clothes and removing all evidence of their passion showed that he wanted to protect her reputation, not ruin it.

'I should get up.' Daisy swung her legs out the bed. 'You will make me into a lazier creature than Mrs Blandish.'

'Webster seemed to believe that you would stay in bed all afternoon. Not my lady, I said. She is used to doing things. We have an afternoon of sewing and altering ahead of us.' Polly tilted her head. 'If you are up to it.'

'After I have had a wash and dressed. My light-green work dress I think. The one with a bit of lace about the neck.'

Polly gave a smile and started bustling about the room, tidying. Daisy's neck muscles relaxed. Polly had not noticed anything different. Nobody would. She could pretend that this morning had never happened.

'Where is Lord Ravensworth?' Daisy risked a sip of the chocolate.

'He has left a note.' Polly returned with her arms full of fresh petticoats and the light-green afternoon dress. Daisy had to admit that wearing that dress was far more appealing than her own dull grey or black dresses she had worn as a governess. That woman was gone for ever. 'I should have mentioned it afore now.'

Daisy saw the cream note, sealed with wax. 'How long ago did Lord Ravensworth leave the note?'

'I am not sure. Webster simply asked me to deliver it. I peeped in a while ago and you were asleep with a smile on your face.' Polly pursed her mouth tightly. 'My lady should get her rest.'

Daisy broke the seal with eager fingers and then began reading with growing dismay. Adam had left for London. Urgent business. He did not expect to return. All danger was over. Brief and curt. The note fluttered from her fingers.

He had used the danger as an excuse to seduce her. She had forgotten all her ideals and rules about being a governess.

Adam tightened his grip on his pistol and looked at the black door of the hut. The last few rays of autumn sunlight gave feeble light. Webster should have been here before now, long before now. He had agreed to watch and to report if anything went wrong. But Webster was nowhere to be seen.

His muscles relaxed slightly when he saw a tall cloaked figure: Webster.

'It took you long enough. We were supposed to meet at the stables, but the head groomsman said you had gone on ahead. It is unlike you, Webster.'

'When do we go in?'

'Are you sure he is in there?'

'One of the stable lads has been watching this place ever since you gave me the map. He knew where it was sure enough.' Webster tapped the side of his nose with a bandaged hand.

'What have you done to your hand, Webster?'

'Scalded it this morning. A bit of bother, but don't you pay it no mind.'

Adam frowned. It was unlike Webster to be clumsy. The back of his neck prickled, but he dismissed it. In a few moments, this would all be over and he would be free to live his life. He could offer Daisy certainty, rather than fear. 'I want the doctor to see it when we get back to the hotel. No excuses. And it sounds as if you are sickening.'

'Yes, sir.'

'Neglecting your health does no one any good.'

'Just didn't want to take liberties.'

'Miss Milton thought you were watching out for her this morning. Thank you for that,' Adam replied smoothly, ignoring the familiarity. There was something about Webster's demeanour, and his speech, something that he could not put his finger on. 'Luckily Miss Milton possesses an excellent brain. The stone hut was painfully easy to find after following her directions. Funnily enough I had thought them vague.'

'If it leads us to the man with the strange eyes like you said…who cares how the directions were given?'

'What man with the strange eyes?' Adam froze, one hand on his pistol.

'Different colours and with an angry scar about his

neck.' Webster licked his lips and stared at him with his cap shadowing his face. 'I am sure you told me, sir. There can't be many like that around here. If he does not show, we are bound to find him soon.'

'I never said anything about a man with strange eyes or a scar, Webster. Only about the hut.' Adam withdrew his pistol, pointed it at his erstwhile valet. 'Explain! What have you done with my valet?'

'I think, Lord Ravensworth, you should reconsider your position before you begin making demands.'

'Had I?' Adam's neck muscles tightened and he cocked his pistols. 'My valet! Answer me now!'

'You are no longer the one asking questions, Ravensworth. You are the one providing the answers.'

Several burly men emerged from the woods. Adam recognised three from the earlier attack. The false Webster reached out and took the pistol from Adam's fingers.

'You have been singularly obtuse. Easy like the other aristocrats. The great nobility who cannot see beyond the ends of their noses.' The man's smile became a sneer as he took off the bandage on his hand and revealed a tattoo. Adam blinked. Not Webster, but an imposter. His head had been so full of Daisy and wanting to return to her bed that he had hurried, not paying proper attention. It was too easy. And he had been trapped by his own desire.

'What have you done with my valet? Answer me! Is he still alive?'

'If you will proceed this way, you can be reunited with your valet. Who knows—maybe he breathes.'

Daisy touched the cream note and looked out at the darkening landscape. The note did not make sense. She had turned it over and over in her mind. She had to think with her brains, rather than with her emotions. Emotions led to difficulties. How many times had she told herself that when she left her employers to start another job?

Adam would not have left with just a note, not without telling her who the culprits had been or if her sister and niece would be safe. He had only taken what she offered. But there was a courtesy about him. He knew she worried.

'Polly, did you say that Lord Ravensworth gave you the note?'

'No, miss. It was Webster. Apparently Lord Ravensworth left early this morning just after first light. He did not even stop to change after the ball.'

Daisy froze. Webster had deliberately lied to Polly. 'But that is wrong. I saw Adam...later.'

She kept her eyes modestly on the floor, but she knew her cheeks flamed. What sort of woman made love to a man mid-morning?

'I've no idea what to make of it, miss, to be sure. I only know what Webster said. He is a man who dislikes to being crossed. My uncle told me that. Last summer when Lord Ravensworth was here, he used to throw his weight around a bit.'

'Lord Ravensworth?'

'Lord Ravensworth is a toff.' Polly gave a small curtsy. 'Begging your pardon, miss. He is by all accounts a perfect gentleman, if a bit demanding. It is why I wanted this job. I can go places if I'm your lady's maid.'

'Then who threw his weight around?' Daisy rubbed

her hand against her temple…there was something here.

'His valet. All smiles and bows unless he thinks you are below him. Overly proud, Wor Davy called him. Mr Webster was particularly nasty today. He had burnt his hand and it was all bandaged. I offered to help and he said no. And he didn't even know that the railway was going to Rosehill.' Polly clapped her hand over her mouth. 'I have been telling tales. Servants' gossip and I promised my uncle that I would learn to keep my mouth shut.'

'No, I am pleased you said something.' Daisy pressed her hands into her eyes. She should have known the note was false. But who had sent it? Surely Webster had to have known… Webster knew all about railways. It was why Adam and he travelled here last year.

She drew in her breath sharply. Webster had been here last year. His eyes might not be different colours, but there was a certain look about him that matched Nella's description. That matched the man who searched for Adam. Perhaps Nella could identify him…if she could find the sketchbook.

It was an entirely slender thread, but it was all she had to go on. And she wanted to be doing something, rather than sitting around, waiting and hoping. Action was required.

Daisy narrowed her eyes and began to look through her pile of papers, sorting as she went. A huge stack needed to be burnt, but there were others like Nella's note and some of the drawings she had done of the woods that Daisy wanted to keep. Halfway down, she came across the old sketchbook. Daisy flipped through the pages.

Various satirical sketches and doodles. The one of Mrs Blandish as a giant tabby cat supping cream was particularly good. She had to admit that Nella had talent for capturing people in a few lightning strokes. It was a pity that, given her class, she would be prevented from putting it to full use.

Daisy sucked in her breath and looked at the series of sketches of the cloaked man. They could have been Webster. Had Adam been harbouring a viper? Or had Webster known more than he said?

'Polly, can you ask for one of the grooms to take me to the Blandishes? It appears that I have found the missing sketch book after all.'

Daisy waited in the vestibule of the Blandishes' house. All about her stood boxes and trunks. Above her, she could hear Miss Blandish sob and wail.

'Was there some reason for the call at this late hour, Miss Milton?' Mrs Blandish waved her handkerchief. 'We are in the midst of packing or otherwise you would have found us dressing for dinner. We have decided to quit the neighbourhood. The air has been less than kind. My nerves will no longer stand it.'

'Nella mentioned that she had lost her sketchbook.' Daisy held it out and kept her voice calm. Mrs Blandish could be managed. A steady manner would do more to ease the situation than anything. Above all things, Daisy wanted the truth. Daisy looked up at the gilt ceiling. That was not strictly true. She wanted Adam back alive and well.

'I promised to return it if I could. I went through my papers one last time, and there it was.'

'Nella will be pleased, I am sure.' Mrs Blandish turned to go.

Daisy drew in a breath. She had to risk it.

'Mrs Blandish, I need your help. I am fairly certain that Adam Ravensworth is in trouble.'

Mrs Blandish raised an eyebrow. 'That is his problem. He should not have been foolish. I do not see what I and my dear girls can do to help.'

'Nella drew sketches last summer. There is one that she wanted to see. A man who had frightened her, and she saw the same man consorting with Lord Edward.'

'That man has no claim on this house.' Mrs Blandish stuck her nose in the air. 'Who he consorts with is no concern of mine. Why Nella should start telling tales again, I have no idea.'

'I believe Miss Blandish had a lucky escape.' Daisy rapidly explained about the conversation she had over-heard and watched the astonishment grow on Mrs Blandish's face.

'Opium, did you say?' Mrs Blandish waved her hand in front of her face. 'When I was a girl in India, I saw some of its ravages. And, yes, you are right—Lord Edward did display some of the symptoms. I have been blind.'

'He would have made a poor husband.'

'What do you want me to do?' Mrs Blandish dabbed her eyes with a handkerchief.

'Call Nella. I want to see if some of her tall tales were actually correct.'

Mrs Blandish went white. 'Could she be telling the

truth? Have I punished my darling girl for telling the truth? You promised, Miss Milton, that she was telling stories.'

'I owe Nella a sincere apology.' Daisy bit her lip. She had to sacrifice her pride and beg. 'Please, Mrs Blandish, Lord Ravenworth's life depends on your assistance.'

Chapter Fourteen

Adam sat on the hard floor of the hut, fuming. The sweet heavy scent of opium hung in the hut, clawing at his mind. He fought against it and the parade of ghosts it dragged from the recesses of his mind. A faint breath of air seeped through a crack behind, giving some small measure of respite.

Such a simple ruse to dress in Webster's cloak. Adam had been arrogant beyond belief, and fallen into the trap. How easily it had been arranged. What made matters worse was that he was not the only soul to pay for his hubris.

Next to him lay Webster's body. Adam laid his head against Webster's chest and heard the rhythmic sound of his heart and soft rattle of his breath. His valet lived. Barely, but there was life. Silently, Adam vowed to do all in his power to keep the man alive. Both of them would survive. He glanced over and saw another figure huddled in the corner. The figure kicked out and gave a faint moan. Heritage. It made a certain amount of sick sense.

His stomach clenched. And Daisy? Would they capture her as well?

One more regret to add to his list. He should have woken her up and said goodbye. He should have told her how he felt, rather than wanting to keep the picture of her peacefully sleeping in his brain.

He clenched his fists, relaxed them, tried to get the ropes to move. He could escape. He would live. He would marry Daisy. It was inevitable now. All he had to do was to keep his brain free from the opium and not to panic.

A footstep resounded in the hut. He glanced up and saw the cloaked man, the false Webster, sneering at him. Ice-cold fury coursed through Adam.

'Who are you?' he croaked.

'You may call me Jones,' the man leered at him. 'You knew me once. We worked together. But then do the aristocracy ever notice the ordinary? Aren't we all just cogs in a wheel?'

Adam concentrated hard. He could vaguely remember a Jones; he had had that Jones punished for sadistically beating an Indian soldier to death. Was it the same one? Or someone else, someone who bore a grudge?

The man tilted his head and pressed his lips together, a small act, but one that brought his features into line. Adam's stomach plummeted. It was Trooper Jones. Adam searched his mind. Jones had been part of the detail guarding the thuggee prisoners.

Daisy's words haunted him—an angry red scar, different-coloured eyes and Sanjay. He doubted then, but no longer. They had all done Nella a disservice. The most dangerous of the thuggee had survived.

His blood ran cold. He had not only survived, but had begun rebuilding. Adam longed to wipe the smirk from Trooper Jones's face.

'You were a soldier once.' Adam glared at Jones. 'It is treason to consort with the Crown's enemies.'

'And you think I am afraid of hanging?'

'You served your country.'

'Aye, and that bloody excuse was my officer.' Jones sent a stream of spittle towards where Heritage lay. 'Do you think he cared? All he wanted was his opium pipe filled.'

'Did he save Sanjay? For opium?'

'Very good, Lord Ravensworth. I knew you was intelligent. I did that on my own. They don't die immediately, you know. I obeyed orders, hanged him and then cut him down. No one paid me no mind. Just put out one of the poor wretches who had died. That piece of dirt never noticed the difference. Just like Sanjay predicted.'

'When did Heritage join you?'

'He were a late recruit. Met him in an opium den, Sanjay did. He owed Sanjay money and, to save his squalid existence, he got us information, information about you and your habits. Think he enjoyed seducing your mistress.'

'That was how you learnt about the ruby necklace.' Adam cursed whichever woman had told Heritage.

'Sanjay already knew you had it. Sanjay makes it his business to know things like that. He is the last one and so they rightfully belong to him. Them and all the jewels. We spent a time collecting them up again. All he wanted from Heritage was information. You are a hard man, Lord Ravensworth. A worthy opponent. We thought we had you last summer when you visited here. But you never let your guard down. Stronger measures were necessary.'

'Why did you decide to join him, Jones? He will kill you in the end. People like that don't share.'

Jones sent another stream of spittle towards Heritage. 'I figured that I weren't going to get rich being in that army. So I left. And we became brothers, Sanjay and me. He's giving me half of all the jewels.'

'You murdered for him.' Adam closed his eyes and said a silent prayer for all their victims. He stretched behind him, trying to find even the smallest shard so he could work on his ropes. If he could keep Jones talking, there was a slim chance, he could work himself free.

'Retribution, Sanjay calls it. I was a soldier in a holy war. We tracked them down one by one, saving the best for last. I'm going to be a very wealthy man, Ravensworth.'

'No, you are a common criminal.' Adam shifted slightly and a loose board poked into his back. For the first time, since he had woken up in the hut, he believed he might emerge alive. 'A cold-blooded killer. And with me, it ends.'

'I thought so, but your friend Heritage told us about the Milton woman and her box. She is unclean. She will have to die. It will be up to you who goes first.' Jones wiped his hand across his mouth. 'Sanjay said that I could sample her as well. I like it when they scream. And she screams beautifully. I had my hands around her neck that day. I nearly did it then, but Sanjay hadn't given the final word, like. I can only kill under his orders.'

'Your quarrel is with me.' Adam began to work frantically at the ropes. If his hands were free, he would tear Heritage limb from limb for putting Daisy in danger. 'Daisy Milton is an innocent.'

Adam fought against the rising tide of panic. Jones wanted this. He and Sanjay enjoyed torture. And when he and Daisy were dead, would they turn their attention to Daisy's sister and the child? He wanted to meet the child, of course. But she was nothing compared to Daisy. There had to be a way of warning Daisy. Somehow. She had to flee from this place. Flee and never return.

'That's right, your worship. Struggle. I made them knots good and tight. I know my job.'

'You are a monster, Jones.'

'I am what the British Army made me.'

'You and Sanjay won't win. They will catch you and hang you for murdering a peer.'

'Ah, but will they? When they find you and your lovely woman, they will think that piece of dirt did it, and then shot himself. A lover's triangle. Quite clever, I thought.' Jones aimed a kick at Heritage's midriff. 'I hold all the cards and you will lick my boots before you die.'

Jones sauntered out of the hut with an echoing laugh.

'Oh, my aching head,' Heritage complained.

'Heritage!' Adam shouted. 'Wake up, you miserable worm! How much did you tell them?'

'Had no choice, old boy. They were going to kill me. And, what was worse—expose me. I would have lost everything.'

'They are going to kill you anyway. You betrayed me, Heritage.'

'Betrayed is a harsh word.' Heritage opened his bloodied eyes. In the dim light, it was clear that Jones had already used Heritage as a punching bag. A trickle of blood dripped down one side of his mouth. 'I needed the money. It was not like they were going to hurt you. They wanted the necklace.'

'Spare me the platitudes. You wanted their opium.' Adam felt the ropes slip the tiniest bit. He started to twist his wrists. 'Why did you tell them about Daisy having jewels?'

'She was just a governess, a person of no importance, you said. What is it to you if she lives or dies? Anyway, I thought they'd go away if they had something.' Heritage gave a ghost of a smile and blood bubbled from his mouth. 'At least that was the plan. Seems I miscalculated. Again. Should have saved us trouble. I should have checked to make sure he was dead the last time.'

Adam clenched his jaw. Heritage had seen service. He probably knew the extent of his injuries and that he was near death. Adam's only hope was that Webster was not as severely injured. 'Miscalculation is the least of your worries. You were a fool, Heritage. You will go to your grave knowing you were a fool and a coward.'

'Jones took me at my word, you know,' Heritage continued in a dreamy voice. 'He went out and found the box. It rattles, Ravensworth. Could it be the jewels? Really a lot of fuss over a governess.'

'The maharajah gave Milton that box. It has nothing of value in it. Nothing.' His wrists had become raw and throbbed with pain. Adam redoubled his efforts. 'I am going to marry Miss Milton, Heritage. My intentions were always honourable. The one thing Miss Milton is not—is expendable.'

Heritage was silent for a long time. 'No woman is worth it.'

'Some are. One definitely is.'

'Are you certain that you saw this man?' Daisy asked Nella.

Nella gave an enthusiastic nod. 'They were using the hut last summer. He is not a nice man.'

'But it is Lord Ravensworth's valet. It looks just like him. Is there anything else?'

'Nella, if you are funning Miss Milton, I shall be very cross.' Mrs Blandish put a hand to her head and straightened the ribbons of her cap. 'Did you see Lord Ravensworth's valet do anything wrong? Anything at all?'

Nella chewed her bottom lip. 'This man had a bird tattooed on his hand. He used to carry a yellow scarf in his back pocket and threaten people with it. He spoke in a foreign language. And around his neck was this angry red scar. Mostly he tried to hide it, but I saw it one day.'

Daisy closed her eyes and tried to remember. Did Adam's valet have a tattoo? She felt certain she would have remembered. 'Webster does not have a tattoo.'

'Then they cannot be the same man,' Mrs Blandish said triumphantly. 'I declare, Miss Milton, your imagination is worse than Nella's. Suspecting your fiancé's valet of wrongdoing.'

Daisy froze. Polly had said something about Webster hurting his hand. The two men looked enough alike. What if...? Her mouth went dry. It was a possibility, a slim possibility, but one nevertheless.

She had to investigate the hut without delay. It was obvious they had been tracking Adam for ages. The hut had to be investigated without delay.

'Mrs Blandish, can I borrow your footmen and butler? I believe Lord Ravensworth may be in danger.'

'Why should I do that?'

Daisy regarded Mrs Blandish. She had to make Mrs Blandish do this of her own free will, much as she would make one of her students. She paused, seeking the perfect reason. She bit her lips and then her gaze fell on the trunk with the brass handles. What was the one thing Mrs Blandish craved? Respectability.

'Because of Lord Ravensworth's connections.' Daisy pressed her fingertips together. She had to play this right. 'Ravensworth's connections are worth having if one is trying to launch one's daughter in London society. His ire is not worth considering. And his friendship can open many doors.'

Daisy waited. She had not actually promised anything, but the implication was there. And the important thing was to save Adam. Afterwards, she would explain. Adam would understand and honour the debt.

'The Ravensworth name is indeed highly regarded.' A broad smile broke out over Mrs Blandish's jowls. 'Susan will need every help. I have no wish for her indiscretion here to cling to her ball gown. She was overly familiar with Lord Edward, I see that now.

Youthful folly. Mr Blandish will have to pay for a truly top-drawer finishing governess.'

'Far too many people speak of rumours, but *on dits* can vanish overnight if the right pressure is applied.' Daisy held her breath and willed Mrs Blandish to agree. 'Lord Ravensworth will apply that pressure.'

'True, true.' Mrs Blandish held out her hand. 'I think it is a fair exchange. I too want to see the end of this gang of ruffians. A body cannot rest safe in bed until they are behind bars. I think you had best have reinforcements from the hotel as well. Hopefully, this time Nella is telling the truth.'

'She is,' Daisy said. 'I promise.'

'How do you open this?' Jones growled, turning Daisy's box over and over again.

'It is a puzzle box. Milton liked codes and tricks.' Adam forced his wrists apart and the last of the ropes fell away. His hands throbbed as the blood rushed back in, but he was free.

'You mean it does hold a fortune?'

'I saw Milton take a pouch of gems from the maharajah's belt. The missing jewels are worth a king's ransom.'

Heritage merely grunted. Adam did not risk a glance towards him, but kept his being focused on Jones. If he could drive a wedge between Sanjay and Jones, he might stand a chance. Divide and conquer. Neither Webster nor Heritage would be of any help in the coming fight. Silently he willed both of them to live. There had been enough death.

How much longer did he have before Sanjay began

his game of torture with them? Had he already captured Daisy?

The tall thuggee glided into the hut, and stopped halfway into his bow. His eyes bulged. 'Keep away from that, Jones. It is not for you.'

'I have no idea what you are talking about, Sanjay. Share and share alike, you said.' A flicker of emotion went over Jones's face. Adam felt a sense of grim satisfaction.

Sanjay's eyes widened. 'There are things you are not permitted to understand.'

'What, that Heritage was right? That the box is full of jewels? You intend to cheat me, Sanjay.' Jones turned the box over again. 'I can't get in.'

'Such things are only permitted for the true believers.'

'There is no honour amongst thieves. He will take all the jewels from you,' Adam said as Sanjay reached for the box. Jones lifted it above his head.

'You ought not to have done that! I would have shared.'

'You stole the treasure! You are unclean! All unclean people must die.' Sanjay began to rock back and forth; spittle foamed from his mouth. 'Give it to me now! You do not know its power. You will destroy it.'

'Come and take it! I want them jewels.'

The box crashed to the floor. Jones cursed, raised his fist and backhanded Sanjay, sending him flying across the room. The man's head hit the stone wall of the hut with a sickening thump. 'I told you not to disturb me when I was busy.'

'Now do you see that I spoke the truth, Jones? He used you.'

All of Adam's muscles coiled, ready to spring. But out of the corner of his eyes he saw a faint movement from Sanjay. The thuggee rose from the dust and advanced towards Jones. He pulled his yellow scarf from his pocket.

'Give that to me! I will do my duty to the brotherhood.' Sanjay lunged for the box again. Jones and Sanjay grappled over it, rolling over and over. Sanjay lifted his hands and showed his thin scarf, and started to wrap it around Jones's neck. Jones's eyes bulged as he fought against the pressure.

Adam reached out and grabbed out Sanjay's legs, trying to get him to loosen the scarf. Jones jerked back with his head. Adam sent the man flying across the room to the fireplace. The mantelpiece crashed down and Sanjay's body jerked as if in death throes and then lay still.

'You are going to regret that, Ravensworth. Your death will be slower and more painful. That man was my friend.'

'A funny way to show friendship.' Adam held out his hand. 'It's over now, Jones. Time to pay for your crimes.'

'Who is going to bring me to justice? You? You are just like him.' Jones spat towards Heritage.

'You know nothing about me.'

Jones leapt forwards, knife gleaming. 'I know enough.'

Adam's hand came up and grabbed Jones's wrist as the knife sliced down on Adam's cheekbone. He brought his knee up, and connected with Jones's stomach. 'I went to Eton, Jones, I know how to fight dirty.'

'You will pay for that.' Jones lifted his knife higher.

Adam reached out and his fist fell on Jones's wrist. The knife arched away from them, landing in the middle of the hut. Jones started to scramble towards the knife, but Adam tackled him, sending him to the floor.

They rolled over and over on the floor. Adam rained blows down on Jones's face, but he kicked his legs out and sent Adam flying backwards, crashing into the table.

Adam fumbled about on the floor, grabbing Daisy's box. He curled his hand around it and felt its weight. Not much of a weapon, but it would suffice. He waited.

As Jones dived towards him again, Adam brought the box down on the back of Jones's head. The connection made Adam's arm reverberate. Jones crumpled, hitting the floor with a thud, alive but unconscious. Adam put his hands on his knees and tried to get air into his lungs.

'What is going on in there?' a voice thundered. 'Answer me. Jones! Sanjay!'

'I believe your leader has encountered a problem.' Adam stepped out of the shadows.

Daisy tried to concentrate on keeping up with the footmen and stable hands rather than noticing how tight her stays were. Adam had to be there and he had to be alive. She gripped a lantern tightly in one hand and in the other she held Mrs Blandish's walking stick. Mrs Blandish had counselled that Daisy wait with her, but Daisy knew that she had to be there.

As they neared the hut, the group seemed to swell. Farmhands came from the fields with pitchforks and suddenly the innkeeper stood beside her, pistol shoved in his belt.

'Raise the lantern a bit higher if you would not mind, miss. Let them see that there are a number of us here. I will not have my business being ruined by thieves! Imagine kidnapping a viscount! And then Lord Edward has disappeared.'

Daisy swallowed hard. Heritage was gone as well. Adam had been overconfident about that man. 'I do not know exactly when it happened.'

'Well, his carriage remains in my stable and his lordship has disappeared. That is kidnapping. My niece doesn't have the sense she was born with.'

'Polly was fooled. We all were.'

'You need not worry, miss. I will see that you come to no harm. First sign of trouble, you go to the back. Let me and the lads handle it.'

Several men had taken off at a run when they had seen the crowd approaching. It was all over far more quickly than she could have dreamt possible. But nowhere did she see Adam's body.

'Adam, are you in there?' she called, unable to stop herself. 'Adam Ravensworth, are you all right? Answer me!'

'Daisy, you were supposed to wait. I should have known you'd disregard my wishes.' Adam emerged from the hut in his shirt sleeves. 'I owe Nella Blandish an apology. She accurately described the leader. He had been hanged once. But it is over now. He's dead.'

Daisy stopped and lifted her lantern higher, trying to see better. Her eyes feasted on his for an instant. His hair was a mess, he bore bruising on the side of his face and he walked stiffly. 'Webster... Lord Edward...'

'Both are severely injured. We need to get them to a doctor,' Adam said, watching her. Daisy appeared like an avenging angel at the head of the horde. Her hair tumbled about her shoulders; in her hands she carried a stout walking stick and in the other a lantern. Most women he knew would be cowering beside the fire back in the safety of the hotel, but not Daisy. She had come to his rescue.

'To a doctor? How badly injured is Webster? Has he been shot?'

'I want them to live.' Adam looked towards various footmen who were milling about, holding up lanterns and exclaiming at a blade of grass. 'Get me a stretcher now! Take the door down now. We need both doors. There will be bodies to carry.'

'Is anyone dead?' The colour drained from Daisy's face.

'The man whom you met on the riverbank and his accomplice. He used Heritage's desire for opium and blackmailed him to provide information. Heritage wanted to keep his hands clean.'

'The one in the card room who was speaking to Lord Edward? But he was the leader, wasn't he?' Daisy glanced up. 'It is dreadfully wrong of me but I cannot help feeling relieved.'

'The man was not the leader. Heritage suffered a severe beating.'

'Did you kill the leader?' Daisy covered her mouth.

'Not by my hand. He hit his head against the fireplace. It's over, Daisy, the gang is smashed.' He grabbed her hand and savoured the way it curled around his. He wanted a few moments more before he told her the full truth. Was it too much to ask? He had gone through hell and the only person who was important to him was standing there, unharmed. Safe. 'We need to speak. There is something that I must tell you. I promised myself when I was lying in the hut.'

'What did they want? Why were you kidnapped? The treasure?' Daisy looked up at him. Her hand touched his face. 'How badly did they hurt you?'

'The leader of the gang wanted me dead. It did have something to do with India,' Adam said.

'What stopped him?'

'The thing that saved me, Daisy, was your box.'

'My box?' Her eyes widened and the lantern swung wildly.

Adam paused and took the lantern from her fingers. He placed it on the ground. The last thing they needed was a fire. 'It was stolen from your room this morning. You were right to go on that walk. They wanted you because of Tom. If you had been in that room, you would have been kidnapped.'

'It doesn't bear thinking about.' She pressed her hands together and tears sparkled in her eyes. 'But, Adam, all this can wait. All I care about is that you safe. We should get you back to the hotel.'

'Look out, Ravensworth!' A hoarse cry came from the hut. Suddenly a wild figure appeared in the doorway, scattering footmen. Adam stared at him in astonishment.

'I will avenge my brothers. It has been foreseen.' Sanjay held up a gleaming knife and captured Daisy's arm. 'I told you, you would bring her to me. She dies. I do this.'

'Adam!' Daisy clawed at the imprisoning arm. 'Help me!'

Adam's nerves coiled. Behind him, he heard vague shouts, and the sound of a pistol being cocked.

'No!' Adam shouted, reaching for Daisy's arm and pulling. 'Get out of the way!'

'I have him, Ravensworth!'

A shot rang out and then there was a soft thump as two bodies slid to the ground.

Chapter Fifteen

Daisy rose from the ground where she had been pushed. She stared in horror at the crumpled figures. They grappled for a long moment and then lay unmoving. Two pools of blood seeped.

Adam's cry of alarm and the pistol shot rang in her ears. She shook her head and tried to rid it of the buzzing. Adam turned the nearest man over. In his hand, he had a bloodied knife.

Lord Edward gave a crooked smile. 'For the regiment, eh, Ravensworth? I thought he would feign death again, but I was wise to his tricks and got him. You said she was worth it. I hope for your sake she was. I didn't die a coward, Ravensworth. Say it.'

'You did well, Heritage.' Adam knelt and closed the now sightless eyes.

'He was going straight for you, miss,' Mr Armstrong said. 'I had no choice like. He had a knife. I saw it in his hand. Oh, my God, I hit Lord Edward.'

'You missed. The bullet hit the door.' Adam's voice

held a note of great weariness. He pressed his hands to his eyes. 'Edward Heritage pushed Daisy away and then went for Sanjay. He did it with practically his last breath. I should have checked the Indian closer. I assumed he was dead by the way he lay. Luckily, this time, Edward Heritage finished the job.'

'I had to act like. He was heading straight for Miss Milton. I warned her to stay away, but she refused.' Mr Armstrong stared at Adam, his whiskers bristled with indignation. 'What do you mean I missed?'

'Are they dead?' Daisy whispered and she started to shake.

'Heritage knew he was dying. They had beaten him too severely.' Adam draped an arm over her shoulders. She leant into him, grateful for the warmth. 'In the end, he proved his worth.'

Daisy cupped her hands about Adam's face. 'It is over now. We are both safe. Nothing is ever going to harm you again.'

He put his hands over Daisy's, held her there for a moment. 'We will have all the time in the world, Daisy. First there is duty. Someone has to tell his great-uncle that his nephew was a hero.'

Faint streaks of dawn shone in the sky giving Adam's room a rosy glow. He stood at the window, watching the changing scene. In his hand, the necklace was a ruby-red rebuke of things he had not done. Even though he had wanted to leave with Daisy, he had stayed until Webster was brought out. Webster, despite his chagrin at being abducted by such a feeble trick, would live. Then he had gone to tell Lord Denning of his great-nephew's heroism. To his credit, the old man had taken it better than he had hoped. In death, Heritage had redeemed himself. And now all that remained was to go to bed and to hope for a better day.

But all that he really wanted was Daisy by his side. Tomorrow. He gave a slight smile. Today, he would get a special licence and they would marry. And then he would tell her everything.

A soft knock sounded. He opened the door and saw Daisy standing silhouetted in the doorway. Her unbound hair shone in the candlelight.

Adam stepped back one step and allowed her to enter. Her green dress brushed his leg.

'What are you doing here, Daisy?'

'I saw a light. I thought perhaps you needed a valet.'

'I can manage.'

She put her shoulders back and kept her head upright. 'You promised to talk to me but you never came near me after... I also wanted to show you the box.'

'The box?'

'Mr Armstrong retrieved it for me. I was able to prise it open. One of the panels buckled in the struggle.' She held out the box, crammed full of rubies and emeralds. Deep rich colours glowing in the dawn light. 'There was a note from Tom...and his wife. They are to be my dowry. Not quite a king's ransom, but enough to live comfortably. It seems such a waste. I had a fortune in my hands all the time and never knew it. That evil, evil man is dead. It is more than enough to start a school...for Felicity, Kammie and me to live on. But I worry. Did he steal them?'

'Did he write how he got the jewels?'

'From the thuggee?'

'From the maharajah. The maharajah thought he could bribe your brother, but he wanted none of it. When he heard that Kamala was to be burnt alive, he attempted to bargain with the maharajah by buying Kamala with the jewels. The maharajah refused. So Tom acted. He took them back after he killed the maharajah.'

'Tom, my gentle brother, killed him?'

'And saved my misbegotten life.' Adam shook his head. 'Tom should have taken Kamala and run. I had arrived at the pyre a few moments too late. But Tom turned back. He joined in. Kamala fought as well.'

'Tom was like that. Kammie will love to hear the full story about her parents' bravery. It sounds like something out of the Arabian Nights.' Her smile turned tremulous. 'They are an excuse really. I waited for you. I wanted to thank you.'

He rubbed the back of his neck as the pit of his stomach sank. He had half-hoped that no matter what had passed between them, she would have no choice but to marry him, but she seemed to be intent on keeping to her ridiculous agreement.

'There was much to do.' He kept his words calm while his mind raced. There had to be a way of keeping her here with him and convincing her of the necessity of their marriage. He needed her and it frightened him. 'Someone had to tell Lord Denning. Heritage's part in the affair will be hushed up. It is for the best.'

'You sound upset.'

'He died saving you.'

'He was a bad man.' Daisy turned her head, but not before Adam saw the shadows in her eyes. He willed her to understand. If she could understand and forgive Heritage, maybe she could forgive him for what he did all those years ago. 'But I can't fault your logic. You owe something to people who save your life. I think you are right to keep quiet about his involvement. It will not serve any purpose.'

'The governess is prepared to bend the rules?'

'A balance needs to be struck.' Daisy pushed the hair from her eyes. 'Mrs Blandish will be praising Miss Blandish's lucky escape. If she had been engaged to Lord Edward, she would have had to go into mourning but now she will be able to have a proper London Season.'

Her grey-green gaze met his. 'Did you allow the doctor to look you over? Or did you simply pretend you were fine?'

'Me?' Adam stared at her in astonishment. 'I will live.'

'I was worried about you.' She reached up and touched his cheek.

Adam forced a tight smile. He was a coward. He knew they should speak about her brother and Kammie, but right now all he wanted to do was to hold her. Selfishly he wanted her to love him and stay with him because it was her desire to, and not because she felt an obligation. He had once thought she would be his redemption, but now he knew that he had no right to her. 'Daisy, you should go.'

'Because of my reputation?' She gave an arched laugh. 'What reputation do I have left? I went tearing after you, demanding people follow me.'

'The heroine of the hour.'

Adam put his hand on her shoulder and her flesh quivered underneath his fingers. He barely retained control over his desire to crush her against him.

Some day he knew he would have to tell her about what had happened in India, but right now he was not ready. He would have to explain. Some might call him a coward, but he needed to see her as she was now. Right now, he wanted Daisy to love him, but he was afraid to ask her. For a man who had never been daunted when confronted with terrible odds, who took instead of asking, this was beyond him. For once, he would do the right thing.

'Why are you here, Daisy?' His voice sounded hoarse to his ears. 'I asked you to go.'

'Hold me, Adam. I need to be held by you. We shared something precious earlier...' Her voice quavered slightly. 'I thought I had lost you.'

Adam gave a groan and pulled her into his arms, settling her yielding curves against his hard planes. He gently kissed her temple. Her hand curved around his neck and pulled his face down.

'I thought you were dead,' she whispered against his lips.

'I should never have left you. I should have said goodbye.'

She placed a kiss on the corner of his mouth. 'That is an understatement.'

He gave into the impulse, lowered his lips and drank from her mouth.

'I want you,' he murmured against her mouth. 'You can leave now, but if you stay...we will make love. No seduction. It will be us two meeting.'

'I'll stay.' Daisy curved her arm tighter about Adam's neck and held him there. She had waited in her room, hoping that he would come to her, but when he didn't, she knew she had to try. She wanted to be with him and only him and she was so frightened that he would reject her. 'Please let me stay. I insist on it.'

'Never let it be said that I refuse a lady.'

She buried her fingers in Adam's crisp hair and pulled him close.

Their tongues met and retreated and then met again.

Furious fingers worked at his shirt, parted it and then her hand encountered his silky skin. She stroked it and felt the warmth under her fingertips grow red hot. Her fingers traced his flat nipples, feeling them tighten.

He captured her hands, holding them against his skin, and she saw the red marks on his wrists.

'Your wrists,' she gasped.

'They are nothing. You are everything.'

He lifted her up and carried her into his bedroom. Like hers, it was furnished in the hotel style, but there was also something undeniably masculine about it.

She collapsed back down on to the bed and looked up at him. With impatient fingers he took off his shirt. In the dawn light, his skin seemed tinged with rose, truly a Greek god.

He picked a tendril of hair off the pillow and smiled. 'Lavender. The smell of your hair enchants me. I kept thinking about it when I was in the hut.'

'It has never had that effect on anyone else.'

'That's because you're mine. All mine.'

His lips nuzzled her neck trailing down to her shoulder. This time her body knew what to expect and arched off the bed towards his questing mouth. His fingers began to undo the little buttons at the front of her dress, pushing aside the material to reveal her breasts. His exploring fingers stopped.

'You did not wear a corset.'

'You told me to take advantage of my maid,' Daisy reminded him. She reached up and wound her arm about his neck, pulling his face next to hers. 'And so I did.'

He groaned and recaptured her mouth. Teasing her. Taking the time to explore until her body thrummed with desire.

His mouth travelled slowly down to her bared breasts. He captured each dusky-rose nipple in turn and feasted on them, licking round and round. Then he moved inexorably lower. His mouth touched the apex of her thighs and then began to explore her inner folds.

With each sweep of his tongue, she felt more alive. Her body trembled on the brink of an abyss. She heard a cry and knew it came from her throat. But it was not enough.

This time she wanted to take an active part.

'Lie back,' she whispered.

He raised his head and looked at her with blazing eyes. 'As you command.'

Her hands undid the buttons on his trousers and pushed away the fabric to reveal his arousal. Her hand reached out and stroked him as she had done before, revelling in the soft velvet firmness of him. She heard the swift intake of breath.

'We can take this slowly,' he whispered in her ear. 'We have all the time in the world, but not if you touch me like that.'

All the time in world? She swallowed hard. It was not what she had. She had nearly lost him today, before she had had the chance to say how she felt about him. But now, looking at his magnificent body, she found no words came. She had to show him what he meant to her.

'I am not sure I can last that long,' she said with a shaky laugh. She touched him again, her fingers encircling him. She bent her lips, testing the heat of him.

'I need you,' he growled, pulling at her shoulders and turning her on her back.

She looked up at him, golden skin gleaming over her and knew that this was what she wanted. This man with her now.

With one hand, he parted her thighs, positioning himself.

Their joining was fast and furious. The tenderness of before was not there. This was a celebration of life. Everything he asked, she gave; everything he gave, she took. Until she trembled on the brink. He thrust once more and she shattered.

In the aftermath, Daisy lay in his arms. She had really and truly fallen. She could no longer deny her nature. She should feel wicked lying here in his arms, but instead she felt reborn.

She had gone to his room to explain about the box and to show him that he should not worry about her. She would more than survive. But this had happened. She had wanted his touch; more than wanted it, she had craved it.

A small movement made her glance over and she saw that Adam was watching her with intent eyes, eyes of caramel, eyes like Kammie's. Daisy's breath caught. The words echoed round and round her brain. Eyes like Kammie's. Then they combined with another thought—the maharajah gave everyone a gift; he was good at finding their weakness; someone had stood next to him on the first morning and told him about the monkey. Kamala?

What if Heritage had not lied at the ball? What if Tom had fallen in love with Adam's mistress?

'What are you thinking about with your storm-tossed eyes?' His velvet voice slid over her skin and enticed her to forget her troubles.

She shook her head to clear it. She had to know now before it started to eat away at her soul. 'Was Kamala your mistress?'

He sighed and flopped down amongst the pillows. For what seemed like an age, he stared up at the ceiling. 'Yes, she was, Daisy. It all happened a very long time before I met you. We do not have to speak of this now. We have the rest of our lives to discuss such matters. You are tired and I have had a long day.'

'Why did she give you the necklace?' Daisy hated how sharp and needy her voice sounded.

'She gave me the necklace so I would have proof to show the authorities.'

'Why did you keep it afterwards?'

'I gave it back to her, but your brother threw it at me. Told me to keep it. That he had purchased her freedom with it and she would be beholden to no one now.'

'You should have told me.' Daisy felt a great space open within her.

'I wasn't aware you needed a complete list of my

mistresses. I have had a number, Daisy. I do not deny it.' He touched her cheek with his hand. 'Know that they are in my past. You are my present and future.'

Daisy forced her body to get out of bed and begin to dress. When she was clothed, she looked at him again. He had not moved but watched her with eyes of rich caramel. 'Is Kammie your daughter?'

'Kamala was pregnant when I left the hill station with the necklace. Her pregnancy gave her the strength to steal the proof I needed. I believe I am your Kammie's father.'

'Did my brother know?' Daisy whispered.

'Yes, he knew.' Adam ran his hands through his hair. The red marks of the rope burns stood out. Her heart twisted at how brave he had been and how modest. 'It is not a time of my life I am particularly proud of. Kamala was the best thing to happen to me until I met you. But I refused to listen to her pleas. If I had taken her with me, she would never have been on that pyre. I knew she carried my child and I left her in danger. All because I cared about the wrong things.'

'And while you were gone…'

'While I was gone, Tom and Kamala fell in love. I had asked him to watch over her. He never touched her because he felt she belonged to me. After the battle, Kamala pleaded with me to free her. I behaved badly like the spoilt aristocrat I was.'

Daisy concentrated on the coverlet. She did not dare look at him. She wished she'd known this before she'd given herself to him. 'What did you do?'

'I beat your brother to a bloody pulp. I would have killed him, the man who saved my life if Kamala had not intervened. She begged me for the sake of our child. I very nearly hit her.'

'It was then that my brother threw the necklace at you.'

'Yes. He married her. He gave his name to my child.'

'And you loved her.'

'More than anyone else in the world at the time. I told her so, but it did not make any difference. She told me that I didn't have a heart and there was a great wickedness within me. She loved your brother. In time, I came to realise that she was a wise woman, but by then it was too late. They were all dead.'

Daisy hugged her arms about her waist. He had loved Kamala more than anyone. The fact hurt far more than she thought it would. She could not compete against a dead woman. 'But why didn't Tom send Kammie to you? Did Kamala fear you would neglect her?'

'When my brother died, I was happy to depart India and all its darkness. But I had left Kamala and Tom in no doubt of my sincerity. If they had any need, they were supposed to come to me. They never did. I assumed Kammie had died. Children often do in India.'

Daisy looked up at the ceiling and tried not to let the blackness overwhelm her. What would Felicity do when she learnt the truth about Kammie's parentage? What would Adam do about the falling sickness? And worse, he had only seduced her after he had known that Kammie was alive. He was wicked and selfish. 'Why not tell me before we…before I lay in your arms? Why not tell me when I first confided about Kammie? Surely I had a right to know. I could have decided.'

'What would you have decided?'

'I don't know,' Daisy replied truthfully. 'You did not give me that choice.'

'I meant to tell you earlier, Daisy, I swear it, but I needed your touch far too much. I wanted to show how much I care for you. How I could take care of you. I wanted you to see the best in me before you learnt the worst. I wanted a second chance with you. Can't you see how hard I have tried to be good?'

Care for her? And he could not even tell her this simple truth? Daisy's heart shattered into a thousand pieces. He had wanted to live a lie and in the background would be his passion for Kamala. 'Why are you telling me now?'

'So you will understand the worst about me and how I have changed.' He leant forwards with eager eyes. 'You and I could give my daughter an excellent home. She—'

'You want to claim Kammie as your own.' Daisy stared at him; the words tasted like ash in her mouth. Her entire being trembled. He did not know anything about Kammie. Would he be so eager when he knew she was ill? So many people were frightened of the illness.

'I can give her a good life, Daisy. She will want for nothing. I owe that to her mother. We will be the perfect family.'

Her mother. This was still about Kamala. It was why he had kept the necklace. If she stayed with him, she would be constantly fighting a ghost.

'Kammie has falling sickness. She has fits. She is far from perfect.'

A light died in Adam's eyes. He turned away from her and his shoulders hunched. 'I didn't know.'

'Do you still want to claim her as your own or will you seek to put her in a home to rot away?' Daisy fought against the tears and the frustration. Whatever happened, she would ensure that Kammie received the best care. It was what the jewels had to be used for— to give Kammie care. It was what Tom would have wanted. This had nothing to do with the jealousy she felt towards his love for Kamala and everything to do with protecting Kammie.

'I will do what is best for her. Those sorts of decisions are for another day.' He held out his hands. 'I am giving you a choice, Daisy.'

'You are seeking to use me.' Daisy backed away from his outstretched arms. 'You should have told me all of this, before…before… You looked at me and saw only an obligation and a duty, a wrong that needed to be righted. And then I was a challenge. Something to show that you were in charge. I am more than that, much more. I am a person.'

'You are cheapening yourself, Daisy.' A muscle jumped in his jaw. 'I kissed you because I wanted to, not because I felt a duty. I could have taken care of you in a thousand different ways.'

'I was a means to an end.'

'You should have told me who your niece was in the first place. But you chose to let me believe she was your sister's child. There is blame on both sides. I accept what I did was wrong. I fight against the darkness in my soul every day, but I am trying to do the decent thing now. We could be a family together.'

'There is no need. Kammie has a family.'

'We did not take precautions, Daisy.' His voice

dripped ice. 'I will not have history repeat itself. I failed once before. I will honour my responsibilities. We will marry. Society will demand it. I will bring *my* daughter up as the lady she should be as I would do with any child we might have. Kammie will have all of London at her feet when she makes her début.'

Daisy drew herself up to her full height. Inside of her, she had gone numb. Kammie would never be able to be in society. Adam had never mentioned one word about loving her or caring for her. He saw her as an object. It all had been about righting old mistakes, making sure that no one else was hurt. He did not love her and she knew after what she had experienced that she wanted love. She needed more. She deserved more.

'I am sorry, Adam, but I refuse to marry you. Not like this and not for those reasons. Marriage has to be about love or it is nothing.'

She blindly stumbled to the door. Her hand closed around the knob, but the door refused to budge. She gave it a little kick. His hand closed over hers and opened the door. 'You walk out on me now, Daisy, and it is over. I am offering you a glittering future.'

'Then it is over.' Daisy kept her eyes straight ahead. She did not dare look at the anger that would be on his face. He would get over it. It was only because she was taking his latest plaything away. 'I am going back to War- wickshire. It is where I grew up. It is where I belong. I would be no good in London, Adam. I am a governess, not a social butterfly. Some day, you will find the right woman for you. Somebody who does not expect more from you.'

She could hear the sound of his steady breathing

behind her. 'I will send you back to Warwickshire in my carriage. There is no need for you take the public stage. But you are wrong about me. I only wanted you to be happy.'

'The carriage would be a kindness.' Daisy forced the words around the lump in her throat. She did not want him to be kind. She wanted to hate him. 'I wish to leave within the hour.'

'Here I took you for a fighter.'

Daisy paused. She knew she was staring into bleakness, but it was better now. 'I fight when there is something worth fighting for.'

'I love you, Daisy.'

The words tore at her heart.

'Love?' Daisy forced scorn into her voice. 'You do not know the meaning of the word. All you know about is desire and desire always fades.'

Keeping her head high, she swept from the room. Behind her the door closed with a decisive click.

Turn around, give me the slightest sign that I have a chance. Let me prove to you that it is more than desire.

Adam watched his carriage roll away from the Shaw's Hotel and silently willed Daisy to look back. It had taken all of his will power and self-control to accede to her wishes and let her go. Even now, he fought against the overwhelming urge to haul her out of the carriage and take her back to his bed.

The place in the centre of his chest felt worse than when Kamala had walked away. Adam knew there was no comparison between the youthful combination of desire and guilt he had had for Kamala and the love he bore Daisy. The words of the curse were wrong. He had learnt what love was and what it was like to lose it.

The carriage began to go through the gates and he saw the barest hint of movement.

Somehow I will find a way of proving my love.

'Lord Ravensworth!' a self-important voice trilled across the gravelled drive. 'We must speak.'

'Mrs Blandish, now is not the best time.'

'It is about the help Miss Milton promised you'd give.'

'Miss Milton promised?'

Mrs Blandish crossed her well-upholstered arms. 'She said you were a man of great honour and integrity.'

Adam glanced towards the gates. The simplest thing in the world would be to go after her, to haul her out of the carriage and kiss her senseless. But Adam knew that this was about more than possession. He wanted to prove to her that he was worthy enough to share her life. He threw one last longing look at the now-empty space.

'Mrs Blandish, whatever promise Daisy gave, if it is in my power, I will do it.'

Chapter Sixteen

Daisy alighted from the carriage and took her small satchel into the tiny cottage in the rural Warwickshire village.

All throughout the journey, she had half-expected to hear the sound of thundering hooves as Adam came to demand that she stay with him. She even had her scathing retort ready on her lips. But no horse and rider came past.

At the first coaching inn, her heart had skipped a beat when she had spied a pair of broad shoulders, but it turned out to be a stranger.

Then as the miles stretched out, her hopes and her anger faded away, leaving only a great hollow place in her middle. And she was forced to concede that he did not think she was worth fighting for. In the quiet of the carriage, she wept until she had no more tears left.

'Daisy, what are you doing here? You were supposed to be in Cumberland? At Gilsland Spa? Have you left the Blandishes?'

'Aunt Daisy! Aunt Daisy has come home!' Kammie danced about, her soft brown curls glowing in the afternoon sun.

'Yes, poppet. I have come home. For good.' Daisy lent against the doorframe as she caught sight of Kammie's eyes. The only wonder was that she had been so blind with Adam. Kammie was a feminine version of Adam down to the curve of her lips and the way she tilted her head. She had always assumed these looks came from her mother.

'Is everything all right, Daisy? You look like you haven't slept in a week.'

'Everyone was very kind.'

'From the letter that arrived yesterday, I understood that you were to marry Adam Ravensworth, Viscount Ravensworth.'

'The marriage has been called off.' Daisy gave what she hoped was an unconcerned shrug. 'We did not suit.'

'Didn't suit or wouldn't suit?' Felicity linked arms with Daisy and drew her into the tiny front room with its horse brasses and John Martin engraving above the fireplace while Kammie bent down to stroke a cat. 'I know you, Margaret Milton. You like to leave before you get hurt. Did he hurt you?'

Daisy winced. Felicity had to be furious as she was using Daisy's real name. 'Not intentionally. It was better this way, trust me. I couldn't have borne it…'

'Did he have feelings for you?'

Daisy put her head in her hands. It was one thing to think up excuses, but she knew Felicity would see through any lie. 'Yes…no… He said so. But I am not sure. It seems far too quick. I had always thought love took a long time. But this seems to be something that burns bright and fierce. I am terrified that it will die just as quickly.'

'Then you are a fool. And that is something I never thought I would say to you, Margaret Milton.' Felicity put her hands on her hips. 'You threw away something precious because you feared for the future. Well, nothing in life is guaranteed. If not for yourself, think of the advantages you could have given Kammie.'

Daisy watched the sunlight play on Kammie's hair as she engaged the cat in solemn conversation. 'Lord Ravensworth will assist with Kammie. He considers it his duty to his lost love.'

'You have lost me, Margaret.'

'Adam Ravensworth is Kammie's natural father.' The words tumbled out of Daisy. 'Not Tom.'

'Kammie was born in wedlock, Margaret. Tom is her father. He gave her his name. Our brother had a big heart. And he loved that little girl as his own.'

Daisy stared at Felicity in astonishment. 'You knew.'

'Knew what?' Felicity went over to the brasses and started to arrange them. 'I knew Kammie wasn't Tom's. But I didn't know the name of the father. All I knew was that he had been in the British Army, rather than in the East India Company. Tom did not confide that. He was in love with Kamala. He was determined that Kammie would grow up with the last name of Milton. Goodness, I might have wanted him to do better, but I accepted his choice. But once I set eyes on Kammie, I knew he had done the right thing.'

'When did you find this out?'

'It was in his last letter. The one I threw on the fire when Kammie arrived.'

'You knew and never told me?' Daisy stared at her sister.

'I wanted a child.' Felicity reached out and covered Daisy's hand. 'Colin abandoned my bed before our baby was stillborn. He was not going to come back. I had so much love to give.'

'You should have told me.'

'You were unmarried. You had no need to know of such things. I didn't even know if you knew where babies came from.'

'Felicity!' Daisy stared at her sister. 'All these years. You should have told me that Kammie was not Tom's.'

'Kammie was born in wedlock. She was our brother's child in the law. That was all you needed to know. And we needed every penny you sent back.'

Daisy straightened her back. She did not know which was worse—Adam's betrayal or Felicity's. 'I was so proud of you the day that Kammie arrived. How you argued with Colin and were determined to keep the baby, despite the vicar's wife saying she was poorly. It was why I agreed to become a governess. To help out.'

'Can you imagine what would have happened to Kammie if she was put into an orphanage? With her sickness?'

Daisy glanced over to where Kammie sat in the dust, pulling a string for the cat to chase. She put her hand over her eyes. Every particle of her was exhausted. Felicity was right. What she had done was right and Daisy knew that the girl she had been then would not have understood. She would have seen it in black and white. She did not begrudge Kammie anything. She was her darling niece. 'You were far better than I could have ever been.'

'Do not judge yourself harshly, Margaret. You were young.'

'There are other things I have to tell you.' Daisy quickly related what had happened to her, leaving out her relationship with Adam as much as possible. 'And the fight must have loosened the puzzle box's mechanism. It contained a small fortune in jewels. There is no need for you to worry about Kammie's health now. I will be able to stay here with you.'

Felicity tapped her fingers together and did not say anything for a long while. Daisy shifted from one foot to another. Surely Felicity had to see that the jewels were really Kammie's. 'Margaret, are you saying that you do not want to have anything more to do with Adam Ravensworth?'

'Lord Ravensworth had no intention of marrying me,' Daisy said quickly. 'He would have been quite happy to have me as a mistress, but I suspect would have soon tired of me and my countrified ways. I wanted more than he could give. I have no wish to speak of him again.'

'I am sorry you quarrelled, Margaret.' Felicity kissed Daisy's forehead as if she was no older than Kammie. 'He must have been someone very special to get through your defences. He will come after you.'

'I don't want him to,' Daisy said and knew she lied. 'If he comes here, I expect you to deal with him.'

'You can stay here, but I won't let you hide behind my skirts. When he comes here, it will be for you and not for Kammie.'

In the days that followed Daisy learnt that she was not pregnant and tried to settle into the routine of the house, helping Felicity out when she could. A great gaping hole had replaced where her heart had once resided. At night, she'd lie awake and wonder if the necklace had been truly cursed and whether she had proven unworthy. Certainly, Adam did not make any attempt to contact her or Kammie. When daylight came, she dismissed her night time thoughts as nonsense.

Twice she started letters and then threw them on the fire. The third time, she finished the letter, signed her name and accidentally allowed a tear to stain it. Angrily she tore it into pieces and threw it on the fire. Felicity made no comment except to look up from her sewing.

In desperation, Daisy went up to her tiny room and started to leaf through her books. Her fingers lighted on the book of Keats's poems that Adam had brought her from Carlisle.

'Let's see what your favourite sonnet is like, then. Maybe that will help end my heartache,' Daisy muttered, leafing through various pages. She came to the words 'Bright Star would I were as steadfast as thou art'. On the last line—'And so live for ever or else swoon to death'—the word 'swoon' was replaced with 'love'. In copperplate handwriting, Adam had written—*how I feel about you, Daisy*.

She traced the words with her finger, reading them

over and over again. She had been the one to make the mistake. Just as she had once used her governess clothes as a shield, she used her hurt at not being his first love to deny her love for him. And his for her. What they had shared was not the passion of youth, but the meeting of true minds, if only she had seen it for what it was. It was not he who was at fault but she. She had made a mistake. *I always took you for a fighter.* His accusation rose in her mind and she knew he was right. She hadn't fought. She'd run. She'd have to go back and try.

Without giving herself time to think, Daisy jammed her clothes into her satchel. Suddenly all her doubts dropped away and she knew she had been hiding, not wanting to face his love. She had run away, rather than risk getting hurt. She would go and explain. If it was too late that was her fault, but she had to try.

'Daisy, Daisy, I have news,' Felicity called from downstairs. 'The hall has been let. They say the new tenant is to be Lord Ravensworth.'

'You will have misheard, Felicity. Adam Ravensworth would not come to a backwater like this.'

'God save us from addle-headed governesses.'

For a long heartbeat, Daisy forgot to breathe. Had she somehow conjured up his voice. Daisy withdrew her hand and stumbled to the door. This had to be some sort of waking dream brought on by lack of sleep. She pinched her hand hard. 'You can't be here,' she whispered. 'Not after how awfully I treated you or the words I said. I was wrong. I was jealous of Kamala. Oh God, I have started talking to myself.'

'Daisy Milton, will you come down or shall I come

up?' The tones were aggrieved, but her heart soared. Daisy knew that it was no apparition. Adam Ravensworth was here.

Daisy hurriedly smoothed her skirt and pinched her cheeks. There was no time to change from her grey dress. Then she halted. Silently she consigned her sister to some dark place. It was all her doing. She had written to him. As quickly as the excitement had come over, it left, leaving her in a state of dull grey numbness.

'Daisy? Aren't you going to answer?' her sister called. 'There is a gentleman who wishes to see you. Six-year-old children have only a limited amount of appeal to gentlemen.'

Slowly Daisy walked down the narrow stairs. He stood in the centre of the front parlour, dwarfing Kammie as he stood in earnest conversation with her about her cat. With his top hat, cream-coloured trousers and form fitting frock coat, he seemed to be a creature from another planet. Daisy risked another step and the stairs' creaking alerted them to her presence. He glanced up and their eyes met. Instantly his eyes became liquid amber pools. He took a step towards her, reached out his hands. Then he stopped motionless and unmoving, simply watching her with those molten eyes.

For several moments, Daisy found it impossible to do anything but stare at him. He was far thinner than she remembered, and there were circles under his eyes as if he had not slept.

'Lord Ravensworth, I see you have met our Kammie,' Felicity said, breaking the spell.

He patted Kammie on the head, but all his attention

seemed to be for her. 'Kammie reminds me of my late brother more than anything. They have the same coloured eyes. You have done a good job, Mrs Fulton.'

'I understand Daisy explained about Kammie's illness. Kammie is having one of her better days.'

'Falling sickness. My brother suffered from it as well. It can run in families. Were you aware that Julius Caesar suffered from the same malady?'

'What are you doing here, Adam?' Daisy asked before Felicity could answer.

He raised an eyebrow. 'I am attempting to meet my new neighbours. I have taken possession of the hall. Kammie will break hearts when she is older whether she is in London or if she chooses to live quietly in Warwickshire.'

'Adam, I—' Daisy felt the tears begin to prick at her eyelids. There were so many things she wanted to say to him and she did not know where to start. How did she begin to say she was sorry for all the things she had accused him of, and for all the things she had said? How could she explain that she had been overwhelmingly jealous? And that she had thrown away the chance of the love of a lifetime on a petty green-eyed monster. His heart was surely big enough for two people. He could have loved both her and Kamala but she had selfishly wanted a whole heart.

'Use mine.'

In two steps he was beside her, handing her a freshly laundered linen handkerchief. Their fingers touched and a brief pulse went through her. He gave her hand a little squeeze before letting go.

'The last thing in the world I want you to do is to

cry, Daisy.' An uncertain frown crossed his face. 'I have no wish for you to be unhappy. You are far too thin. Have you been eating properly?'

'I am not unhappy.' Daisy dabbed her eyes.

'Are you certain you are quite the thing? Are you sickening?'

Daisy took the handkerchief from her eyes. Her heart sank. He thought she was in a delicate condition. He was here to make sure that he didn't make the same mistake twice. 'No, no, I am very well. Very happy to be home. You must not worry about me.'

'I always worry about you. I will always worry.' He looked at her with a solemn face. Daisy wanted to reach out her hand and smooth the creases away. She wondered that she had ever thought his face arrogant.

'Come along, Kammie, let's see if we can't find a saucer of milk for your cat,' Felicity said, leading Kammie and the cat out of the room. 'I believe your aunt wants to be alone.'

The mantelpiece clock ticked loudly. Daisy held out the handkerchief. 'I have recovered. You may go, Adam.'

Adam swore. 'I once listened to your speech, now listen to mine. Please.'

'Your speech?'

He knelt down on one knee. His eyes burnt into hers as if he were trying to see into her soul. 'Please, Miss Milton, would you do me the honour, the very great honour, of becoming my wife?'

Daisy stared at him in surprise. Of everything she had expected him to say, he said the words she most wanted to hear. And he was asking! 'Are you certain about this?'

Adam grasped both her hands in his large one. 'I have spent the time away from you rearranging my life so I can be here in this backwater with you. I have leased the hall from Chesterholm.'

'From Jonathon Ponsby-Smythe?'

'He practically gave it to me once I told him of my plight. He agreed that I should have my chance at happiness with you. He wishes he had had a second chance with his governess.'

'Did you tell him about Louisa?'

He shook his head. 'I thought you should make that decision. He thinks she died.'

Daisy stared at him. He was allowing her to make the decision. 'I will have to write to Louisa first.' She stared at his highly polished boots. 'Where is Webster? You can't be rattling around that hall on your own.'

'Polly and Webster are both here. It would appear that Polly is quite the nurse. And Webster is content to forgo the lights of London for Polly's ministrations.'

'Webster and Polly? That is impossible. Or rather improbable.'

'Hush.' He laid a finger across her lips. 'For a change, listen with your whole being. The first thing I have to say to you is this. This is why we should marry.'

His fingers tilted her chin upwards and he gently kissed her lips. The kiss was filled with a sweet loving intensity. Then he stepped away.

Daisy looked up into his eyes with wonder. The ache in her heart had ceased.

'I love you, Daisy Milton.' He cupped her head in

his hands. 'I want to marry you. Not because society says that we must, or because you think it will mean your sister can keep Kammie, or whatever excuse you want to say. I want to marry you because I am selfish. I want you in my life and at my side. I need you and I desire you in my life. My life before I met you was an empty shell and when you left, I found the loneliness impossible to bear. That is the only reason. It is the right reason to marry.'

'You need me.' Daisy stared at him. Adam never needed anyone. He had changed his life for her. 'After everything I said to you when we parted. I left you, rather than fight. That was wrong.'

'I always said that I wanted a woman with an independent mind.' There was a new humble note in Adam's voice as he continued. 'What I need to know is can you come to care for me? If you think you can never care for me, I will bow out of your lives. I will provide for Kammie, of course. That is my duty, but you need to understand what I felt for Kamala pales into insignificance compared to what I feel for you. But if you think there is the smallest place in your heart for me, I want to marry you. My heart is steadfast.'

Daisy pulled his head down.

'Yes,' she said against his lips. 'For I too love you unto death. I found the sonnet, Adam, and what you describe was not your love for me, but mine for you.'

Adam brushed her lips and then reached into his coat pocket. 'Then it is well that I procured a special licence.'

'A special licence?'

'You have no idea the difficulties you have caused me, Daisy. First you lumber me with the Blandishes, preventing me from going after you. Then Webster and the move. All of these responsibilities. I am not about to let you slip away again and therefore it is a special licence. There will be no long engagement.'

'I didn't mean to,' Daisy sought to explain. 'I had to give Mrs Blandish a reason to send her footmen with me. I wanted to save your life.'

Adam's forefinger touched the corner of her mouth. His eyes danced with mischief. 'It was the one thing that gave me hope. You would not have made promises to Mrs Blandish that you could not keep. You are not that sort of person, Daisy Milton.'

'Why did you need a special licence? I would have been willing to wait.'

Daisy touched his cheek. He had obtained a special licence. He turned his face into her palm and kissed it.

'Because I was determined this time not to give you the luxury of changing your mind. We will be properly wedded and bedded before nightfall.'

'Adam—'

'I was merely existing before I met you.' Adam tightened his arms about her as if even now he was afraid she would go. 'I had allowed my anger and guilt at what happened in India to dominate my life. In my own way, I was as dead as everyone else from the hill station. You brought me back to life. You challenged me and I fell in love with you. I tried to show it, but now I will say it.' He stopped and looked down at her. 'What I felt for Kamala was a combination of infatuation and guilt. A beautiful woman in jeopardy who I failed to save. You were different. You refused all offers of protection and wanted to stand alone. You made me want to be a better man. I want to be your partner, not your master. My heart belongs to you and to you alone.'

'And you have made me a better woman. My heart has been inclined towards you ever since you freed my boot from the bramble.'

'You were very late in falling, my love. I knew you were the woman for me when you took such pleasure in defying me and screaming. Shall we marry today? The vicar has agreed. It is time we went home.'

'A home with you.' Daisy rested her head on his broad chest and listened to the steady thump of his heart. 'That is all I want in the world.'

'Those are the truest words you have spoken, Daisy Milton.'

'Daisy Ravensworth, if you please.'

'I very much do please, my very proper viscountess.'

The Shocking Secrets of Regency Rakes

FIVE SEXY HISTORICAL ROMANCES

The Unmasking of Lady Loveless
by Nicola Cornick

Disrobed and Dishonoured by Louise Allen

Libertine Lord, Pickpocket Miss
by Bronwyn Scott

The Unlacing of Miss Leigh by Diane Gaston

Notorious Lord, Compromised Miss
by Annie Burrows

Available 16th April 2010

www.millsandboon.co.uk

millsandboon.co.uk Community

Join Us!

The Community is the perfect place to meet and chat to kindred spirits who love books and reading as much as you do, but it's also the place to:

- Get the inside scoop from authors about their latest books
- Learn how to write a romance book with advice from our editors
- Help us to continue publishing the best in women's fiction
- Share your thoughts on the books we publish
- Befriend other users

Forums: Interact with each other as well as authors, editors and a whole host of other users worldwide.

Blogs: Every registered community member has their own blog to tell the world what they're up to and what's on their mind.

Book Challenge: We're aiming to read 5,000 books and have joined forces with The Reading Agency in our inaugural Book Challenge.

Profile Page: Showcase yourself and keep a record of your recent community activity.

Social Networking: We've added buttons at the end of every post to share via digg, Facebook, Google, Yahoo, technorati and de.licio.us.

www.millsandboon.co.uk

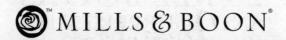

2 FREE BOOKS
AND A SURPRISE GIFT

We would like to take this opportunity to thank you for reading this
Mills & Boon® book by offering you the chance to take TWO more
specially selected books from the Historical series absolutely FREE!
We're also making this offer to introduce you to the benefits of the
Mills & Boon® Book Club™—

* **FREE home delivery**
* **FREE gifts and competitions**
* **FREE monthly Newsletter**
* **Exclusive Mills & Boon Book Club offers**
* **Books available before they're in the shops**

Accepting these FREE books and gift places you under no obligation to buy, you may cancel at any time, even after receiving your free
books. Simply complete your details below and return the entire page
to the address below. You don't even need a stamp!

YES Please send me 2 free Historical books and a surprise gift. I
understand that unless you hear from me, I will receive 4 superb new
books every month for just £3.79 each, postage and packing free. I
am under no obligation to purchase any books and may cancel my
subscription at any time. The free books and gift will be mine to keep
in any case.

Ms/Mrs/Miss/Mr ———————— Initials ——————

Surname ————————————————————
Address ————————————————————
————————————————————————
———————————— Postcode ——————
E-mail ————————————————————

Send this whole page to: Mills & Boon Book Club, Free Book Offer,
FREEPOST NAT 10298, Richmond, TW9 1BR